Edited by
David M. Fitzpatrick

Epic Saga Publishing
Brewer, Maine

SPECTRUM STORIES #1:
A QUIET BLUE WHEEL

"I feel within me

a

peace above all
earthly dignities, a still and

quiet

conscience."
— *William Shakespeare*

"Artists can color the sky red
because they know it's

blue

...Those of us who aren't artists
must color things the way they
really are or people might
think we're stupid."
— *Jules Feiffer*

"Fortune's

wheel

is ever turning."
— *Polish proverb*

Contents

Introduction

In the fall of 2009, I began teaching a class through Bangor Adult Education called "Creative Writing: The Short Story," which was based on my philosophy that anyone with three things could become a published writer. Those three things are a basic command of the English language and its mechanics, an imagination, and a love of writing.

With a love of writing and an imagination, but no basic command of English, the writing might well be unreadable.

With a love of writing and a command of English, but no imagination, the stories would be dull and bland.

And with a command of English and an imagination, but no love of writing, the writer's apathy would show, and his readers will care no more than he does.

Luckily, there has been no shortage of imagination or love of writing in this class. And the command of English has been good—and when that command has weakened, it's my job as editor to fix it.

This anthology is the first in a series with a formula for the title, which follows a format of "Adjective/Color/Noun"—such as *A Quiet Blue Wheel*. After several weeks of class, the students began writing their main project stories for the semester, with only a few rules. The main one is that their stories must reflect the title in some way, so that the object of the title becomes integral to the story. I do this to keep a general theme to the anthology, so there's some connecting idea, lest the anthology become a discordant collection of completely unrelated stories.

But that's where the similarities end. Each contributor has created a story featuring five basic factors: protagonist, antagonist, plot, resolution (in which the protagonist participates), and change (in the protagonist).

Aside from those requirements, and each author featuring a quiet blue wheel of some sort, they had free reign. And they did a great job. They worked hard on their stories, peer-reviewed their classmates' tales, submitted them to me, underwent further editing, and polished their work.

If nothing else, I hope this anthology serves as an example to everyone who has ever wanted to write but never seems to do so. If you want to write, just write. There's nothing stopping you. It might be a difficult challenge, but it will all be worth it in the end.

It has been my pleasure to work with the writers in this anthology, and share with them the few nuggets of wisdom I've gained through years of stumbling through the publication process. For some, this class was just for fun; if so, I hope they had plenty of it. For others, it was with an eye on submitting other work elsewhere; if so, I wish them the best of luck.

Special thanks to student Greg Westrich, the guest editor who reviewed and accepted my submission to the anthology and introduced it, and to student Anette Ruppel Rodrigues for offering a fresh pair of eyes proofing this book's layout.

A portion of the proceeds from this anthology will benefit Literacy Volunteers of Bangor. If you enjoy this book, consider reading other titles in this series, which will also benefit LVB. The next one is *An Odd Red Puzzle,* and its contributors have done an equally admirable job.

David M. Fitzpatrick
Brewer, Maine
April 2012

Dedication

This book is dedicated to the memory of someone who made a profound difference in my writing life.

George McCutcheon was my Creative Writing teacher in high school, around 1985, and he taught me more than I realized at the time. He insisted on strong plots and three-dimensional characters, demanded solid storytelling, and worked to teach me what made good fiction. He didn't expect perfection, but he expected me to strive for it.

But at that time, I was far too busy being a self-centered teenage boy, thinking I knew everything and he was just a silly old man, focused too much on my own perceived talent to understand the importance of what he was trying to teach me. It didn't matter that he was a close friend of Stephen King's and proofed all of Steve's novel drafts (and, in fact, was echoed by a character of the same name in the short story "Uncle Otto's Truck" from King's *Skeleton Crew*). Such is the way of teenage boys, I suppose.

Mac flunked me in Creative Writing. And he should have, even if I didn't realize it at the time. I was furious when he did, because I thought I was the next Stephen King. Later, I realized what lessons Mac had thrown at me—those lessons I'd skillfully dodged, unwittingly, to my detriment. Better late than never, as they say, and today I know I'm a much better writer today because of him.

The fact is, Mac probably wouldn't have remembered me

after I left his class. I was one of countless students who came through his classroom, and although I probably thought I was special back then, I'm sure I was quite forgettable.

Mac died on April 26, 1987, the victim of leukemia. I'm sure there are many students who remember his name. Many will do so with a grimace, as he could be the tough teacher everyone hoped they didn't get, and those who took Creative Writing just to earn half a credit but didn't have that passion for writing probably hated every moment of it. But I'll gamble that any of the students who had a passion for writing will remember him fondly, either for the successes they found in his class or, like me, for the failures from which they learned.

I know Mac would be the first to approve of the stories in this book, written by students who tried hard and wrote hard and polished hard. And he'd certainly approve of my focus as a teacher, because I followed in his footsteps in that regard. I insist on strong plots and three-dimensional characters, I demand solid storytelling, I work to teach them what makes good fiction, and, while I don't expect perfection, I expect them strive for perfection.

The first writing exercise I ever did was in Mac's class, when he wrote down several columns of nouns on the blackboard and challenged us to choose one item from each list. Right there in class, in fifteen minutes, we had to write a story using those things. My students recognize this exercise, because, twenty-seven years later, it's the first exercise I do on the first night of class.

When I was a high-school kid, I wanted to be the next Stephen King. Today, I strive to live up to George McCutcheon's standards, both as a writer and a teacher. It's sad that Mac can't appreciate this dedication, because he's been dead since 1987, but this dedication is intended for the potential writers who read this. Mac isn't here to teach you what he taught me, and I don't presume to be him. But I hope that, by reading this story, you might gain some insight into what writing fiction is all about.

It's about plot and characters, and good storytelling, and all that. And, as in my class, I could go on about protagonists, antagonists, character motivations and flaws, rising action, theme, resolution, and so forth. But let's boil it down to the one thing that should be woven through all of that.

It's about striving for perfection. That's at the heart of writing fiction — hell, writing *anything*. In the introduction, I mentioned that I believe there are three things you need to be a fiction writer: basic mechanical knowledge of the English language, imagination, and a love of writing. Now, anyone can learn basic English mechanics, and everyone has an imagination that can be sparked and stoked and ignited into something powerful. But if you don't have a love of writing... well, that's the deal-breaker. Maybe you can learn to love writing in the way that you can learn to love a style of music you never thought you could, or love a food you used to hate, or love a person you never thought you could. But I think the chances are pretty good that either you have an innate love of writing or you don't, whether you know it or not. And it's the hardest part to fake.

Mac didn't teach me those three points; I came up with them on my own. But I did so thanks to the ball he started rolling for me. I only wish I'd realized what a great and inspiring man he was before he passed out of this world, because I'd give anything to go back in time and let him know.

Let's honor his memory, and honor the writers in this book, and honor the spirit and passion of writing anywhere, by enjoying the tales that follow.

*A*manda Updegraff doesn't waste any time letting us know what her quiet blue wheel is, but this metaphorical wheel permeates the life of the protagonist throughout. Most of us have those moments of desperation and futility in our lives, and we each deal with them in our own ways. Some of us run away from our problems; others of us face them. Perhaps the protagonist in this story does a little bit of both.

Appaloosa Night

Amanda M. Updegraff

She imagined all of life to be nothing more than the tragic turning of a great and silent blue wheel. Some days she imagined a tyrannical child obnoxiously spinning it, while others it seemed only the lackadaisical spiraling of a tide pool. All she really felt was that whatever this madness, it was beyond her understanding or control and it made her feel sick, exactly as she did as a child on a carousel riding a pretty horse on its infinite and absurd journey. She could not tell you if she wanted to get off the carousel. She loved her horse, she loved to ride; she just couldn't stand the queasy feeling that always resided within her, had become her constant companion, her very own self.

Sickness is another self, she thought. She desperately hoped for sickness because all diseases had cures — even those that hadn't yet been found. In the meantime, people wore brightly colored ribbons pinned to their chests in your honor. They donated money in order to help you and your helpless, pitiable cause. You had doctors who had gone through years of tortuous training, so that one day they could meet you — this unique and desperate patient who would make all their late, sleepless, coffee-stained nights spent trying to feel up nurses in the back office worth it. Worth it to be in a loveless marriage and drive a big nice car, live in a big nice house. To say, "I did do something after all. I did not just consume the world around me. I gave another human being life, if only for a brief and futile forty more years. I bestowed that utmost of gifts on another and for that I am godlike. I am charitable. I deserve not to die."

From earliest childhood she remembered feeling off-kilter, tilted, a dread of spinning, and the utter torment of the tire swing. She did not understand the other children holding hands and turning together in those awful circles, laughing and giggling until some poor meek one of them — the one who would assume he would inherit the earth but would really only inherit a life of making up, trying to be big through other means — a lawyer, a cop, a wall-street banker, whatever predilection he could turn into career — and watch out, here comes the big man now — would puke on his shoes. She knew she sounded cynical, she sounded bitter. Bitter at forty is acceptable; bitter at thirty is just lazy. A bitter flavor to cover up the rot.

Immersed in the water in her bathtub, s.She stared at her painted purple toes against the lime-green 7tile of her bathroom wall. Water covered her ears. Better to hear herself think — if "better" could be that distended gobbledygook, so much a perfect imitation of thought. The water was cold, her skin wrinkled.

She lay there.

The phone rang, loud and angry against the walls.

She lay there.

Then she got out and lay in her bed.

Another night passed and a day. Light marked the movement of time, the passage of worldly life. Dust specks traveled from one end of a shaft of light to the other. Her cells died and were reborn. She exchanged the entirety of her molecular self with all that is the universe. She lay in her bed. The phone rang.

The alarm buzzed. She walked to her car. A purple car, a green car—no, just the dull grey of reality: her car. She drove her grey car down the road and watched the breeze play frenetically with the tops of the trees. She thought, "They must get sick swaying back and forth like that. Never in control of their motion, except the steady quiet upward thrust of growth, until the quick, loud, resounding down of death."

At the stable, the horses had been fed. Their heads stuck out of their stalls, quietly watching her, each other, the distant activities of what she could never tell. She loved the quiet of the barn before the clients arrived. The loud stomping and whinnying of horses was movie myth. She liked knowing the truth of this one thing, of being able to see beyond what is told.

She opened her locker, dust matted to everything inside it. She thrust in her purse, hung up her keys. She took out her new helmet and stared at it, just for a moment, but long enough to remember.

When she had fallen, when they had fallen, she meant to say "No, I didn't mean it. I didn't mean all that suicidal ideation, not really, I was just tired. I want to try. I won't be so sad this time. I did feel something once, something that was more than the daily atrocities."

But now she knew those moments were few and far between, mainly in dreams, the dreams you don't want to wake up from. And as far as being sad—well, honey, nobody can make promises like that. Sadness just is. Learn to sit on it.

And perhaps in reply to her plea, the fire engine had come, small children gawked and parents ushered them away while turning their own heads to see. She had lain in an ambulance, a hospital bed, a gurney within the ambient blue cylinder of the MRI. A mere concussion, the ones people forget about, reduce to nothingness despite the lingering notion of something that should have been remembered being forgotten.

So she put on her helmet though she hated it and all it reminded her of. She hated that day plastered in fear against her insides, the day the one thing she had always trusted had betrayed her. But, of course, the horse hadn't betrayed her; he had just tripped, stubbed a toe like the clumsy adolescents she taught, so near her own childhood and so far away, their rainbow assortments of colored hair flowing by like a river of melted crayons. Sometimes, when she watched them, she wondered why she had never been like that—overflowing with what exactly she could not name, that thing that allowed them to put on their affectations like armor and wear them so steadfastly into the world. She tried to pick them out: this one to college, that one to the bars, this one to a nameless life of drugs and rehabilitation, that one to marry a man not-so-secretly gay.

But she was always wrong. This one turned up looking chic with a job in New York; that one worked as a secretary, a paralegal; that one married a guy, got pregnant, was never seen again and never rode again. Leaving the horses, she thought, never feeling the warm side of another creature, never giving oneself up, one's life completely to another without thought, without hesitation—so simple, like the putting on of clothing, like the taking off of clothing, a simple daily necessity—she could not imagine leaving that. And that lack of imaginative leap was precisely why she had never left, whether this was good, bad, or beyond the scope of either is nothing that can be judged. Some things in life are like truths: big, heavy objects to be walked around.

And so she went on with her day, the seemingly endless stream of children, her well practiced stance, her harsh and encouraging voice thrown out to them, to guide them on in this moment, in their future. She watched their legs flap against the sides of their horses, their feet dangling in stirrups, and she hoped for them not to fall. She hoped for the horses to be good and trustworthy. She was glad the sun stayed out all day. She did not mind the sweat. As the dirt filled the cracks of her skin and her voice grew tired, she forgot the nighttime, her barren kitchen table, her sagging couch, her ever-enticing television.

And eventually with the depth of heat came the quiet afternoon. The children and their doting parents had gone off to practice some other sport, some other life-enriching activity about which they could tell their own children. Another form of structured positivism to ward off the evils of sloth, diabetes, creativity.

The idea of these schedules, all the endless timekeeping, the ticking off of this hour for the next even in the early fog of childhood aroused her dizziness, and the only cure for dizziness was motion. If she just ran atop the wheel, her brown hair blown back by the wind in her face, she might not notice the turning, like we forget the turning of the earth, the revolutions of orbit, the full and incomprehensible wheeling of the galaxy, the expanding universe and what impossibilities might lie beyond it.

She walked to the stall of her favorite horse, Dallas, who was not her horse and would never be her horse. He was too fancy, too expensive, the arbitrary movements of his legs placing him in a category of importance, because anything having is worth judging. She groomed him, running the bristled brush across his delicate fur and not-so-delicate hide. She ran her other hand behind it, feeling for any leftover speck of dirt, any errant molecule to harm him beneath the tack she so unceremoniously put upon him. She wished to ride bareback, with no halter, no bridle, in a loincloth. She wished to gallop across the city park, her breasts bared to the world as an affront to their reasonableness, the iniquity of their prudence, their modesty. But she was modest. Or if not exactly modest, she was shy. And she was afraid. Fear was her new suitor. She tried to ignore him, like a man at a bar who will not get the hint.

So she would use saddle, bridle, and cold metal bit, all

intimations of control. She rode out into the field beyond the barn, the ten acres that substituted for openness, wildness, freedom. Today, Dallas was excited. She could feel his back arched, pressed up against the saddle, his energy jittering up his legs and into her body. She was glad for him to feel this way. She felt empty, neutral, a lack of anything particular. The particularness of something was the essence of a thing itself. She didn't mind borrowing.

She and Dallas walked their routine path of the perimeter of the enclosure. She played voyeur: She peered into the unoccupied houses, she dreamed of the lives they contained but found them as uninteresting as her own, and rode on. They trotted, cantered. She asked of Dallas to let her mold him, for him to give her control of this muscle, that movement; and through his excitement, his barely contained energy, he consented. She jumped the solid wooden obstacles interspersed among the field, the sparse trees. She smiled; she knew she did, but she forgot it quickly too.

When she had worked him, as his owner would have liked—a slight sweat beneath the saddle, supple foam in his mouth—she walked him again near the fence. He stretched his neck out and down, ears pricked, relaxed, attentive. They walked around once but she did not want to get off, to go and work the small pony that had run off with its child the week before. She did not want to fight with it, to reprimand it for its naughtiness—for its inability to conform to the whims of the very creatures that had stolen it from the moors of Ireland and replaced the beauty of soft, verdant, and rolling fields with the sweltering Texas heat and dry, brown, brittle hay. So she began her circumnavigation again and saw a break in the fence bordered by two trees. Her first thought of surprise that the horses left out to graze had not escaped was quickly replaced by a calculation of width and possibility.

Dallas squeezed through the opening and they sat on the other side, amidst the mown lawns, the manicured scrubs, the watered plants that had stolen the life of the Colorado, the Rio Grande, the ancient limestone aquifers.

She blinked in the sunlight. Faint whispers of "Go back" rustled in her mind. But she was reminded of her childhood home, the dark backyards that abutted her own, and the cover of their trees. She would climb her fence, crawl within the shadows down the side yards, and run, bursting forth onto the street. Only then would she glance back at the home she had violated. She would laugh and feel dangerous.

So she rode on, picking her way through flowerbeds, gravel walkways. Eventually, she tired of this game and steered Dallas out onto the concrete road. Each of Dallas' steps echoed with the metal ringing that has been so perfectly reproduced on the sound stages of Hollywood. Old women opened their screen doors to peer at her riding by. Some children momentarily paused in comical repose, water streaming from garden hose. They, of course, had heard the occasional distant whinny from the nearby stable but dismissed it, as part of the many dreams grownups said were not real. Horses belonged on farms, on ranches, on desert stretches with men in cowboy hats and leather leggings. But there she was in the August sun, a summer's afternoon in the city.

For the first time in her life she did not mind people staring at her; they were not her subjects, but they were not of her world either, just strange creatures. When she looked at their dark and gleaming eyes, she saw only blankness, a stale passivity that surprised her. She thought Dallas magnificent though she had never gone in for the "majestic beast" sort of thing that non-horse-people seemed to imagine — fairy-tale beasts, like dragons or unicorns. Dallas, though, with his shining red coat, his thick arched neck, his massive size — she had fallen in love with him.

For the first hour she hardly thought about what she was doing. No one would think about her. They would just assume she was out working a horse somewhere else on the property.

But after two hours, two hours of riding away, she wondered what exactly she was doing, where she was going, but did not turn around.

Dallas seemed unperturbed. They crossed a simple creek. He drank. The sun sank lower in the sky, a hand's width above the horizon, a finger's, and then only the fading ambient glow of light traveling for eight minutes to the eyes of earth. They went on.

The darkness came before the city turned on. For a brief and wonderful few minutes, the skyline, the road, the houses around her, Dallas below her were all covered in the heavy stillness of night and dark. The moon still hid below the horizon. Her eyes hurt and strained to see grey delineations of this thing or that. She turned away from porch lights, glowing kitchen windows.

The steady rolling hills lay ahead. Rocks and brush to be ridden over and around and no light, nothing to feed the eyes, her vision where she instinctively felt that all of consciousness might lie. Because with eyes closed there were only dreams; she did not trust her unworthy nerves, their unreliability so proven in moments of pain or pleasure. What vision held seemed the only true testing ground, for only eyes had no ulterior motives.

But soon enough, the moon rose and the city said hello to the nighttime. Girls in tight black pants, red high heels, and draped and fragile tops would totter out into the world, claiming it not only as their own, but feeling so... so something about all those regular people who got up with the sun and lay down with the moon and had forgotten the wonders of the night and all its human possibilities. The Texas clouds gathered to reflect all of this light back down in a pale and glowing purple.

The night was not cold. The heat merely faded and she was comfortable in her tall boots, her breeches (ones made to ride in, not to attend gallery openings in New York in), her plaid long-sleeved shirt—her silent rebellion and quiet harkening to the West. Dallas nibbled politely a bit of fertilized grass here and there when she stopped to decide where to turn. Generally they were partners in their journey. A hint of motion this way, a suggestion of that and so on they rode, vaguely south, southeast. Perhaps in the recesses of thought, they heard the ocean waves.

In this way they travelled past the city and into the suburbs, the land of palatial houses, the substitute for American nobility; the quaint farmhouses, now havens for metropolitan refugees. And then out into the open acres, preserved by millionaires, their own private Africas. And indeed they rode by antelope, kudu, aoudads, and zebras, their white stripes aglow in the bright moonlight. The exotic animals came out to their high and impenetrable fences to watch the interesting specimen of girl and horse in the night before the coming of the day to await once again the fate assigned to them by the great hunters who stocked them like fish in a pond.

She rode on the side of these pastures, but sometimes the limestone would break free from its earthen blanket and she would take again to the two-lane highway. When at last they came to a barbed-wire fence in disrepair, they set out away from the road through the mesquite trees that tried to tear her clothing from her, the small and viscous cacti, the gramma grass.

She fell into a dazed rhythm, oblivious to everything but the steady back and forth of Dallas' shifting legs. She thought of nothing. She dreamed of nothing. She only rode, becoming nothing but her body, until Dallas stopped abruptly, neck stiff, head up, a quick deep exhale, watching. For a moment she saw nothing, and then she could pick out between two cedar trees a blurry, light-colored something. Dallas whinnied. The white spot whinnied back. And so they circled slowly closer to the small and dirty appaloosa.

Mud was caked on his legs. His mane and forelock where

thick and full, matted into dreadlocks. His dark tail was short and rubbed off nearly to its base. She could not tell in the darkness where the mud ended and his spots began across his white hair. She dismounted Dallas and walked to the appaloosa. He held his head low and only tilted his chin slightly at her approach. A thick nylon halter, once red, now faded pink, hung on his head, cactus spines large and small embedded in the fabric. She reached out to his shoulder. His skin rippled and shuddered slightly at the approach of her hand, but quickly quieted. She took off her two-hundred-dollar silk pink-and-green polka-dotted ribbon belt and pulled it through the metal ring and the base of his halter. She petted him, scratched him, reached under his mane to the warm smooth fur untouched by grime. She let go of the belt briefly to mount Dallas and then picked it up again. She noticed how calmly he stood.

Tired Dallas balked and dragged himself, in all his eloquent movement. He became petulant and pawed the ground. He did not appreciate this little ugly thing walking so closely next to him. The appaloosa took no notice or offense.

Over this scene of girl and horses, the first rays of morning broke up and over the hillsides, the tentative omens of another day. And now, with her new companion, they rode home. Slowly.

Eventually, Dallas gave up his adolescent grumbling and acquiesced to his new companion and on they went. He was hungry for grain, lonely for his stall and the horses beside him. The appaloosa seemed almost oblivious to the activity and merely walked patiently, stopped patiently, and continued, stretching his legs to meet Dallas' stride. She watched her new horse walk beside Dallas through the morning. She decided to name him Bodhi .

And this was the night, just another passing of a night. Drunken adolescents fornicated and then crashed their cars headlong into soccer moms driving home late from unhappily ended affairs. Pregnant women gave birth, girlfriends called boyfriends, teachers unfairly graded papers, and judges longed for fairness but knew they would awaken only to a courtroom and the cruelty of humanity's judgment. This was just another turning of the wheel, its blue silence deposited into all things.

For her, she could not tell if this night were any different. Had she ever truly spent a night otherwise? It could have been that she had lived her whole life this way, riding the endless plains. Or it could have been that her dreams had become life. Or that she had merely awoken and now could see that there had never been any real difference to begin with between dreams and reality. There was only a veil laid over her eyes by her parents, her well-meaning mentors, teachers, coaches, and librarians, who too wore veils. And now she could become like those atop the mountains—the men with long beards and crazed eyes, the women hidden under cloaks with strained and screeching voices—like those for whom madness had come not like a mask but a revelation.

She reached the barn road near sunset. Again she snuck through yards and fences. This time she had no audience, except a cat perched atop the back of a couch, watching with the same disinterested stare with which it watched the entire world go by, on the other side of paned glass. When she reached the small stand of oak trees that had hidden heir initial escape, she did not bother to tie Bodhi. She just let the belt hang from his halter and he stood still with only the slight swish of tail or twitch of ear.

She undid Dallas' tack and laid it on the ground. She held his head and petted him, whispered in his ear as he stared ardently towards home, and then she walked him back into the open pasture and let him go. For a moment he looked back at her and she thought she might have been wrong about the animal heart, but then he turned and galloped towards the barn, his evening grain hours late.

She leaned against Bodhi's warm body and unconsciously

worked the caked mud from his mane with her fingers. When heavy darkness descended she walked across the pasture herself.

She went back to her barn locker that for years had marked her territory. She pulled out her oversized purple leather hobo purse and emptied it, keeping nothing but a twenty-dollar bill. She replaced billfold, cell phone, appointment book, and pink shimmering ChapStick with brush, hoof pick, and a bag of carrots.

She went to the medicine room and put gauze, vet wrap, butemine, banamine, and antiseptic in her purse. The jacket of one of the Mexican barn workers hung on a hook. She put it on and pushed the twenty-dollar bill onto the hook. She draped her purse over her shoulder and across her body.

During her gathering rounds she heard a loud squeal from the far ring, and then peals of hysterical laughter. Some of the teenage girls, drunk again, were chasing around their horses, or falling off into water troughs. They would not notice her. They would not care. She did not enter into their consciousness anymore than starving children in India, the denial of homosexuals' rights, the extinction of the polar bear.

She walked assuredly through the barn aisles, one more time past Dallas in his stall, already groomed, placidly eating his extra alfalfa treat. He did not raise his head; she did not stop to pet him. But she did stop at the Irish pony's stall. Hanging next to the door was a halter made of the softest leather, and from it a long luxurious purple lead rope. She took this too and marched back to where Bodhi waited as still as when she had first left him, only his rear left leg cocked for comfort. He perked his ears at her and gave a slight nicker. She gave him a carrot.

She tacked Bodhi up. The white of his coat looked yellow next to the clean white of her saddle pads. She briefly calculated the monetary value of her saddle against that of the horse on which she placed it, but stopped. And with her polished tack atop Bodhi, halter for bridle, she set out again across the city, this time south and west.

If anyone saw her that night, they never said. Or perhaps they could not believe it. She had become an apparition in the night.

Her apartment stood empty, her car unmoved. Her cell phone, battery long dead, did not ring. People wondered where she was but not in earnest for many days. Dallas' disappearance and reappearance had caused a stir but mainly of insurance paperwork and the drying of eyes of little girls who would never ride him, or any horse like him, but took lessons nonetheless, acting out the books their overweight mothers gave them and dreaming of a gallant steeds to steal them away. The two disappearances were not connected. Eventually, though, too many lessons went untaught; too many parents wondered why their children's teacher could no longer bother to show up. A mental breakdown day here and there was one thing, but they had tennis lessons to go to. Phone calls were made to the barn owners, and eventually to old emergency-contact numbers.

Divorced parents unearthed themselves from careers, flew down separately, flew home after a week. Police were called but no one knew how to describe her, what to relate to the well -meaning but perhaps over-earnest young officer. They described her shiny long brown hair, her authoritative posture, her well-fitting jeans. They described her aptitude for tardiness, her not-infrequent sick days. They described her darkly tanned skin, her brand-name sunglasses. They did not describe her eyes. They did not describe a helmeted woman in an oversized coat, breeches, tall leather boots, laden with heavy bag, astride a red-spotted appaloosa.

For a brief time, she was news, a five-minute spot on the local television station. There were pink-and-green polka-dotted ribbons pinned to a few ample breasts: Bring Andrea

Home. A high-school boyfriend broke down in uncontrollable sobs and embarrassed himself at work only to go home to his girlfriend who petted his head and praised him for his compassion. Candles, wreaths, and teddy bears were set out in front of her barn locker only to be removed as a fire and tripping hazards.

After a time, a friend cleaned out her apartment. Sad little baskets of tampons, unopened makeup cases, and fingernail polish. Unread, overdue library books, coffee-stained bills, unvacuumed floors, laundry baskets full of clothes imitating the ones of twenty-something college freshmen. Photo albums full of people she no longer knew, horses she had ridden. Maybe there had once been a journal, but it was lost or ignored or overlooked in the shuffle.

Sometimes people talked, shook their heads at the waste of it all, a young life taken. Potential, they said. Potential for what exactly, they could not say. Sometimes Dallas wondered about the lack of the familiar feel of her legs, her particular tension from reins to bit. Someone said something about a turning wheel. Some people looked west into the sunset and didn't know why. But mostly, people didn't.

And things like this happen in cities; women disappear while jogging, while driving to work, while shopping. They are never found again. Questions go unanswered, and people eventually accept it, like the disappearance of their socks from the dryer.

If Philip Marlowe were an Irish cop in Boston, the character you're about to meet might well be him. But unlike Chandler's larger-than-life detective, this hard-boiled cop isn't quite as invincible, as he's been hit with a pair of traumas that forever changed his life. Charles O'Leary lets us ride along for the journey his damaged hero takes, which quickly moves from its opening detective-noir feel to a more relaxed mystery in Maine, where a work of art might feature a blue wheel... and it isn't talking.

Her Room

Charles J. O'Leary

I was a cop. My father and his father were cops, too. This was the way with the Boston Irish. You followed the trade. If your father was a plumber, you were a plumber; if your father was a brick mason, you were a brick mason. Well, my father was a cop. I'm not complaining; there were advantages. You never lost your job because of market conditions and you never lost your job because they invented something new. You didn't have to worry about the color of your tie or the cut of your suit. We always wore blue, and humanity hadn't changed in a million years. People still beat, murdered, and stole from each other. Murderers, rapists, and thieves were our stock in trade.

I was a cop, but for the last seven months I've been a civilian—or, to be clear, a retired cop... a retired cop with a disability. I have post-traumatic stress disorder. There are a lot of veterans of the Iraq War or Afghanistan that have PTSD. Theirs resulted from road bombs or violent combat. Mine was the result of a dispatcher's mistake.

On February 4, 2009, I was working out of the Bureau of Domestic Services of the Boston Police Department. At 2:57 a.m. I received a call from dispatch sending me to an address on the Boston-Brookline line for a domestic disturbance. When I arrived at the address there was a car with blue lights flashing; I was not the first on the scene. Sergeant Bill Riley, a cop I knew from the old neighborhood, was standing by the entry to a basement-level apartment, the kind that has three windows at sidewalk level and three at the back that looked out on an alley. As I started down the stairs, Riley said: "Lieutenant Foley, this is a bad one."

I should have known when he called me by grade that he was sending a signal. A mick cop never addressed another mick cop by grade. This was as bad as it gets in police work.

I walked into a large room that served as a dining room, sitting room, and kitchen. In the dining area was a female, mid-thirties, Caucasian, her hands tied with electrical cord and the bottom half of her face missing. As I looked closer, I saw that it was not missing but spread on the wall to her right. She had multiple wounds on her torso, probably stab wounds. To her left and in front of the kitchen sink was a male, Caucasian, late thirties, with a large and bloody hole in his chest. This was not a domestic disturbance; this was double homicide.

I went to the rear of the apartment and found a room that had been decorated as a child's room. There were Disney murals on three of the walls; Donald and Mickey were looking straight ahead, but Goofy was drawn facing the children's beds. There was a nightstand with two glasses of water and a Dr. Seuss book, the one he wrote about green eggs and ham. The blue walls and the nightlight gave a glow to a boy, maybe age twelve, and a girl of about seven. The boy had been shot once in the back of the head. The girl, wearing pajamas with a sailboat design, was on the bed opposite the boy. Both were covered with blood. Her carotid artery and jugular vein had been cut with such violence that the small muscle above them was hanging apart from her body. A pool of blood had accumulated on the floor.

I looked at the wound and the blood, thinking that she probably bled out in three or four minutes. I had to get out of the apartment. I sat in my car. First I vomited, and then I cried.

Why had I been called? This was not domestic violence — this was a multiple murder. Fate and a mistaken dispatcher had left me with a vivid, traumatic memory I would not forget.

* * *

Depression is worse than death. Death has finality to it. It's over. Depression goes on forever. At the very least, you think it's going to last forever. It is a detached loneliness that immobilizes you.

For five days after I visited the homicide scene, I played solitaire on the computer. I didn't answer the phone, I didn't watch television, I didn't go out, and I didn't eat. Well, I didn't eat much. A stale doughnut, a piece of cold pizza, or a peanut-butter sandwich would do. I didn't choose to be that way; it was just the way it was. Sitting in my house on the Cape waiting for the world to go away.

On the fifth day, I woke up and started thinking of Ann and how this would have been our twentieth wedding anniversary if that miserable bastard hadn't killed her. Just a guy drinking all afternoon with his buddies who gets in his car and arrives at the Bourne Bridge precisely and on time to kill the woman I loved. As I tried to cope with this day, I thought to myself, *Oh Jesus how I would love a drink. God grant me the serenity to accept the things I cannot change... Oh Jesus, Jesus, Jesus how I want a drink. Ann, I miss you. Help me, dear Jesus, help me...*

Then I heard one hell of a racket coming from outside the house. Somebody was pounding on the door and calling my name.

"Pat! Pat, are you in there?"

Shit. There was Charlie Boyle pounding and yelling. Charlie is my oldest friend — maybe my only friend, but not someone I wanted to see right now. He wasn't going away, and I'd have to make some kind of a response. I thought fleetingly about getting my service revolver and scaring him away. There was no escape; I had to answer him.

"Charlie, stop your goddamn pounding," I said, throwing open the door. "I'm right here."

"Right here, my ass," he growled as he pushed past me and into the house. "If you were right here you'd answer your phone. If you were right here you'd answer the door when someone rings the bell."

Charlie went into the bedroom, opened the closet, picked up a suitcase and started packing my clothes. "You're going on a trip."

"What are you talking about?"

"I'm talking about you and your schedule," he said as he latched up the suitcase and turned back to me with that hard look on his face. "This is the way it is. Your friend, Alley McFarland, wants you to meet with a woman named Ellen Stratton at four o'clock this afternoon at Prouts Neck in Maine. Reservations have been made for tonight at the Kimble Inn. That means reservations just for you, not the woman. The next day you'll go to Rockland to meet with Alley."

Charlie was acting like the drill sergeant he had once been, and directing his orders at me. At least, for the moment, I wasn't thinking about drinking; I was thinking about Charlie kicking my ass if I didn't do what he said.

Alley McFarland is director of one of the most respected small museums in New England: the Farnsworth in Rockland, Maine. He is a Rhodes Scholar and an expert on American artists. I've known him since his undergraduate days at Harvard. At that time, I was a patrolman taking night courses and he was a student getting an extra credit. The course we took was American Artists of the Twentieth Century. We formed a friendship that has lasted all these years.

The McFarlands of Jonesboro first came to America in the

early eighteenth century. They were the Scotch-Irish who settled in Maine, hunkered down for the winter, fought the Indians, and stayed. They became the old Yankee establishment. Alley's father and his grandfather had both gone to Harvard, and that was the route they had chosen for Alley. That's what old Yankees do.

I got in my 1997 Ford Explorer and started for Maine. I was too tired to fight this assault by my friends and I had several nagging questions that were picking at me. How had Charlie and Alley planned this trip? Who was Ellen Stratton, and why did Alley want me to meet her? Questions that needed pondering, and this was the time to ponder, because the drive from South Yarmouth to Scarborough is not a scenic one. As you pass through New Hampshire, you see one golf course that breaks the monotony. The state of New Hampshire gets your attention by charging a toll for using all sixteen miles of their interstate highway. This toll has increased over the years, and after I paid it I spent the rest of the trip being pissed off about it.

The Kimble Inn imitates the grand hotels that were common to the coast at the beginning of the twentieth century. When you first see it, you're impressed by the size and awed by that many cedar shingles. It has a weathered and welcoming façade. The grand motif continues as you enter. Thick red carpets and shining brass are common. There is a large fireplace in the lobby and a print of *Eight Bells* by Winslow Homer, depicting a pair of sailors taking their bearings on the deck of a ship amidst a growing storm.

I checked in and went to my room just in time to answer a ringing phone. It was Ellen Stratton saying she'd meet me in the lobby in fifteen minutes. She said I should look for a middle-aged woman in a gray suit. I should have looked for a very attractive woman in a gray suit. Ellen Stratton was tall, thin, and beautiful. She had black hair, shoulder length, tied back with a white ribbon. She was not what I expected.

"Hi, I'm Ellen Stratton," she greeted me with a smile. "Alley described you perfectly. He said you'd look tired but carry yourself like a Marine."

I liked her greeting and loved her smile. I was nervous and a bit awkward. I hadn't talked with a woman for several months. The last one I talked with was my sister Doris. Not a very good prep for this occasion.

"I'm... I'm pleased to meet you, Ellen," I stammered. "But I have no idea why Alley was so eager for us to get together."

"Alley knows that I was a docent at the Winslow Homer studio," she explained. "He knows that you're interested in American artists of the twentieth century, so he put those two together and asked if I would be your guide for what he thought would be a real treat for you. So, are you ready to take a short walk with me?"

I saw that the November shadows were getting longer at this time of day, but I thought I'd go anywhere with this woman, even if it were completely dark.

"It would be great to walk with you," I said, "and I appreciate your thoughtfulness."

We walked a short way and found the shore path to the Homer studio. As we walked on the fine-gravel trail, the saltiness of the ocean air in my nose, Ellen talked of Homer and his time at Prout's Neck. She told me two stories she said were urban legends.

The first story was about Homer being very poor when he first came to Maine, and he gave some of his canvases to his landlord to cover the rent. The landlord, being a kind man but not especially interested in art, told his son to take them to the dump. Rather than discard the paintings, the son saved them, and in later years sold them for a small fortune.

"If you believe that, you'll probably believe this," Ellen said as we passed a stand of white birches amongst the pines. "Supposedly, there's a missing Homer painting called

Blue Wheel. It's not known whether this painting was stolen or lost, but people have described it. There's a farmhouse and barn in the background, and a long drive with a great blue wheel at the entrance. Can you imagine what it would be worth today?"

"Probably a lot more than the kid made from the paintings he was supposed to take to the dump," I said.

Ellen smiled at the remark as we arrived at the studio. She showed me the table where Homer had mixed his paint and pointed out the sextant that had been the model for *Eight Bells.* In a private part of the house, she pointed to a wheel that Homer had salvaged from a wrecked ship. It's said that he kept this wheel over his mantel.

I closed my eyes and tried to imagine the grand master working in this place. For a moment, I felt a reverence and tranquility I usually associated with a cathedral.

It was dark when we started back along the shore path and, in several narrow spots, I offered my hand to steady Ellen. She took it and each time thanked me. There was something about Ellen that made me feel good. She had a manner and way of moving that made her attractive. Feeling good was a new experience for me

When we returned to the inn I thanked Ellen for the tour and her stories of the artist.

"Alley thought this would be a good break for you and a way to start thinking about art and artists again," she said. "Get some rest, Pat, and drive with care." She leaned forward and kissed my cheek.

Blushing like a schoolboy on his first date, I managed to thank her, and walked her to the car.

I had a good feeling as I got into bed. I looked forward to sleep. I hadn't slept well for a month and I welcomed this surrender. There were no dreams for the first seven hours, but toward morning the dream came.

In the dream I was looking into the room. I could see the characters Donald, Mickey, and Goofy. Goofy was telling me to look at the girl. The girl in the sailboat pajamas was sleeping on her stomach. Ann came into the room and turned the child over. The wound was horrible and the muscle was just hanging there. I turned toward Ann for comfort but she walked away. Then she turned back to me, and she was covered in blood. I screamed

I woke with a chill and felt disoriented. The room was unfamiliar.

"Where the hell am I?" I said aloud.

The phone was ringing. I looked at it, still disoriented, and picked up the receiver.

"This is the front desk. Are you all right, Mr. Foley?"

"Yes, I'm fine. I had a bad dream."

"We were just checking. Have a good night."

I looked at the digital clock. The only thing that was out of place at the inn was that clock. They should have clocks with hands. It was 5:05 a.m.—too early to get up, and I had too much anxiety to go back to sleep. I went to find some coffee. There was a big silver pot in the lobby and I had two cups. I packed my bag, checked out, went to the Explorer, and sat behind the wheel. I thought of the events of the last year. A drunk driver had killed my wife, a schoolteacher at the Braintree Middle School, as she came off the Bourne Bridge. Some guy who spent Friday afternoon in a Hyannis bar drinking while Ann was correcting papers. Was it fate that brought these two together, and was it fate that sent me to the blue room and the child?

I knew I was in bad shape. The depression, the dreams, and the loss of appetite were all bad signs. Yet for a few moments last night I had felt good. I had enjoyed Ellen's company and our talk of art. Art had saved me many times as I walked the corridors of the Boston Museum of Fine Arts on Huntington Avenue. It was my refuge from police work; I called it my sanctuary. Maybe there was hope. The therapist had said it would take time, but there was hope, and I would get better.

It was early, and the time of day and the time of the year meant light traffic. I drove through Scarborough, South Portland, and Portland, anticipating the scenery on Route 1. It wasn't until I got to Bath that I saw wider vistas. As I crossed the bridge, I saw two Navy destroyers docked for repairs at Bath Iron Works. The Kennebec River widens at this point, and I could see several sailboats at their moorings. Continuing on through Wiscasset, Newcastle, and Damariscotta, I saw many places an artist might place his easel. I realized the driving and scenery were having a calming effect. Was this all part of Alley McFarland's plan? If this was the prescription that had been written for me, it was starting to work. Thinking of the artist and the woman, and looking at this magnificent place, was okay. I felt good and I would enjoy the feeling. Capture the moment.

I drove until I came to Thomaston. At that point I needed to stretch my legs and get a fresh cup of coffee. Caffeine was the last of my addictions. I found a diner called The Mariner, where they still had barstools. I ordered a coffee and slice of blueberry pie, the house specialty.

It came, as it always had, without warning—a mood change so sudden it seemed as if the sun had set. I felt that I was in a dark place isolated and alone. I sat staring at the untouched blueberry pie.

"Is there something wrong with the pie?" asked a waitress who looked like she might have served the original settlers of Thomaston.

"No, there's nothing wrong with the pie. My stomach just felt a little queasy."

"I'll get you some water. Should have got it when you first

sat down, but this place has been so darn busy. Parent conferences at the school. Mom and Dad come in for pie after they hear how bad their little Johnnie has been doing."

But I was gone before she could return with the water.

It was late in the day when I realized I was looking at the dashboard of the Explorer. I had no idea how long I had been in the parking lot of a Renys department store. Disoriented and confused, I fumbled for my phone and called Alley McFarland. At the sound of his voice I felt an immediate and pleasant sensation.

"There are only two people who have this number," he said. "Pat Foley, you're one of them. Where are you?"

"I'm in Thomaston, Alley. Sorry I didn't get here sooner, but I've had some problems."

"I know you've had problems. That's why I want to see you. Where are you in Thomaston?"

"I'm in the parking lot of a discount department store called Renys."

"Stay right there. I know exactly where you are. I'll pick you up. You can leave your car right where it is. I know the manager there, and the chief of police is a Lodge brother of mine."

Fifteen minutes later Alley, driving a black Lexus, pulled in next to the Explorer. Fifteen minutes after that we were sitting on the deck of a small white cape looking out at the bay. Alley was enjoying a glass of bourbon and I was sipping on a Diet Coke.

"Pat, you can stay here tonight, and tomorrow we'll get you settled in a place with a bay view," he said. "I have an apartment we use for visiting artists. November is a good time to be apartment hunting. There aren't many people that want to stay in Maine for the winter. You'll have your pick of some beautiful views, and if you sign a twelve-month lease the price will be right. In the morning, I want to have a talk with you about your illness and what we can do."

Why was everyone telling me what to do? First it was Charlie, and now Alley. I wondered, too, why Alley was talking about a twelve-month lease. With a house in Massachusetts, why would I need an apartment in Maine?

I went out to dinner with Alley, who explained that his wife had been gone for several days visiting a friend and the meal would be better if he didn't cook. The dinner was what Alley called home cooking: meatloaf and potatoes. We talked about baseball, the weather, recent exhibits at the museum, and a book Alley was working on. It was light conversation and as relaxing as it could be.

I was exhausted when we returned to the house and looked forward to some rest. Alley had a fine guest room with a king-sized bed and a private bath. There was a painting by a local artist that presented a bird's-eye view of Rockland, and I admired the detail. I started to read a bedside book on New England but soon fell asleep. Then the dream came.

In the dream, I was looking into her room, seeing the child. The wound on her neck was bleeding, and I could see her chest rise and fall as her heart continued to pump blood. I reached for her and tried to stop the bleeding. But I couldn't—I couldn't stop the bleeding. The blood on the floor was rising over my shoes—

I woke up and sat upright in a panic. My heart was pounding in my chest. I was sweating and my hands were shaking. I turned on the light next to the bed to orientate myself to the room.

I got up to go to the bathroom. This nightmare left me feeling drained and depleted. After walking around the bedroom, I went back to bed thinking I would never sleep. To my surprise, I closed my eyes and slept soundly and without another dream.

*　*　*

Alley had cleared his calendar. Today, there were to be no interruptions; today, he had some business to conduct with me. We sat in the director's office. The décor fitted the title of museum director. It was a small office with two leather chairs and a small leather couch. There was a colorful antique oriental rug on the floor. A large, colorful scene of the ocean at sunset, done in oils and in a gold frame, was the only decoration on the white walls. It was a plush, elegant space. I sat on the couch, facing Alley.

"Let me start by asking you about Ellen Stratton," I began. "I enjoyed meeting her, and I'd like to know more about her."

"Ellen is a widow," he told me. "Her husband was a fisherman who was lost at sea four years ago this past September. Ellen went back to school and finished her degree. I met her when she took a class I was teaching at the University College at Rockland. She's a delightful and talented woman. Occasionally I ask her to do some work for me; she writes a very good press release and has helped the museum. She works part-time in the Scarborough school system teaching art. When she's not doing that, she works at the inn as a Jill of all trades. She gives directions, recommends restaurants, and gives guided tours to my friends."

"She's delightful, and I enjoyed her stories," I said. "She told me one about Homer's poverty when he first came to Maine, and another about one of his lost paintings. As you know, the first one's bunk. Homer's family was quite wealthy, and by the time he came to Maine he was a successful artist. What do you think of the lost painting?"

"Anything's possible, but there's no historical evidence to support the story. There are rumors of preliminary sketches, but no one has ever seen any. Now, having said that, some private collector could be looking at *Blue Wheel* as we speak — but I doubt it. All of Winslow Homer's paintings are accounted for."

Alley paused, collected his thoughts, and went on. "The art world is full of imitators, fabricators, thieves, and murderers. It's not a place for amateurs. Remember, it was only nineteen years ago that the largest art theft in world history took place. On March 18, 1990, thieves stole thirteen pieces collectively worth five hundred million from the Isabella Stewart Gardner Museum in Boston. A five-million-dollar reward is still offered for information leading to their return. Only last year, paintings including a Van Gogh and a Monet were stolen from a foundation in Zurich. Their worth was one hundred sixty-three million. Museum guards have been killed during art thefts—and do you realize that international terrorists often use art pieces as collateral in gun smuggling and drug deals?"

"Why are you telling me this?" I asked.

"I'm telling you all of this by way of background and because I want you to come to work for the museum," he said, then held up his hand. "No—I want you to come to work for *me*."

I must have looked as if I had seen an apparition; it was as if the Holy Ghost himself had appeared to me. I hadn't expected a job offer. I hadn't come looking for a job and I wasn't sure I could accept this offer.

"Jesus, Alley, I'm not sure I can come to work for you or for anybody else," I said. "I'm not in very good shape. Oh, I'm not drinking or anything like that, but I've been pretty screwed up. I've had severe depression for the last year. I have trouble sleeping, and when I do sleep I have horrible dreams. I'm exhausted most of the time. Are you sure you want to hire someone like that?"

Alley had clearly anticipated my response, and I sensed he was choosing his words carefully. "I know this has been a difficult year for you. Ann's death must have crushed you." He looked long and hard at me. "And Charlie told me about the child's murder in Brookline. This job and a change of scenery will help you to move on. Because it's time to move on. I've arranged for you to see a psychotherapist who deals exclusively with PTSD — she's one of the best in the country, and she lives in Camden. I want to do everything I can to speed up your recovery. I'll help you, but you've got to help me. Tell me you'll take the job at least for a year."

"I'll take it," I said, and I was surprised at my response and my eagerness. I extended my hand, but Alley would have none of that, instead wrapping his arms around me.

"Thank you, Pat," he said. "You have no idea what a relief this is to me. Now that you're an employee, I can show you something, and not violate regulations or jeopardize our insurance. Follow me."

Alley led me out of the office and down a stairwell to the basement. There was a steel door that required a security code. Alley punched in the code and we entered a room. Several hundred paintings, all numbered and arranged neatly in rows, ran to the back of the building. Except for one: It rested on a stand and was carefully covered with a cloth. With a flourish Alley removed the covering.

"Behold!"

I was stunned. Before me was a magnificent watercolor with a farmhouse, a barn, and a long driveway rich with the golden colors of autumn. At the end of the drive, a blue wheel stood at the entrance.

"Oh, my God!" I exclaimed. "Is it real? Is it the missing Homer?"

"No, it's a fake. But a pretty good one; the artist knew his Homer, and he used old wood and paint that mimics those from the turn of the century. Unfortunately, the canvas has a Portland name on it, and it's dated June 2002. I was tipped off that it was over at a farmhouse in Lincolnville. I went over and bought it; not for the asking price of a hundred thousand, but I did give him a hundred bucks. I thought maybe I'd hang it in my living room and we could invite Ellen over for dinner."

I laughed and thought of the surprise Ellen would have when she saw it.

Alley excused himself. "I've got some paperwork that has to be finished today. Why don't you walk around the museum and check the other buildings? It will be your responsibility. No time to start like the present."

Late in the day, the museum was empty. The November cold and the hour had kept patrons away. I walked to a room that held a single painting. It was *Her Room* by Andrew Wyeth. In 1965, the directors of the museum had purchased it for sixty-five thousand. At the time of purchase it was the highest price every paid for the work of a living artist. It would cost much more today, but I wasn't thinking of the value or the history of the painting. I was paralyzed by its beauty. The simple lines and the soft tone Wyeth captured with his use of tempera and the pink curtains that seemed to blow with a gentle breeze. The view of the ocean and the brightness of the day presented a panorama of peace and quiet. A painting that gave me a feeling of peace, I stood for several minutes seeking sanctuary in the scene. The feeling reminded me of the days when I was a young patrolman who had gone to the Museum of Fine Arts to find quiet from the everyday turmoil of his shift.

As I stood there I realized that I had gone from despondency to joy and then to fear. I had revisited the death of my wife and the horror of the homicide. But for the first time I was beginning to feel that perhaps I could move on. The demons were still there, I knew that. They would haunt me during the day and then again at night. But there was something else now; I felt joy and the goodness of friendship. I was returning to life, no longer alone. I whispered the serenity prayer:

"God grant me the serenity to accept the thing I cannot change, the courage to change the things I can, and the wisdom to know the difference."

As I repeated the words, they felt real this time. I was learning acceptance. Ann was gone. I had seen death at its worst. I felt hope. Hope not only for myself, but for a world that might have a lost painting called the Blue Wheel—and someday that painting would be found and bring us all joy.

*J*osh Updegraff knew from the beginning his story would involve a miniature elephant, and having a miniature elephant for a protagonist isn't like having just about any other character as a protagonist. Raja's quiet blue wheel is a security blanket of sorts, giving him a place of rest during the good times and a place of comfort during the bad. And as this little pachyderm embarks on his adventures in a human world, he'll find plenty of both.

The Elephant in
the Corner

J. D. Updegraff

The small, furry elephant stood in the opening of the living room door. Looking outward he saw houses, planted in a row, conjoined at either end, not one dissimilar in size or color. Above the interminable joinery of rooftops the elephant, squinting his small eyes in the discordant glare of the morning sun, strained to see the distant hills not yet touched by backhoe or excavator. He stepped outside onto the concrete door slab, adorned with a coarse welcome mat, and breathed the cool air, heavy with the scent of drying leaves. It was autumn. He shook his hair, matted by time and listlessness. It fell slightly from his body and hung in disheveled blond locks. This short fleece coat atop wrinkled pewter skin was indeed disparate from the usual pachyderm as well as his unusual proportion, similar in size to that of an armchair. This elephant, emerging into the bracing light of morning, was indeed unique. But none would ever know just how much.

His tangled tresses once fell upon a throne of sorts, if one could believe: a downy round bed adorned with tassels, jewels, and thick rope stitching; it sparkled brilliant blue when shafts of light spilled through the skylight above it. The hemming was sewn into the fringes of the bed with eight straight pieces of rope connecting to the center, forming spokes like that of a wheel. These ropes, pregnant with flecks of gold, added to the luminescence of the bed. It was truly remarkable craftsmanship, assembled by the most skilled of artisans. Surrounding this bed was a room, vastly open and ascetic in furnishings, containing only a wooden bookcase and a red, wingback chair, which sat abreast of the blue bed. The floor was granite, cut into large tiles and jointed by carefully smoothed plaster. The meticulously laid stone was silver with flecks of pale-white feldspar; unshined, it had a dull veneer that drew little attention. There was glass both above and next to the bed. Skylights stretched across the ceiling, giving way to the insipid blue vespers of fog eddying overhead — common to the London firmament. To the side, an entire wall of plate glass separated the room from a massive, enclosed garden. Within this garden was a cobblestone walkway that meandered through raised beds, containing fruit trees, high arching palms, and ferns, all under a milky canopy of glass.

From atop the bedecked pillow the elephant would sit and listen to his master ruminate on literature, poets, and playwrights, invoking the sonnets of Shakespeare in heady, verbose dialectic. One particular night the elephant watched in silence as the aging Englishman, his face drawn downward by time but uplifted by gaudy narrative, acted out a scene from Macbeth. He used the full extent of the vast floor space. The elephant's small dark eyes blinked in quiet observation from behind wisps of tan hair. "Double, double, toil and trouble..." the man squealed, his elbows arched high into his armpits, his wrists and bony fingers luridly stirring an imaginary kettle. He then turned and shifted his character—straightening his gait, puffing his chest into a proud posture, personifying the poise of Macbeth.

After hours of play, the man collapsed, his face red from his great reenactment of amorous gestures, and raucous evocations, into the wingback chair, like an exhausted child. His hand stretched out and touched the thin tips of the elephant's forelocks. "Raja..." the man said in a quiet, receding voice, thick with English brogue. His head slowly tilted to the left as his hand slipped from atop the elephant's head. His speech melted and gave way to deep guttural snores. Raja readjusted his trunk and lowered his head onto his downy, blue bed. The furry elephant drifted into dream beside his master, under darkened skylights.

Nights within the house were often spent this way, with the Englishman gleefully telling stories or acting out plays. During the day, however, their time was spent in the garden—the only other room which Raja would ever see inside the London compound. The man would walk with the elephant at his side and speak with fervor regarding one thing or another. As he spoke, the man would ring his hands and occasionally gesture, his arthritic fingers outstretched into the humid air. Raja, would listen as they shuffled along the cobblestone walk, noticing the peaceful stillness of the garden sanctuary. The recirculation fans, impelling tarnished city air through filtration before being dispensed into the enclosure, were unequivocally silent and supplied meager airflow, providing an immersing tranquility. This allowed Raja to fall deeper into watchful observation of the carefully planted world and the aging Englishman to stray deeper into thought. As Raja's four padded feet fell against smooth, cobbled stone he watched leaves of great trees and smaller ferns fall under the weight of insects. Once close, Raja's eyes would blur and the world would become a blank fog of colors, commingled with the slight impression of indiscernible movement. The sound of the legs of the insect, however, clinging through hooked, spindly feet, resounded in Raja's large ears as the insect edged its way across the green leaf.

Days would stretch into weeks and the garden would show only small changes in growth or decay. A nectarine might birth from a blossom and bow the knuckled branch that it clung to. Once ripened, the man would pluck the fruit in one lurching yank and hand it to Raja. Clutching it with his trunk, Raja would hold it in the air, in the miasmic, milky, filtration of light, and then curl his trunk under, feeding it into an open mouth.

Much like the garden, little changed within the compound from one day to the next. There were times that the Englishman would leave, but these times were few. Most of his time was spent at home with the quiet elephant, spooling about the open floor, walking in the garden, and reading antique books held with care by his vein-lined hands. Eventually, though, the Englishman began feeling his chest heavy and his breath labored. A man toting a clichéd black-leather satchel began coming to the house weekly. He would press his hands against the Englishman's chest and call for him to draw deep, elongated breaths. Raja would sit atop his blue, cylindrical pillow and watch with a deepening gaze as the man drew crackling inhalations and expel loud, vociferous respires. Raja would wince when the noise grew loud, and edge closer to where the Englishman sat, raising his trunk to meet the man's quivering hand.

It had only been a year since the elephant had come to live with the Englishman. It was merely coincidence that their paths would cross or that anyone would ever behold such an extraordinary being as Raja. At the Englishman's first sight of the elephant, he thought him only to be a larger deposit of stacked shale amidst a field of smaller, shredded scree on the hillside. It wasn't until Raja stirred that the man saw him for what he was, an aberrance within the setting. The Englishman stood, high in the Himalaya, under weight of backpack, bearing witness to an elephant the size of a coping stone. The man was staggered, not knowing what to do—whether to move, talk, or simply continue staring. He unwittingly chose the latter. Raja returned his gaze, moving his trunk in small arcs, his ears lightly flapping in the stagnant, tepid air.

The Englishman eventually sat, slumping to the cobbled path with little regard to where he fell. The elephant continued to stare back. The man had read of elephants climbing onto the shoulder of Mount Kilimanjaro to die, or walking solitarily through the Sahara on a death march, but this seemed even more incomprehensible. Eventually, the incredulity that surged through the man's body began slipping beneath a sheen of doubtful dread. He was sure this was an elephant, a furry, small, goddamned elephant. But he alone stood witness to this little brown creature, sitting amongst the stone like a stuffed animal. He doubted his senses and his ability to discern the reality of what he saw. He quickly referenced a disheveled traveler's guide for greater insight and thumbed through until he found reference to high-altitude sickness: a condition that afflicts mountaineers and old men stupid with ideas of high-altitude venture. He felt none of the symptoms.

Not knowing how else to quell his thoughts of psychosis, he dropped his backpack and took out a length of climbing rope and tied an adjustable loop at one end. He climbed carefully upward, until he was close enough to smell Raja and run his fingers through his long wispy locks of hair. He was surprised that his coat smelled somewhat herbal. Raja, with watchful eyes, failed to move as the loop fell down over his head. Unclear to the Englishman if the elephant was acting in aid, Raja raised his trunk and allowed the rope to slip beneath his chin. Now, the astounded man had a small furry elephant on leash and it was time to lead him. Below the hillside was a village, composed of herders, yaks, and very little else. Still, the village offered an alternate set of eyes to displace the man's fears of infirmity. With the slightest of pulls, the elephant rose alongside the man and they began to walk down the hillside.

The village that they descended into was simply utilitarian. Situated in a deep crease of the Himalaya, it consisted of terraced, stacked rock houses, not one equal in roofline to the other, each different according to the hands that fashioned them.

Once they arrived, they were met by a local woman on the outskirts of the village. Her face was dark and enveloped by wrinkles that encircled her eyes and framed the corners of her mouth. She wore a loose white dress and a circular, woven hat that sat on the back of her head. In her hand she gripped a knife, tacky with blood. She was not smiling, not polite like others the Englishman had met along the way in tea houses. The man wondered if he would be able to speak with the woman, or anyone within the village.

At once the woman muttered, "Hello," in a somewhat questioning tone.

Aghast, the man fumbled for words within his own language. In the absence of anything better he contrived, "Do you see this elephant?"

"That yak behind you?" the woman spoke, this time revealing that her initial correspondence was not questioning, but an inflection caused by her accent—seemingly Cockney, if the Englishman would guess; perhaps educated by an English philanthropist in one of the villages to the east, if he would further speculate.

"Yak?" the man asked, glancing back at Raja, reevaluating the initial thesis of his pachyderm identity. Again, he saw Raja's trunk, quietly undulating, occasionally brushing against the back of his pant leg, and his ears, small fans of skin, protruding out from either side of his head. The man sighed in quiet desperation. With the slight raise of the man's hand, pulling tension on the lead, he and Raja continued deeper into the village, leaving the woman to her knife wielding. As they walked, Raja kept equal pace with the man, as he later would in the garden, under palm branch and fruit tree. They walked the narrow, crushed-dirt pathways, deeply recessed between shambled houses, in search of another set of eyes to nullify or confirm the man's ideations.

From an entryway emerged a short man. His skin, also dark, was less creased, giving him the appearance of youth. He wore pants and a long-sleeve shirt, fashioned from woven yak and goat hair. He was a porter, strapping goods to the fur draped backs of ungulates, driving them over steep passes. Some would call him a Sherpa, but Sherpa is a cultural identifier rather than a job title; this man was merely a herder. Once they made eye contact, the Englishman delved into questioning only to be met with a despondent stare. After a few lines of English, the man realized his folly and muttered an apology in a somewhat pensive tone. He switched to what Hindi he knew—contrived and derived from the starched pages of a book, filled mostly with platitudes. After a few moments of this, the man simply gestured toward Raja. Oblivious to why the white man so fervently motioned toward this young, marred yak, the porter waved for the Englishman to follow him, along the pathway, towards the hovel an elder.

Stepping into the hovel was like entering a dark tomb, with only small shafts of light spilling through gaps in the stacked stone. There were no interior walls, just an open dirt floor, a bedroll, and an altar crudely fashioned from wood and stone. The Englishman followed the porter's movements inside, taking careful assurance to mimic the young man's rituals, such as taking off his shoes before entering. The elephant, after much persistence from the porter, stayed outside. Huddled in the corner of the darkened room sat an old man, ancient within the harshness of the Himalaya. The porter kneeled before the huddled elder and spoke softly but briskly in a language that the Englishman could not identify. The young man rose and stepped aside as if beckoning the two to commence their interaction. It was not the educated white man from London who spoke first, but the elder, in an unpredictably deep and steady tone. "What do you want?"

Unsure how else to state it he spoke, "Pardon sir, I found an elephant on the hill and..." his voice drifted away as he noticed the old man's barely lit face fill with confusion. "He is resting outside if you would like to see," he said, attempting to appear assured despite his own doubts. After exchanged words between the elder and the young porter, the porter helped the old man to his feet; the old man wobbled on thin, crooked old knees. The porter led him to the doorway, out into the lurid glare of the high afternoon sun. Through squinted eye the old man stared at young Raja, seated languidly against the exterior wall of the house.

"Yak?" the old man spoke, looking at the foreign traveler for assurance that this is what he wanted.

"Yak?" the Englishman retorted. "No, no, sir. Elephant!" he resounded, this time more desperate, picking up Raja's trunk, articulating it in a circle. Raja blinked listlessly. Exasperated as to what the white man wanted, the elder took in a deep breath of the arid, thin air and leaned against the same wall as Raja. In concordance they stared at the Englishman.

In futility the Englishman began a line of questioning with the elder, asking such nonsensical realities as whether yaks have flat feet, or tusks, or long trunks, or spindly, wagging tails. Mixed with flamboyant gestures, palpation of Raja, and verbose English, the man grasped for recognition from the elderly man who nodded and appeared thoughtful. Once out of anything more to add to his defense the man drew quiet and waited for the old villager's response.

"Bad yak"

"Bad... what, what does that mean?" the Englishman asked, both startled and confused.

After a momentary conversation between porter and elder, the porter led the white man from the hovel, bad yak in tow, briskly retracing the recessed pathways toward the town outlet, where they first entered. It was here that the Englishman saw the woman again, this time hacking tenaciously into a slab of meat; bits of tan fur still clinging to the fringes. The young porter spoke hesitantly to the aging woman in their native tongue, his arms pulled to his chest, his voice sullen. The woman nodded and the young man walked away, not back into the village, but toward an outlying cairn of neatly stacked stones, on which several lines of prayer flags were strung. Once there he collapsed to his knees and began throwing bits of rice onto the altar—rice that had been placed there by others before him. The Englishman, glancing between the woman and the humbled porter, questioned what was happening.

"What you have, mate, is a yak. An ugly little bugger. All disfigured from birth," the woman said, her accent almost too stilted for the Englishman to discern. "It's a bad omen. Terribly bad."

After some explanation the man came to realize that the elder had ordered the man from the town and that this small, shag-coated creature was destined for slaughter in order to purify the town from its curse. At once the man was flabbergasted at the troglodyte barbarism he had descended into —to needlessly butcher in the fear of difference. He thought for a moment to flee with the elephant; he could give a quick yank at the lead and they would run into the hills, the high, mighty Himalaya, rescuing the elephant from its cruel fate at the hands of this female butcher. Instead, the man erupted into ardent pleading to have mercy on the small, defenseless animal. As his performance grew in zeal he was halted in mid-sentence by the raise of her knifed hand, and the Englishman froze, paralyzed.

"Just get that bloody thing out of here," she gashed in an irritable tone, leaning over once again to hack at the animal already slain. Ignorant in how to thank someone customarily, he gave an overly extended bow, gave a tug on the lead, and elephant and man were once again alone, walking side by side.

The Englishman and Raja ascended from the town and made hasty effort to navigate the terrain as to reach the closest sizeable village unnoticed. The man deeply feared for the small animal's life—a life that could be taken if the bigoted denizens extended their surly, superstitious grasp upon the elephant's misconstrued disfigurement. In a wary fit of travel, in which the Englishman brutalized his shins over sharp stone, and Raja tripped over his long trunk, they met the village within the cold chill of night.

Under darkness they entered and found refuge in a small inn, where Raja stayed, sequestered in a small room, with cracked plaster walls and mats rolled onto the dusty floor. The man, after stowing his elephant, questioned the innkeeper and was able to locate an American mountain guide who was staying in the village. After conversing with the shaggy-haired young male, who was adorned with a red goose-down jacket and a prickly beard, the Englishman borrowed his satellite phone. He made a quick call to London, making arrangements for a helicopter to transport them, man and elephant, to the nearest airfield, where they would rendezvous with a private plane, bringing both to London. He referred to the elephant as "discrete luggage." The plan was set in motion.

The helicopter landed in the midst of a Himalayan sunrise, the sharp yellow glare of morning alighting the fields of ice that spilled between edged spires of rock. The lifting of dirt from the barren earth, caught in the up-wash of rotor, obscured the Englishman's view of the Himalaya until they were safely overhead, above anyone that sought to hurt the small elephant. He gazed out his small window and looked into the surrounding Himalaya Mountains which were like a tempestuous, torrential sea turned to stone. In their journey to safety and their winged passage home, the seeds of their brief but ultimately revelatory friendship had been planted.

As time passed aboard the small plane, amidst the screaming of jet engines, the Englishman began to converse with the elephant, as the small, furry creature lay in the narrow isle. It was in this conversation that the man began seeing the elephant as not a vagabond within the Himalaya but as a creature of elegance—a displaced king, fallen from the throne to live as a beast in the field. In attribution to the elephant's rightful place, the man named him Raja—the king.

It was in the presence of this unlikely pairing, this uniting of unique souls, that the Englishman would leave this world, taken by the cough that eventually left him gasping heavily beneath the hiss of a plastic mask. He forcefully coughed, hacking, groping for oxygen amidst lungs brimming with fluid. With one hand clenching the rung of the hospital bed that his doctor had placed in the large room, and the other pressing against Raja's flat head, he secreted foam from the corners of his mouth. Raja stared with intensity as the man exuded vociferous rasps until he drew silent, his hand slipping from atop the elephant's head. Raja listened for the guttural tones of sleep to ensue—the snores that accompanied the man as he fell limp in times past—but he heard none. The doctor would not arrive until morning to find the man who died alone in the night, with only a small elephant to watch over him. Raja waited by the man's side until that time, atop his circular, bejeweled, blue pillow. The immersing quiet enveloped Raja, and he felt a stillness within the room that he had scarcely felt before. It was uncomfortable and unnerving. He grasped at the man's stiff hand and pawed at his wheel-shaped bed. He knew nothing else to do with this unease that he had never felt before.

The Englishman's death came as no surprise to the Englishman. He had known that he was suffering and that the affliction would take him steadily. In accordance, he had enacted a will, corresponding with his lawyer by phone, but failing to contact the beneficiaries to their claims or even the nature of his illness. His sickness even escaped the lengthy conversations that the man had with Raja, who wouldn't have understood regardless.

The weeks following the Englishman's death thrust Raja into an unimaginable existence: people coming to take him away, sticking a needle into him, and taking him on a journey that crossed an ocean and placed Raja into a fold of reality that he could scarcely imagine.

Eventually he awoke in a place under the bewildered glare of a different man, a round-faced, mustache-wearing man, and into a world imbued with humming madness of humanity's material assertions of power. Raja's vision cleared slightly and the world appeared less blurred. Straw was scattered in front of him, drifted out from the open side of the crate. Raja lay on his side within the box, his legs slightly bent towards his stomach with his trunk curled downward. He felt stiff, his appendages heavy. In front of him, on a concrete door slab, atop a coarse welcome mat, stood a man, starring, scratching his small, dimpled chin. A woman of the same age stood beside him, holding a letter in her hands. Appearing bereft of comprehension, they gaped in disbelief. Raja, unable to return their stare, slipped back into a deep oblivion.

When he awoke again, he was laying on his side, atop his opulent, blue wheel bed in the corner of a room. As he opened his eyes, he winced, and slowly grew accustomed to the saturation of artificial light. In front of him, two figures stared at him. Seated across a couch sat the man and woman that the elephant had earlier seen only briefly. Without moving, the elephant used his eyes to look around the room, to see in what strange place he had awoken. He noticed the ceiling, white, lacking skylight. He saw the room around him cluttered and small, which made him feel contained and anxious. He saw the floor, tan carpeting stretched to each corner of the room. It smelled of something fake. A putrid flower, rotten perhaps. He wondered where the garden was.

He felt like sleeping. He could feel the deep pull, the undertow of the drugs still lingering in his bloodstream, lulling him back into blank dream. As his eyes began to shut, he heard subtle utterances from the couch, which grew louder as he forced himself to become more alert, more aware to what was said. He was barely able to make out their scuffled exchange of language. A slight raise of a voice here, a harsh intonation there, punctuated by brief inordinate gestures towards one another. The bout continued between them, becoming more consuming, until Raja lifted his heavy head and attempted to sit up. Silence reentered the room and they all exchanged unwitting stares.

At once, under the cold stare of strangers, Raja missed his Englishman, his life within the expansive room, his walks in the garden, the spinning vespers of insipid fog above his bed. He drew deeper into his bed, pushing himself lower as if to surround himself with the anodyne nature of the object, to feel fulfilled by its deep, embedded comforts. In that instant Raja cherished his bed and sought to never leave its safety. He became beholden to the soft, bejeweled pillow.

Day became night and night became day. The initial drama that came with the arrival of Raja eventually drifted into the undertow of the couple's lives, their oblivious entrapment within the milieu of contemporary society, lulled to sleep by material effects. Clinging to keys and a yoga mat slung over her shoulder, the woman hastily walked past Raja's bed everyday. The man, grunting, clutching coffee and briefcase, lumbered by in concord. Both scarcely recognized Raja or one another. The elephant felt entombed by the indifference within the household. He despised the woman and man for this, their ineffectualness and blurred ideations. He felt trapped between the suffocating white walls of the room cluttered with furniture, magazines, and hopelessness. Raja saw the great discordance between this life and his last, and became deeply embittered as a result. He could feel this caterwauling life driving him deeper into a melancholy shell. No longer taking notice of the world beyond his bed, he became despondent. He felt that all that was once perfect was now lost.

One night, Raja awoke to screams emanating from the top of the stairs. The woman yelled in a vociferous rage, her tone high and piercing, her words incoherently slurred. A sharp burst of shattering glass terminated her shrill outburst, which then led to female sobs and turbulent vibrations of feet steadily descending the staircase. Once at the bottom she grabbed her purse, her cell phone, her keys, and turned back toward the stairs. She screamed once again—a violent, short burst two syllables long. She cried and marched out the door. Its closing was thunderous and seemingly rocked the house off its foundation. From the top of the stairs no one stirred, and the house once again fell silent.

Raja felt restless, unhinged by the chaotic uproar that had just occurred. He did not know that this had happened before, that she would go to her mother's and wail about the life she could have had. How this man had deprived her of her inner soul, stifled her, kept her from attaining her fullest potential of… she could never say. But this time was different. This moment would result in the consultation of lawyers, the drafting of documents, and the resulting division of property. To the woman: the small sedan, alimony, and their joint savings. To the man: the house, payments, the old pickup truck in need of a head gasket, and Raja, the displaced elephant once exalted by the man's estranged uncle.

It was in these days confined with the man that Raja began watching once again. He watched the man devolve into a pit of dejection. The man allowed himself to disintegrate into a shameful mass of disrepair: his shirt stained, his face covered with stubble, his breath heavy with fermented rye. No one entered or exited. The man holed himself within the dim, dank house, like a hermit on a hill. But the man's loss and torment of guilt—the angst of losing a piece of oneself—kept him in seclusion. He became fixated on his emotions, and they enveloped him.

Raja grew thin in the absence of food, but drew all his perceptual sustenance through his observances of the man pulled into shambles. As he fixed his eyes on the man who stared distantly into the recesses of the dark room, raising a brown bottle to his mouth occasionally, Raja reflected on his own absences—his own fixations that he clung to so desperately. His bed, now matted, muted, and dingy from his own corpulence weighing on it for some time, had become his only solace. He never wanted to leave its ethereal comfort. He clung to the memory of the aging Englishman who showed Raja a world of only beauty. He longed for the days in the garden and wished, above all else, to see the Englishman's whirling gestures as they walked the cobbled paths. He wished not to remember the cold hand of the Englishman slip from his head, but to become immersed within the contentment that he once had. He wanted to know why he was deposited here, astride all the ugliness that he never knew existed in the world. Above all else, he wanted to abandon the restlessness that he espoused within his small elephant stature. He no longer wanted to cling or to be stuck. He simply wanted to drift into the ether, for which his only master left him.

It was morning, and glancing light filtered through the drawn curtains. The man, in all his despondency and disregard, lay upon the couch, his eyes half open. Raja, seated on his bed, had not slept, but remained in a state of revelatory acumen. Within the stillness of night his mind became unlatched from the impermanence of this place, and in doing so he found he did not have to stay. He could seek a life beyond the plastered walls, the neatly squared corners, the Scotchgarded carpet. He could find fulfillment without existing within the memories that he resurrected of a past life — and so, in this uprising of the furry elephant's inner self, Raja resolved to leave.

In the awakening of morning, he stood from his bed, his feet pressing against the fabric of the pillow, nearly to the floor. He stepped, reaching out his padded left foot, planting it on the carpeted floor just beyond the blue pillow. After a moment of pause, and a brief closing of his eyes, his other three followed, and he slowly made his way over to the couch, to the feet of the half-comatose man. Raja stared at him and, in a moment of compassion, outstretched his trunk and slowly touched the man's left cheek. Aroused from his stupor, the man opened his eyes and gasped, instantaneously sobered by the sensation of the elephant's trunk. The man retracted and placed himself in a fully seated position on the couch, his arms locked at his sides, his posture tense. The elephant pulled his trunk into his body and began gently swaying it back and forth. The man's posture relaxed, and they locked eyes. The man became engrossed at the sight of Raja, enamored by this small elephant whom he had forgotten, unacknowledged in the corner of the room. At once the man momentarily strayed from his afflictions and found peace within the simple exchange. Raja remained in this tacit colloquy and then turned away, beginning the steps towards the front door to the home.

It was in this moment that Raja failed to look back at his once opulent bed, a blue wheel compressed against the carpet in the corner of the living room. Alone in the corner, the bed, now soiled, threadbare, and unremarkable, bore little resemblance to what it once was, the seat of a great king. In the immersing quiet of the house Raja made his final steps toward the door, extended his trunk, and grasped at the brass of the knob.

*C*hristopher Olsen's blue wheel seems very not-quiet at first. It's set on a backdrop of local Bangor history, thanks to Olsen's first-person familiarity with local history and the Bangor Historical Society. But he's changed names and situations to protect the innocent, and perhaps the guilty, while working up a good, old-fashioned ghost story. It's worth noting here that Chris wins the awards for "Hardest-Working Student" and "Most-Improved Student," having diligently worked through seven drafts in a die-hard bid to produce his first story so that it would be publishable and engaging. He's done an exemplary job, and has never known the meaning of the word "quit."

Ten Grand

Christopher Olsen

Jack Kendall sat waiting for the interview with the Historical Society's board of directors in their museum's Grand Army of the Republic room. Jack was originally from suburban New Jersey but had ancestors with roots in New England. He found the history of Bangor fascinating to say the very least. The city was a thriving and prosperous community at the end of the nineteenth and early twentieth centuries, due in part to the lumber and logging industry but even more so because of the spirit of its people and the desire to compete with and even surpass Boston. A job here would be perfect.

A white-haired gentleman, who Jack assumed was one of the organization's volunteers or board members, was sitting in a high-back chair in the corner of the room, smiling at Jack. "History fascinates me," Jack said to the man, returning his smile. "I've lived in Maine since I was twelve, but I grew up in a house that was a stop on the Underground Railroad in northern New Jersey. All these Civil War artifacts you have here are awesome."

"Rehearsing your 'hire me' speech?" said the board president, Sally Hallett, as she entered the room.

Jack turned to face her, momentarily wondering why she was being rude to the gentleman, but he politely replied, "Just making conversation," he said. "I'm always up for talking about the Civil War." He turned as Sally found a seat, and realized the white-haired man had left.

"Sometimes we have visitors from the south," Sally said. "They call the Civil War 'The War of Northern Aggression.'"

"I've heard that," Jack said, shaking his head. "But there are a lot of fascinating things about that war that you'll never find in the history books."

"Such as?" asked Sally.

Jack pointed out a visored infantry cap in an exhibit case. "This hat, for instance, was likely the basis for today's baseball cap. There were even accounts of ball games played on Sundays between Union and Confederates. They had such thick leather visors because the majority of new infantry recruits had never fired a musket, and unlike the Spencer repeating rifles that came out later in the war, the muskets had one hell of a kick, very much like a shotgun. Many of the recruits could only get off one shot. The kickback was so powerful that a lot of them got knocked out cold when the barrel snapped back and hit them in the head."

"I think you'll like one of the upcoming exhibits that talks about the advances made in nursing because of the women getting involved by helping the wounded."

"They made a real difference. I've read that they saved many lives acting as nurses and some women even went to battle, passing for men. It wasn't until they applied for benefits following the war that they came forward as soldiers." He enjoyed talking history with her. He really wanted this job.

"Well, you clearly have the right mind set for this position," Sally said with a smile, as if reading his mind.

* * *

One by one, the rest of the board filed in. Jack was surprised that the white-haired man he was talking with earlier wasn't among them. The seven members gathered around the long wooden table, and the interview got underway.

It was long, and Jack didn't get the sensation that he was making much of an impression on the group; they seemed bored with him and the interview. The pauses got longer and more uncomfortable, and although he really wanted the job, Jack realized he wasn't getting it. His confidence lost, he decided to ask a question that would ensure the deal would be blown so he could just get out of there and move on.

He blurted out, "So... who died in here?"

Surprisingly, the tension in the room dissipated as the small group broke out in laughter. When the laughing stopped, he asked again, "Seriously, who died here? I feel like we're being watched."

Sally smiled. "You have to be the most unpretentious candidate we've interviewed yet. If you read the Godfrey Journals, you'll find the only one who actually died here was the home's second owner, Samuel Dale, the city's mayor, after a scandal."

"What sort of scandal?"

"In 1871, the Great Chicago Fire destroyed much of that city. Communities all across the country raised money to help the people in the city as they worked to recover and rebuild. Bangor raised ten thousand dollars, which was quite a large sum for that time, but it disappeared."

"And the mayor was involved?" Jack asked.

"His wife, too," Sally said, "It's all in the Godfrey Journals. The man who founded the historical society was a probate judge named John Edwards Godfrey; our next exhibit is based on his view of the city. He wrote them like a journal, as letters to his sons. The money never arrived in Chicago. But the investigation was delayed; the railroads had linked up, allowing trains to go all the way from California to the Canadian Maritimes, and President Grant was visiting Bangor. By the time they opened the investigation, Dale was found dead in the bathtub—reportedly from poisoning himself."

Jack's curiosity was in overdrive. "Any chance of getting a copy of the journals to read?" he asked, his excitement building.

"Certainly," Sally said.

The next leg of the tour was through the rest of the home with one of the veteran docents, which Jack learned was the proper term for a museum tour guide. "My name's Glenna," the elderly woman said as she offered her hand to Jack.

"Jack Kendall," he said, shaking her hand. "Nice to meet you."

"Likewise. I heard part of your interview. It was refreshing."

"What was?"

"To hear someone down to earth, someone who isn't a bag of wind!" she said, and they shared a laugh.

There were paintings everywhere. Jack was standing in front of one depicting three small children cuddled up on an overstuffed chair, all reaching down to pet what looked like a black Labrador retriever. "I love all the paintings. This one's especially interesting; I don't remember seeing too many paintings from this period with kids with a pet."

"You're right. In fact, when the museum first found that painting, it was so old and covered with grime, you couldn't even see the dog. It appeared when we were having it cleaned up. We did a little research and found that black Lab was a hero. There was a fire in their house late one night and the dog managed to wake everyone up, including the kids, and helped them to safety."

Each section of the double parlor had handsome, black-marble fireplaces. Glenna led him down to the other end of the double parlor, gesturing to two large Corinthian columns on either of side of the room. "Everything here has a story. These were put in back in the 1870s by the second owners of the home, the Dales."

"Dale — as in the mayor?"

"The same. The Dales had a rivalry with the neighbors; Isaac Farrar built the mansion across the street as a wedding present for his second wife, and shortly after Dale saw the inside of the home, the 'keeping up with the Joneses' began. Mrs. Dale headed over to Italy and brought back not only the new marble, but also craftsmen to rebuild them."

"These are fascinating stories," Jack said. "Whether I get the job or not, I want to read those journals. Dale sounds like an intriguing guy."

"He sure was. Here, we have a painting of him."

Jack followed Glenna to the end of the room and she swept her hand up toward the portrait on the wall. "This is Mayor Dale," she said.

Jack looked up at the face and froze. Chills ran down his spine. The man in the painting could have been a twin to the man he had seen in the Civil War room just before the interview started.

"That's Mayor Dale?" Jack said, eyes wide.

"Yes. Why do you ask?"

"Uh, well," Jack said as he shifted nervously. "He sort of looks like Andrew Jackson with that wild hair, doesn't he?"

"That he does."

"Is there a volunteer here who portrays him?"

"Like a re-enactor?" Glenna said. "No, we have a volunteer from Hampden who portrays Hannibal Hamlin, President Lincoln's first vice president, and another who portrays General Joshua Chamberlain. But no one I know does Mayor Dale. Why?"

Jack paused, worried he might look like some sort of nut. "There… there was a man in the room just before the interview started," he said quietly. "God help me, but I swear he looked exactly like the man in this painting."

Glenna's eyes widened—not with disbelief or shock, but with obvious child-like glee. "You saw him?" Glenna whispered excitedly, grinning like a ghoul and rubbing her hands together. "Don't worry—I've seen him, too. Other volunteers and staff have mentioned seeing or sensing something. Hell, ask any of the previous caretaker families that lived here before the alarm system was installed and they'll tell you about the noises."

He couldn't shake the chill as he looked back up at the old, painted eyes of Mayor Dale, who seemed to stare back at him. "Sally said he died up here. Where did it happen?"

"Closer than you think," Glenna said.

Jack spun on his heel to face her, but his foot abruptly slipped wildly out from under him and he almost went down. He caught himself with a flailing hand on the wall as Glenna frantically reached out to help him.

"Jesus Christ," Jack said, looking down to see what he'd slipped on. But the floor was bone dry and clear. "That's weird," he said. "I slipped, as if the floor were wet."

He looked up to see Glenna staring back at him, her lips tightly pressed together, shaking her head, and realization dawned on him. "Don't tell me," he said, "the tub was right about here?"

Glenna nodded.

There was no turning back from his curiosity about this story. "What can you tell me about that scandal?" Jack asked.

"It's in the journals, but the short version is this: All the work in the double parlor wasn't just to piss off the Farrars," Glenna said. "President Grant was coming to Bangor for a special ceremony as the railroad system connected both coasts, and the final stretch from Maine to the Canadian Maritimes, called the European and North American Railway, was completed. President Grant was staying at the Bangor House Hotel and there was a big shindig here in his honor. According to Judge Godfrey, all was going well until someone realized they had forgotten to extend an invitation to the president. Dale himself went down to the hotel to get Grant. When they arrived and Grant saw the party in full swing, he wasn't too impressed. The president and one of his aides went through shaking hands along the way, from the front door to right out the back door and back down to the hotel."

Jack shook his head, "That probably didn't do well for the Mayor."

Glenna laughed. "Nope, not at all. But the real scandal involved the missing ten thousand dollars that Sally told you about. The rumor, according to Godfrey, was that Dale's wife Matilda had used the money to spruce up the house for President Grant's visit."

"Too bad it wasn't locked up in something like that," Jack said as he walked across the room to see what must have been the largest floor safe he'd ever seen. It sat on the hardwood floor, cordoned off by rope barriers like one might see in the lobby of a movie theater. It was big and black, save for the big spindle wheel on the front, which would be spun once the combination lock was properly turned. The wheel had six spindles from a central hub, with an outer ring near the spindles' ends, and the metal was blued. It looked a lot like a sailing ship's wheel.

"So what's the story with this behemoth lock box?" he asked.

"It was custom built for the home's original owner, Thomas Hill. He handled the finances for several of the lumber businesses and he had a fascination with the sea and nautical items. They wanted to open it last year, like a time capsule, but nobody has a combination. They've had a few locksmiths try to figure it out over the years, but they've never had any success. And nobody can come up with a way to get it open it without ruining it."

"Yes, nitro would be a bit loud and messy," Jack said with a grin.

Glenna laughed and shook her head. "You'll fit in here just fine!"

"Something bothers me about how Dale died," Jack said. "It's odd that a man in that time period would poison himself. Usually women use poison as a way out; men usually shoot or hang themselves."

Glenna nodded. "That story has bothered a lot of people, but it was so long ago—and without any proof otherwise, it's always been classified as a suicide."

"If it *was* murder, perhaps his wife was the killer," Jack said, almost mesmerized as he approached the big safe and reached out for the big blue wheel. He was half tempted to grab one of the handles and give it a spin.

"Go ahead—give it a whirl," Glenna said.

Jack grinned and did so, as if it were the wheel on *The Price is Right*. It made a high-pitched squeal, startling Jack, who jumped back. Glenna burst out laughing.

"Gotcha!" she cried. "Don't worry—it's one of the few things here that's okay to touch. So do you think you can handle the job?"

"I'm sure I can, but it will be a while before I know."

Glenna grinned and waved her hand. "Hogwash. You'll get it. I feel it."

"Thanks for the vote of confidence."

But Glenna was right. As they came down the stairs, he saw Sally grinning from ear to ear. "So, did you enjoy the ten-cent tour?" she asked.

"Very much so."

"Good! If you'd like the job, it's yours."

Before the interview, Jack had figured he didn't have a snowball's chance in Hell. But after he learned a little bit about the organization and the home's checkered past, it had become interesting to the point of obsession, especially after meeting the late mayor—so to speak.

Meeting the rest of the staff was the next step. The person who really knew the museum and was truly focused was a woman a few years older than Jack named Nicole, who took him to the small museum store. Jack asked how well the shop did.

"Not bad, between the sales of map reproductions, and books, including the Journals and the book about Bangor's lumber boom, *Whigs & Woodsmen*. We've also had a lot of luck with little items like these," she said, holding up a couple of painted slices of pine wood cut in the shape of the museum house and other area landmarks. "I especially like this one of the Farrar Mansion across the street."

As she reached for it, Jack caught a glimpse of something out of the corner of his eye and the small rendition of the mansion popped off the top of the glass display case, falling to the floor. Nicole crouched to pick it up—and Jack looked up to see a faint wisp of the white-haired man gazing down at her lovingly, smiling all the while. As she stood up, the apparition quickly faded . "That Samuel is a scamp!" Nicole said with a laugh.

Jack gave a start. "Pardon?" Had she seen him?

"The model falling down—around here, we blame little things like that on Sam Dale. A lot of folks believe he haunts the place, you know."

"So I've heard," Jack said.

"We all joke that he fancied himself a ladies' man. He likes to pull things with the girls. Maybe you'll see what I mean next Thursday, when the Ladies' Junior League meets here for their fortieth annual meeting. Sam might get a little playful."

"Sounds like fun," Jack said.

Learning the workings of the museum was a lot different for Jack, who had most recently worked as a fund raiser for a shelter that helped alcoholics and addicts get sober and back on their feet. He still kept in touch with some of the staff and would occasionally run into some of the guests. While taking a break outside one afternoon, on the sidewalk in front of the museum with his camera, he met with one of the guests. Jack was trying to get a decent photo of the house that he could use in a fundraising brochure he was designing when he heard the familiar voice.

"Hey Jackie Boy! How's it going?"

Jack turned to see one of the shelter guests he only knew as "Bear," a nickname the man had earned because of his large build.

"Hey, Bear," Jack said, reaching out to shake Bear's hand. "You look great. What have you been up to?"

"Staying clean and sober," Bear said. "As they say, one day at a time. So, how do you like it here?"

"It's good. Pay is okay, and it's an interesting place."

"I bet it is," Bear said, looking a bit pensive. "You know, I've seen things some strange things here."

"What kinds of things?"

"Weird shit, like lights coming on late at night—and not electric lights. More like flickering, like a candle but brighter."

"Like gaslights?"

"Yeah—I'd seen some like 'em on my grandparents' farm up north in Aroostook County. They look like regular chandeliers or wall lamps but they had a flame dancing around inside the glass chimney. One of the few times I ever tried to sack out on the porch here, the curtains would move and I'd hear some real old-timey music, but real faint. Almost like it was in the distance, but it was coming from inside the house."

"Had you been drinking?"

"As matter of fact, I hadn't. I didn't think much of it when it happened, but when I drifted off, I had a dream, except it wasn't really a dream. I was in that place between being awake and being asleep, and I looked over there towards Union Street and it didn't look right. It looked like gravel and dirt instead of asphalt. I figured it was my eyes playing tricks on me until I saw it."

"What was that?"

"A horse and carriage going up the hill. The buildings across the street looked different too, except for that one," he said motioning towards the Farrar Mansion. "And that place," pointing to a newer bank ATM, "wasn't there. There was this really big oak standing there, and that lot was vacant."

Jack thought on the story for a long moment. Bear said, "When I shook myself awake and cleared my head, everything was back to normal. I'm sure it was a dream and all, but... well, I got out of there. And I haven't been by here at night since. I guess I just have a funny feeling about this place."

"Me too, Bear," Jack said.

Jack couldn't stop thinking about Bear's story. It was as if the man had seen a glimpse of the past but hadn't realized what he'd been seeing. Later in the day, Nicole and Glenna pulled out some large manila envelopes with old photos in each one. The museum's photo collection was sizeable. They had tintypes, black-and-white prints, negatives, and even glass-plate negatives.

Jack started looking through the files and came across a section labeled FARRAR MANSION, UNION STREET. He pulled out a thick sheaf of folders and started looking through them. Several folders in, he found a wide-angle shot of that section of Union Street with the mansion on the far right.

The road was dirt, and where the little bank ATM now stood was an empty lot with a magnificent oak tree. It was just how Bear described it. Had he seen this photo before, or had he had a brief glimpse into the past?

Jack was looking forward to meeting more of the volunteers, and to the society's annual meeting and dinner, which was barely a week into his tenure there. It was a very relaxed affair, with the food being potluck from the board members and other volunteers. Although the house was built in the 1830s, the kitchen looked like part of the Ozzie and Harriet set. It was a decent-sized kitchen but when it was full of people it got a little tight.

"What can I do to help?" he asked.

Board secretary Kay Leavitt spoke up. "Find us a colander. The peas are almost done."

"Check!" Jack said, grabbing one from the counter, but the sink was full of dishes. He grabbed the pot of peas in his other hand and hurried out of the kitchen to the closet-sized bathroom around the corner, where he poured the steaming peas into the colander. Steam filled the small room and fogged up the mirror as Jack gently shook the colander to strain out the last of the water. He set the colander in the pot and turned to leave.

Behind him, he heard a squeaking noise.

He turned back and froze. Above the sink, the mirror was still steamed up, but to his amazement, letters began to appear, as if an invisible finger were writing them on the wet glass. Jack's mouth sagged open as three words appeared.

OPEN THE SAFE.

He stepped closer to the mirror, a feeling like a rush of cold air cut right through him, making his heart race and bristling the hair on the back of his neck. "What the hell is going on here?" he whispered. "What's in that damn safe?"

The evening of the Junior League was at hand. Jack wore his best suit and tie. The ladies in attendance were mostly college graduates working in professional fields. The funds they raised supported self-esteem-building programs and scholarships. Many of the women Nicole introduced him to had very familiar names, names that Jack had come to realize had been in the area for generations.

The evening went well, and the house ghost seemed to have been well-behaved. Jack wasn't sure if Samuel had been watching from the sidelines or was absent for the evening. It became evident it was the former as Jack was closing up the museum for the night.

He said good-night to the president of the Junior League and sent Nicole on her way, shut the double doors, and breathed a sigh of relief that the night was over. As he turned away from the door, his ears caught a faint, faraway sound. It was a haunting melody, sounding as if it were coming from outside. He unbolted the doors and pulled them open again, and the music disappeared. But no sooner than he'd once again locked the place up did the distant music once again begin wafting through the night air. He bent down, trying to follow the sound... and it was almost as if it were whistling through the keyhole.

He was getting more nervous being there alone, so he hurried back into the double parlor to turn off the lights. The room's large windows were sealed up, and there was no draft or breeze in the home. Jack stepped over to one of the fireplaces and reached up to pull the chain on the lamp. The lamp was decorated with long glass prisms around the base and Jack couldn't help but make them jingle when turning the light on or off. It gave off a sweet sound that made him smile, reminding him of the wind chimes his parents had had when he was a kid. He shut the door from the inside and moved to the opposite end of the long room to shut off the other lamp, hearing a similar jingle. He then headed out the far door and pulled it shut, sealing up the room for the night.

Walking down the hall past the first door that he had shut, he heard the same jingle again. Comforting moments before, now it was startling.

"Good-night, Sam!" he yelled as he hustled through the dining room, through the swinging door into the kitchen. He grabbed his coat and punched in the alarm code so fast the small LCD screen started to flash 'SAFE' over and over.

It certainly referred to the safe mode for the alarm

system—or was it Sam, going on about the old safe?

"I'd love to help you Sam," he hollered to nothing, "but not if you're going to be an ass and scare me like that!"

Jack rushed out the door and ran for his car.

Several nights later, the ringing phone woke Jack from a dead sleep. It was one in the morning. He cursed as he fumbled for the receiver and angrily answered. The caller was from Maine Coast Security.

"Sorry to wake you. Mr. Kendall," the man said.

"Alarm's going off again?"

"Yes, sir. Shall I have the Bangor Police Department meet you there?"

"Yes, please... thank-you," Jack managed. It was the third night in a row. The night before it was at two o'clock, and the night before that it was at three. All false alarms.

After a few nights of romping back and forth to the museum at all hours and introducing himself to several of Bangor's finest, Jack was more than happy to eat his lunch alone up in the tiny office. He'd bought his own copies of the Godfrey Journals and spent his break looking through them yet again. He was tired from his frequent late-night forays, and it caught up with him. He kept nodding off and jumping himself awake, his mind balanced on that invisible boundary between being awake and asleep.

He snapped himself back to consciousness once again— and there was Dale's disembodied face floating in the air above him, looking down at him. He let out a cry, leaping from his chair and coming to his feet even as Dale's face faded away before his very eyes.

"What the hell do you want from me?" Jack cried out.

There was no answer. Downstairs, he heard hurried footsteps, and then Nicole's voice called up, "You okay Jack?"

"Uh, yeah... just fighting with my computer," he called

out.

He listened as she walked away, and suddenly the keys on his computer keyboard began depressing by themselves. He stared in disbelief as words formed in the document open on his screen.

LEARN THE TRUTH.

Jack felt a chill as if someone walked right through him and he watched in amazement as as the keys continued to depress.

OPEN THE SAFE.

"Is this about the missing money?" Jack whispered.

Keys tapped.

YES.

Preparation for the exhibit "Judge Godfrey's Bangor" was almost complete, and Jack did what he could to help the board members and other volunteers in readying for the big public opening. Sometimes it was making calls and moving tables; other times it was learning when to shut up and get out of the way.

Jack decided to offer up an idea to Sally Hallett after talking to an old friend of his. "He's been with the Air National Guard for years, a decorated officer and he's from a long line of locksmiths," he explained.

"We've tried that before," she said. "Nobody has been able to open it, and we don't want to damage the safe."

"This guy is different. He has some high-tech equipment that's like an electronic stethoscope to listen to the tumblers — better stuff than your average safecracker. If he can't open it, he can't open it, but what do we have to lose?"

"What the hell," Sally said. "Either way, it will add some excitement to the evening. Which reminds me, Adeline wants to come in costume as Mayor Dale's widow for the event... for the whole evening."

Adeline was interesting when she was lucid and not in the

middle of one of her spells. Jack couldn't help but groan, "Oh boy. What do we do?"

"Not much we can do. She's one of our top donors and her family connections go way back. We'll just have to keep a close eye on her."

What Jack had hoped would be a smooth event now had the potential of turning into a scene.

The evening arrived and the challenges mounted, especially the logistics of using high-tech equipment with a house full of noisy revelers, but amazingly enough, everyone cooperated.

"Sergeant Dave Windsor has studied similar safes for tonight's special event," Sally announced to the seventy or so people gathered up in the large room.

The crowd was hushed as the sergeant hooked up the audio sensors and started in, rotating the dial, slowly to the right.

"There's one," he said with a smile.

Slowly back to the left... Jack looked over toward the corner of the room behind Windsor and the safe and, like a mist, getting sharper and more defined, he again saw the apparition of Mayor Dale. Dale was smiling, holding his hands together and beaming as if he were watching a treasured gift being unwrapped before his very eyes. Jack realized that Dale's spirit was happy and knew something that no one in the room knew.

All as silent in the room as the sergeant turned the dial slowly back to the right to the third and final number. Turning to the crowd, he raised his arm and stuck up his thumb, like Little Jack Horner finding the plum. Adeline, fully in character as Matilda Dale, shrieked, "Samuel! Samuel Josiah Dale!"

But Adeline started towards the apparition and Jack marveled as he could see the specter's eyes widen. Apparently Glenna could see the spirit as well when she muttered to Jack, "Crazy bitch! In all my years, I never thought I'd see someone scare a ghost!"

"Are you going to let them do this?" Adeline shrieked. "They'll ruin it! They'll ruin everything!"

Jack watched as Sally launched herself from the opposite corner of the room and pulled Adeline aside like an unruly child. "Do *not* do it!" Adeline growled.

"Do what?" Sally asked quietly, trying her best to calm Adeline.

"The money! The God damned money! That son of a bitch stashed it in that big metal box and wouldn't let me have it!"

"What money, Matilda?" Sally asked, playing into Adeline's delusion.

"The money for Chicago. We could have done *so much* with that money!"

The guests were stunned as they watched what they at first assumed to be a skit become strangely real. Even Sergeant Windsor's eyes were wide as he stepped away from the large safe. It wasn't just Adeline's outburst; Jack now realized that Windsor could see Dale, too. Jack's mouth hung open as he, Glenna and "Matilda" watched the apparition of Mayor Dale kneel before the safe, grasp one of the six handles of the big blue wheel that now spun around quietly, almost as if it were new, unlike the squealing it had made before. Dale then released the door of the safe.

The whole room again hushed as they saw objects hidden so long in the safe tumbling out onto the hardwood floor: documents, a pocket watch, a penknife, and some coins. Only Jack, Adeline, Glenna and Sergeant Windsor, saw the vision of a man, Mayor Dale, riffling through the interior of the large, wood-lined metal box, tossing the items out as he hunted. The specter turned, his face all twisted up, holding his stomach as if he was in pain. Those who could see his vision suddenly realized that the mayor, the late Samuel Josiah Dale, wasn't in any pain at all. In fact, he was laughing, laughing very hard. He again turned to the crowd, and like a magician, grinning like the proverbial cat that ate the canary, held up his index finger high in the air, made a fist, and brought his arm down and then back up again like an uppercut. Like a wrecking ball, his fist soundly smacked the wooden ceiling of the safe. The small trap door in the safe's wooden ceiling swung down like a slack jaw and banknotes fluttered to the floor like confetti along with a folded-up piece of yellowing parchment.

Mayor Dale stood up and with a wink, pointed to Jack, and curled up his index finger to beckon him. As if in slow motion, Jack strode forward and bent down to pick up the brittle paper. He looked up and their eyes met and Jack could read the mayor's lips just before the apparition faded. Two simple words: *Thank you.*

Jack stepped back as he unfolded the parchment and the back wall turned into a brilliant, pure white light as Dale turned and walked into the glare only to disappear.

"What does it say?" Glenna blurted out.

Jack held the single sheet in one hand and covered his mouth with the other. "Oh, my God!" he gasped and began to read aloud.

> "*To Whom It May Concern:*
>
> "*If you should discover this missive, my demise must have come. These funds were raised in a gesture of charity for the people of Chicago. While suffering greatly from a massive conflagration, the losses were unbearable. Equal to me is the loss of my beloved Matilda's sanity. Insistent that this gifted money should be used in anticipation of President Grant's visit to the City of Bangor, I fear she will try to abscond with it and cause great scandal for Bangor and my family's fine name. Please set my soul at rest by delivering this gift, and the generous spirit in which it was given, to the fine citizens of Chicago.*"

Sergeant Windsor walked up to Glenna and Jack while the crowd cheered. The people were celebrating the safe being opened, but they were clearly oblivious as to what had really just happened. "It seems that nobody else in this room saw what we did," Windsor said. "Who's going to believe it?"

Glenna smiled "It's the energy. When souls have unfinished business if they can find the right energy, that is the right people with the same energy, they can get their message across. I've seen it before. Dale knew when he first saw Jack come in he could be the one to help him complete his business, I think Mayor Dale can rest now."

The people in the room were murmuring excitedly about the discovery, Glenna and Adeline, once again seemingly herself, began picking up the bank notes.

"Maybe we should include an insert in the Godfrey Journals," Adeline suggested.

Glenna, never one to ever stay serious groaned as she picked up the last of the money, "Maybe in the future they can just Google it!"

Jack smiled, walked over to Glenna and gave her a big hug and whispered "Yahoo!"

Glenna snorted, "I was right; you'll fit in here just fine. Now, about the other spirits here…"

Editor's Note

The people depicted herein are inspired by, or composites of, real people, but bear no real-life resemblance. The exception is the character of Glenna, who was a real person, and remains so named here as a tribute to her memory.

As for historical facts, Mayor Dale did appear to have died by suicide, although some have conjectured he was murdered. There is no evidence of that, or that his wife had anything to do with his death.

Ten grand was raised with the intention of sending it to Chicago, and the money did go missing. Its ghostly discovery here is wholly the product of the author's imagination… but, like him, perhaps we could all wonder just where it went to, and whether there is an intriguing reality behind the events of Bangor's past.

*A*nette Ruppel Rodrigues is German by birth, a German instructor by vocation, and a historian by avocation — or perhaps by fate, given her devout commitment to the history she pursues. For her inaugural fiction story, she has drawn on her extensive knowledge of the history of German participation in the early days of the United States, particularly in Maine and the Maritimes, to craft a tale based on fact, with richly drawn characters who were actually real people. But the particulars of the story are from her imagination, including one important object in the title character's life, which serves as her quiet blue wheel.

Margaretha

Anette Ruppel Rodrigues

The darkness of the lower deck which had frightened Margaretha in the beginning of the journey had become rather comforting. The tight bunk enveloped her like a cocoon. No matter how rough the ocean was, she felt safe among the wooden planks of the bunks hugging the wall of the troop transport ship. She was so excited when Georg told her that he was signing up for service with the troops of Margrave Carl Alexander of Ansbach-Bayreuth. The Margrave had promised his cousin, the King of England, a detachment of excellent soldiers to help quell the rebellion in America. These were already the fifth replacement troops, and it seemed to be a war which never wanted to end.

Margaretha's father had been quite pleased to see that Georg found reasons to continue to come to the Wunderlichs' new mill after he had helped build it. A brick and stone mason would make a good son-in-law, and the young, pretty Margaretha definitely was a good catch. The dowry that she would bring into a marriage was more than what could be expected of the tenant farmers' daughters. Being the miller's daughter placed Margaretha socially higher than others in the village. But, most importantly, she could read as well as any of her brothers. Her father had seen to it since he needed her to decipher the names on the grain sacks and write in the ledgers in the small room off the mill entrance. Reading and writing came easily to Margaretha who exhibited a very independent nature even as a young girl. Her parents often wondered what the future would hold for their bright determined daughter.

When Georg started courting Margaretha, she happily agreed to follow him to the ends of the Earth, or at least as far as North America where the troops would be sent. Even Margaretha's parents gladly entrusted their daughter into his care when he asked them for her hand in marriage. All women in the Wunderlich family started wedding preparations for the three-day festivities while Margaretha busied herself adding to her trousseau. How she enjoyed spinning on her grandmother's spinning wheel! Many years ago, Grandmother had found a way to run her wheel very quietly. When she spun wool from the fleece of her sheep, and her hands were covered with lanolin from the wool, she coated the moving parts of her wheel with the oily substance to silence any squealing spinning usually caused. Since she liked to do her spinning after her children, and later her grandchildren, were put to bed, she did not need to fear waking them while she enjoyed her spinning. When Margaretha was a little girl she had begged her grandmother to paint the wheel her favorite color, sky blue. Grandmother gladly agreed, and there it was, a blue wheel quietly humming along, the treadle powered by Margaretha's little foot. Margaretha and her grandmother spent many happy hours talking and perfecting the little girl's spinning. How Margaretha wished she could take the spinning wheel with her, but on the journey to the New World they were limited to the absolute necessities. The military would supply Georg with his uniform and other clothing, and the wives were expected to bring clothing they needed, and pots and pans to cook in. The knitting needles and wool, and the sewing boxes and cloth, could easily be packed, but a spinning wheel was too bulky.

The whole village came to see off the Jäger troops who relished the thought of being feared by the rebels as elite sharpshooters. Margaretha was glad that her older cousin Elisabeth was able to talk her husband Michael into joining up. Michael had been in the service during the Seven Years War and joined the troops as vice-corporal. Tears were shed, and the older people were fearful for the young who were going into a world strange to them. But what they dreaded most for the troops was the ocean voyage. For their concern the elderly only earned laughter from the young. And young they were. Even the highest ranking officer was not yet forty years old and all his junior officers were only in their twenties.

Regardless of the fears, the send-off was tremendous. The ten musicians with the troops played as if this were a village dance and not a march into the unknown. The eight women and one child with the troops wore their traveling clothes and the women carried their Sunday-best dresses in the packs on their backs. The weather for the march to the river was not as pleasant as springtime can be, but as long as they were moving the cold did not bother them. Only after they were packed tightly onto the river boats did they feel the biting chill of April. How glad they were when they arrived in Bremerlehe, and the troops passed review in front of the British commissioner William Faucitt, and were found satisfactory.

Finally on June 10, 1782 the fleet set sail for North America. Margaretha's churning stomach discomfort had let up, but almost everyone else was ill with seasickness. She actually enjoyed eating the daily pea soup with salt pork. She did not understand the chuckles from the older women when she told them about her food cravings. When her cousin Elisabeth reminded her of Georg's last furlough, before he reported to the

barracks in Ansbach, she smiled thinking of how they had cele-
brated their last weekend alone. Only then did she understand
the knowing smiles of the other women. How was she going to
cope with an ever-expanding midriff in those tight quarters?
Six people—three couples—to a bunk, and she with child.
Georg brushed aside all worries. He was as proud as those
peacocks his father-in-law had strutting around the mill back
home.

The voyage progressed very slowly. The troops, and the
women and child accompanying them, expected to arrive on
solid ground in New York after about six weeks at sea. By their
tenth week they received word that their immediate destination was not New York but Halifax, Nova Scotia. At least there
was a safe harbor and no worry of war action. The condition
aboard the ships had become unbearable—spoiled food, rotten
water, and no beer left which would be safe to drink. At last—
land!

Disembarking took days. Margaretha and the other
women were glad to have solid ground underfoot and glad to
finally be able to cook and not having to eat the ship rations.
Being with child had some advantages. Since she could not
bend down easily the other women and the older child supported her as much as possible. After the work was done, the
women sat outside the tents overlooking the harbor and doing
the mending while they enjoyed the summer evenings. Margaretha did not share the yearning for their village at home that
seemed to plague some of the women. She was instead almost
giddy with the excitement of seeing some of the places she had
read about in her brothers' geography books. Might they even
encounter the Indians? Some books had described them as sav-
ages and others as noble lovers of nature. Whatever this journey had to offer, Margaretha intended to learn as much as she
could. While the women were gazing across the ocean they
could see the sails of ships, but could not make out if they were
British supply ships or Continental privateers ready to attack

the ships. Or could they even be French ships ready to attack to regain their North American provinces, which they had lost barely nineteen years before? The British in charge created plenty of confusion from time to time by making the Ansbach-Bayreuth troops pack up all tents and get on board ship to be sent to who knows where, to fight who knows whom. The French? The rebels? The women all did as they were told, packing up the cooking utensils, packing all belongings, calming each other, and instructing the child how to help, just to be told it was a false alarm. Just as well, as long as the war did not come to them they were glad to get on and off the ship.

Summer turned to fall and fall to an early winter when definite word came to sail to Penobscot. Spies brought news that the French may attack Fort George, and Britain intended to defend the fort. Many Loyalists had arrived, expecting the King's protection, on the east side of the Penobscot. There were rumors that the river would be the border between British North America and the expected United States of America. None of this was of particular interest to Margaretha and the other women. They just hoped to have solid roofs over their heads, strong walls around them, and a warm fire in the fireplaces. The disappointment of seeing the dismal living arrangements left to them was indescribable. Even the women who were used to living in poor cottages and sleeping on straw mattresses near the stoves during the winter were shocked to see the drafty, thrown-together huts which were to be their homes for the winter. And even though it was only mid-November, it was spitting snow.

Finally, the meager possessions each family had brought were unpacked in the hut which was to be the home of all six couples and the older child. The women then went about to give the miserable hut a little touch of home. Elsbet, who was also great with child, had brought a beautifully embroidered tablecloth which now hung in front of the only window to keep the cold draft out. Marion, who was expecting her first child and was still suffering from morning sickness, contributed an etching of Ansbach to hang on the wall. Käthe, who was dealing with a queasy stomach, shared the wooden board and her best bread knife so the hard bread rations could be cut and shared among the women and their husbands. The miserable hut which the six Jäger shared with their families started to feel more like home, if only the fireplaces at each end would provide more warmth against the drafty construction.

Now that they were actually at the military outpost it became clear who was in charge. The Ansbachers thought they were valued allies of the British crown, but the Scots, who commanded Fort George, let them know that they considered them just hirelings. If it had not been for the Brunswick troops who had arrived a few weeks before they did, the Ansbachers would have been at an even greater disadvantage. Captain Cleve, commanding the Brunswick troops, who had served in the Seven Years War and had also served in North America before, was self-confident and experienced, and a decade older than Captain von Wurmb, commander of the Ansbach troops. Captain Cleve took on the senior position of the German troops and through direct demands of the Fort's commander Brigadier General John Campbell, and diplomacy when needed, he provided what was possible.

Yet the one thing causing the greatest misery even Captain Cleve was not able to change — the horrible weather conditions. Margaretha could not remember ever having been as cold as she was this November. Her euphoria of experiencing the new world was wearing thin. She tried to remind herself how fortunate she was to see more of the world than she ever imagined growing up in her village, but it was hard to let her mind appreciate the experience when her body was craving creature comforts. If she was desperately trying to stay warm in November, what would the weather be like once winter actually set in? She knew she should be grateful that her husband, as a brick mason, received additional pay to work on the construction of the fort. When he came home at night she spent much time mending his clothing, which he had torn to shreds at work. The extra pay he received allowed her to buy candles so she could work into the early-evening hours. The prices at the Scottish store were continually rising, but it was the only place where they could shop.

There were advantages to the miserable cold and the early darkness. Margaretha and Georg retired early to their bed, cuddled under the blankets, and spent time quietly talking. Margaretha was glad for the privacy this rough-hewn bed provided them. Speaking in the dark seemed to help both of them confide their deepest thoughts to each other. Margaretha was glad no one could see how she blushed when Georg told her how proud he was that she had the courage to join him on this outpost which could at any moment be the center of great danger. As a proper Christian woman she had been taught humility, but came to realize she did enjoy being curious and daring. As long as Field Chaplain Erb did not hear about her enlightened thought of trusting in herself, she was glad to accept her husband's admiration. Georg shared with Margaretha that he had overheard the field chaplain and Lieutenant von Massenbach speak about their plan to travel the country once the war was over. Georg had offered to be their servant and, knowing how much Margaretha enjoyed adventure, had offered her services too so they could travel with them after the child was born. Thinking of such an exciting future helped Margaretha forget the howling wind and the numbing cold outside, if even for a short time under the warm blanket with Georg by her side.

Margaretha's thoughts, however, were not dealing with the future; she was living in the present. When she confided in her husband that her dearest wish was to be spinning again, to give her life a familiar feel, he knew what she wanted: her grandmother's blue spinning wheel quietly humming along under the rhythmic push of the treadle. How he wished he could provide it for her. But they were at a military outpost surrounded by locals who had sworn an oath to the King, though even the Scottish commander doubted their loyalty. No soldier was allowed to leave the post. Margaretha just knew the spinning wheel would have to remain a dream.

Life at Fort George took on a feeling of normalcy. Field Chaplain Erb held regular Sunday church services which were attended by the religious members of the Brunswick and the Ansbach troops. For many of the soldiers this was the time to sleep off their drunken stupor instead of attending service. The families enjoyed the quiet, festive Advent season that reminded them of home. Being surrounded by scrawny little fir trees was an advantage. Plans were made to cut one down and bring it into the hut on Christmas Eve to decorate it as they always did at home. The women even conspired to make little presents for the child and for each other.

Just a week before Christmas, Margaretha knew her time had come. How grateful she was that her cousin Elisabeth was there, and the other women who helped her bring a healthy boy into the world. The very evening of December 17, the field chaplain baptized him and gave him the name of his godfather, Michael Peter, Elisabeth's husband.

Celebrating Christmas with a newborn seemed a blessing and Margaretha had no wish for any other present. But Georg had conspired with another Jäger, who was an excellent carpenter, to build the spinning wheel Margaretha missed so dearly. And there it stood next to the child's bed on Christmas morning, as perfect as her grandmother's quiet blue wheel.

Perhaps it was the letdown after the festive holiday, or the long dark days, or the unrelenting miserable cold which affected everyone. Georg brought back news about a duel two Ansbach officers had fought, a deadly fight among Ansbach and Scottish soldiers, and the frightening news that a Scottish officer had wounded Captain von Wurmb. The field chaplain held special prayer services as he believed that only heavenly intervention could save the captain from certain death. Why were so many frightening events happening?

The snow drifts covering the paths between the huts, the blowing snow even inside the huts, and the numbing cold took its toll on Margaretha. How she wished to be warm! She even caught herself being careless with the fire; once, sitting too close to the open hearth while spinning on her new wheel, her shawl brushed against the hot embers, which singed it slightly. Only Marion's frightened outcry made Margaretha aware of the imminent danger. Often, when no one was looking, Margaretha threw another piece of the precious wood on the fire, using up more than was allotted per day. The other women did not seem as affected by the cold. They were willing to brave the temperatures and go outside, bundling up against the elements to supervise the child at play, and to make attempts to socialize with the Scottish wives and children. Communication was difficult, but a smile and the mutual interest in the children created a bond for which language was not necessary.

January brought more snow than any of the Ansbach or Brunswick troops had seen in their entire lives. What a desolate place they had been sent to! The officers who cared about their assignment wondered out loud why the British King even wanted to keep a land as inhospitable as this province. They had hoped for some action to prove their military skill, but the enemy did not even care to attack. No wonder they picked fights amongst each other. Though the Scottish and the German troops should have been cooperating, there was enough strangeness between them to see their dissimilarities, and not the fact that they were on the same side.

After giving birth Margaretha felt like she could not shake her sadness. Even Elisabeth noticed that Margaretha was more withdrawn and unresponsive than could be attributed to the normal sadness of a young mother. When there was finally calm between the snowstorms Elisabeth asked permission to visit the local doctor's wife. The doctor and his wife had spent time in Göttingen where the doctor had been studying at the university. They both spoke German quite fluently and were regular guests at Brigadier General John Campbell's house where they met the Scottish and German officers and spent many a pleasant event being entertained by the Ansbach musicians. Elisabeth had taken a plate of Lebkuchen made from a recipe her mother had learned from her mother. Katherine, the doctor's wife, was delighted to have company and the two women spent an afternoon over tea and cakes discussing how to help Margaretha shake the sadness that had enveloped her.

Visiting the housing of the families of the German enlisted men was only slightly out of Katherine's way. She regularly checked on the local and the Scottish wives when they were with child and their times came close. Politics was not the women's interest; they let the men deal with that. Caring for children and their men was enough of a daily struggle. Worrying about putting food on the table, which was getting more and more scarce and more and more expensive, occupied their every waking hour.

It was not unusual for Katherine to pay a visit at the Ansbach family hut. To find Margaretha in such despair shocked Katherine. She had seen her before the birth and enjoyed speaking with her about her time in a German town, and about the joys of motherhood, which Katherine had been denied. Katherine had even been invited to witness the baptism of little Michael Peter. Katherine's gentle prodding finally unleashed a flood of tears and with it the admission that the weather in this province was so disheartening that the only comfort for Margaretha would be to pull the covers over her head and hope for spring. As this was not a reasonable option, being the mother of a newborn, Margaretha shared that she had withdrawn into herself and refused any attempt of interaction with the other women.

At first, Margaretha was offended by Katherine's burst of laughter, but then she was more puzzled and finally curious what would have brought on such a reaction to her admission that the weather was her greatest nemesis. When Katherine finally caught her breath and could speak again, she admitted that just about everyone in the province experienced the same affliction. If people could imitate the local wildlife and hibernate like the bears there would be less fighting among the families, less drinking among the men, and less grumpiness among the women, Katherine told her. Since hibernation was not an option, there had to be other solutions. Her own answer to the dilemma was getting together with other women to quilt. Sitting with friends stitching a quilt and sharing all the news they knew about, some more charitable than others, provided all the gossip to keep the women entertained, which helped pass the long winter days and evenings. Walking through the snow on a moonlit night, laughing about the juicy bits of gossip just heard, should let anyone forget the misery of winter for a while.

Margaretha had bundled little Michael Peter up in the soft woolen blanket Elisabeth had given her after the boy was born. Margaretha and Elisabeth had a pleasant walk to Katherine's house at the outskirts of the village on the peninsula. It had snowed the night before, and the sun brightened up the day. The full moon that night would provide enough light for the evening walk back to the hut. Katherine had set up the quilt stand in her front parlor, bathed in the sunlight streaming in through the windows on the south and west side of the house. Friends from the German settlement of Broad Bay had arrived the day before and planned to spend a few weeks with Katherine. They brought the latest gossip about the three Brunswick deserters from Fort George who had made their way south until they reached Broad Bay. One of them had already found a wife. No wonder, since the men from the village were away fighting with the Continental Army. Any eligible man was welcome and, before he could object, was wed to a local girl. The story that he had been hidden in the cellar by the new wife's family, and fed through the floor boards, sounded so ridiculous that all of the women burst out laughing and were unable to stop until Elisabeth caught her breath and became rather serious.

She posed the question whether someone knew why two Ansbach officers had fought a duel. Katharine had heard from her husband, who was called on to bandage the wound, that Second Lieutenant von Bubna was badly wounded. The other officer, Lieutenant Busch, was obviously not to blame since he was not reprimanded. Were the officers as restless as the enlisted men? As long as they were stuck in this seemingly forgotten outpost without any realistic chance of military action, there was no hope for advancement. But what was the reason for the duel? For the officers there was enough distraction in this post, which had grown tenfold in just a few short years. Ever since the British were victorious in the Penobscot Expedition over the Continentals in 1779, the village around Fort George had grown by leaps and bounds. Loyalists from regions to the south kept arriving, expecting the King's troops to protect them and the King's store to supply them with necessities, since they remained true to their royal ruler. The sleepy little village of Bagaduce had turned into a hotbed of vice, commerce, and culture. The musicians with the Ansbach troops were in great demand playing at festivities for the locals, as well as play at the Scottish and German military balls. Even though none of the German officers had brought their wives, the Scottish officers' wives added a civilizing flair to the events. Could Lieutenant Busch have had to defend the honor of the troops by fighting the duel with Second Lieutenant von Bubna? Who had challenged whom? Tongues were wagging, von Bubna had made many enemies, and some people even said he had it coming. But as good Christian women, the wives

of the Ansbach regiments tried to see the good in everyone—
though in some it was easier to find than in others.

But the greatest mystery was the whereabouts of the Scottish officer who had wounded Captain von Wurmb. Whatever
possessed the captain to invite such a scoundrel? Was there no
honor among gentlemen? It was rather common that the
enlisted men among the Scottish and Ansbach soldiers started
a fight now and then. With nothing to do, generous rum rations, and no enemy to fight, it was no wonder they fought
each other. The officers finally had to put a stop to it; they gave
the order that no man was allowed to carry any type of
weapon, not even a knife, except on patrol.

The gossiping while quilting could have gone on for hours,
but Margaretha and Elisabeth needed to return to the hut to
prepare the evening meal for their husbands. Margaretha
nursed the baby once more before they bundled up to walk
back to the hut. Katherine walked her guests to the door, and
looked worried at the white circle around the moon. Elisabeth
was surprised that even on this continent the weather forecast
agreed with their predictions back home. How bad would the
weather be, which the ring around the moon in the starlit sky
foretold? Fortunately, Margaretha did not see the ominous
sign in the sky. Her spirits had been lifted by the camaraderie
of the women at the quilting, and she almost forgot the dreari-
ness of the winter in the District of Maine, Commonwealth of
Massachusetts. It was already mid-January. Back home on the
south side of her parents' mill, near the stone foundation, the
crocuses would soon poke the tips of their green shoots out of
the cold soil. Perhaps the winter could not last too much
longer, even here at Penobscot. Field Chaplain Erb kept talking
about his plan of starting a garden near the house that he
shared with Captain Cleve. Everyone expected that their time
at the fort would last well into the next years, because here at
the far northern outpost, they did not hear of any talk of a
peace with the rebels. Field Chaplain Erb fancied himself a

good gardener and intended to grow many vegetables to become less dependent on the meager supplies the locals were willing to sell, or on those overpriced goods the Scottish store sold.

As the ring around the moon predicted, a heavy snowstorm blew into the area. It dashed any hopes of an early spring. It also kept everyone indoors. No desertions were reported; it would have meant certain death in that weather. The officers knew that some of their men were only waiting for an opportunity to leave. If it were not for the fact that they had to uphold discipline, which included punishing those soldiers who attempted desertion, they would gladly have done without some of them. Knowing that the deserters might have a better chance at a successful life on this continent, which their poverty back home would never provide, the officers wished they could give permission for some of the men to leave. But as long as they were garrisoned at Fort George, and in the British service, every man needed to remain on the roster, and therefore draw pay from the British.

By early February the weather had improved enough to venture out again. The soldiers had cleared paths through the snow so the women could again walk to the Scottish store. Elisabeth and Margaretha made plans to accept another invitation from Katherine. This time the women planned to do some spinning and needlework. Margaretha took almost as much care wrapping up her blue wheel as she did bundling up little Michael Peter. She placed the wheel on the small sled Georg had built for her and she carried the baby in a sling around her body, protecting him with her cape so only his little nose and curious eyes looked out.

The spinning wheel received the expected admiring glances from Katherine and the two Scottish corporals' wives whom Katherine had also invited. At first Elisabeth and Margaretha were taken aback to find strangers in Katherine's house, since they had hoped to meet the German ladies from Broad Bay again. But soon all five women were deeply involved in their needlework and spinning. Katherine had brought out the soft fleece from her sheep, which had been shorn last spring, and which she had carded but never found the time to spin to yarn. Margaretha was deeply honored to receive the wool as a gift, and spinning it on her blue wheel was pure joy. The quiet hum while Margaretha worked the treadle sounded like familiar music from her childhood.

The visit with the two Scottish ladies turned into a wonderful opportunity for them and for Margaretha and Elisabeth. Whenever either of them wanted to know a new word, Margaretha wrote the German word on a sheet of paper and Katherine added the English word to it. Trying to pronounce each other's language was difficult in the beginning, but it seemed to get easier as the conversation became more fluent. Laughter over tea helped loosen the tongues, and the walk back from Katherine's house turned into a very pleasant stroll for the two German and the two Scottish women.

They waved good-bye when their paths divided as they reached the living areas. The Scottish, who had been at the fort since 1779, lived in much more secure houses than the Ansbachers, who had to move into huts which were thrown together in a hurry without taking manpower away from the building of the fort. The British had not expected that they would need to reinforce the fort to make it as secure as one of military importance would be, but when they caught wind of an attempt by the French to regain Quebec, the Fort had to be strengthened to secure the military presence in order to fight off an attack. The men in the area, from as far away as Broad Bay had been lining up to take employment with the British. Even one of the German prisoners of war of the Convention Army troops from the surrender at Saratoga, who had hired himself out to a Broad Bay merchant, was glad to earn pay by building the fort. The war had made the attempts of the local population to earn a living as fishermen and as shipwrights even more uncertain, and most of them believed that at least now the future was secure. Being back under British protection was not such a bad life; it had served them and their ancestors reasonably well for generations. Not knowing if it was safe to believe in the old order or join the rebels was dangerous. The threatening of tarring and feathering did not endear the rebels to most people who just wanted to be left alone.

Change was in the air — and not just the subtle change in weather noticeable by the melting of the snow on the roofs of the huts and barracks. There were rumors that there would be a peace agreement signed between the British government and the new United States. What would it mean to the settlement around Fort George and the eastern boundary of the Penobscot River? Would they belong to British North America, as the new Province of Ireland, or would the area be ceded to the rebels? This District of Maine in the Commonwealth of Massachusetts had always been an integral part of New England, securely bound to Massachusetts and the other New England colonies, which now would be independent from the British crown.

Change certainly had come to the attitude of the local population. Suddenly they were glad to sell their wares to the British and the Germans, and to the many Loyalists who had moved here in hopes of having found a new home. These plans were now changing. Soon only the locals would remain. What will future generations know about the peaceful cooperation among the British and Germans at Fort George and the locals who enjoyed their friendship?

Margaretha first noticed the chirping of birds in the morning when she was nursing little Michael Peter before she had to get up to make breakfast for Georg and herself. Could it be possible that spring would at last arrive, even if much later than any of the Ansbachers expected it at home? The sun became warmer; patches of muddy soil were visible around the huts. Finally, even blades of green grass poked through the mud where the sun had melted all snow. Spring had triumphed over winter. Margaretha caught herself smiling and humming songs she had enjoyed since her childhood. When Elisabeth asked her why she was in a better mood than she had been in a long time, Margaretha thought for a moment before she burst out her answer: The chains of her imprisonment by the elements had been broken. Spring promised new life. But then she became more thoughtful: When and why had she started to look at her situation with more hope in her heart?

Lieutenant Busch, the new commander of the Ansbach troops, had orders to abandon Fort George. Captain von Wurmb had succumbed to the wound inflicted on him by the Scottish officer and would forever remain buried in North American soil. Dreams by some of the junior officers to travel the young United States would be left unfulfilled. They needed to return home and await new assignments by their Margrave. At least Field Chaplain Erb had a chance to see a little more of the American continent. He was to carry orders from Captain Cleve to New York, and Erb intended to make the most of this opportunity before he had to join his flock in England to accompany them on their return to Ansbach.

Soldiers and their wives were busy packing their gear and belongings. The women made sure the soldiers' uniforms were mended as well as could be so when they proudly marched back into Ansbach they could hold their heads high. How they planned to regale their friends with stories about their time in the New World! If some of the facts were embellished, how would those who have never seen North America know the difference? The women knew their friends back home were eager to hear about the New

World. Those evenings getting together spinning or weaving or doing needlework would provide ample opportunities to share their experiences.

Margaretha and Elisabeth had one bittersweet visit ahead of them. Katherine, who had become a dear friend, had invited them to one last tea before the Ansbachers embarked on the troop transport ship *The Brothers*. While drinking tea, spinning, and talking, their time passed pleasantly but too quickly. Little Michael Peter was lying contentedly on the woolen blanket on the floor while Elisabeth and Katherine said their last good-byes. When it was Margaretha's turn, she looked at Katherine with tear-filled eyes and spoke.

"Without you, I do not believe I could have found the strength to fight the sadness, this winter has plunged me into," she said. "Your friendship has been one of the greatest treasures I have been given. You and my husband's gift of the spinning wheel have rescued me from the depth of my melancholy. Ever since Elisabeth had asked me what had broken the spell of sadness that had taken hold of me, I have thought about the answer. I finally knew what it was: It was your friendship, and also the joy of spinning."

Margaretha gently ran her hand along the outside of the wheel before she spoke again. "When I first stepped on the wheel's treadle I felt like running away, to escape from this wintery hell. But when I saw the even strands of soft wool I had spun, I saw that through my work my family will be dressed warm. I remembered sitting with my grandmother, listening to the quiet hum her wheel made with every step on the treadle."

Margaretha paused before she continued. "I had to remind myself: I wanted a life of adventure, and this certainly is an adventure. And no matter where I am, I can decide how happy I will be."

All three women nodded in agreement. Then Margaretha turned to Katherine again and spoke:

"As a reminder of our friendship, please, accept this spinning wheel. Whenever I spin on my grandmother's blue wheel at home, I will send my thoughts to you in deepest gratitude. And think of me when you do your spinning on this wheel."

Author's Note

British troops had been stationed at Fort George, Penobscot Bay, since the Continental troops lost the battle during the Penobscot Expedition in the summer of 1779. Rumors of a possible French attack convinced the British to send reinforcements in 1782. By September 1782, Captain Henrich Urban Cleve who commanded slightly over 200 Brunswick troops was sent to Fort George with his troops. Captain Ernst Friedrich von Wurmb, who commanded slightly over 200 Ansbach-Bayreuth troops, arrived at Fort George in November of 1782 with his troops. By then approximately 1,000 troops were stationed at Fort George at Penobscot Bay; about 40 percent were those from the two German principalities (belonging to the so-called Hessians) and about 60 percent were Scottish.

All officers and the Ansbach Field Chaplain named in this story, and actions surrounding them, are historically accurate. The names and military ranks of the other Ansbachers mentioned, even little Michael Peter, refer to real people. Margaretha and Elisabeth did live at Fort George, but their relationship to each other is pure conjecture. So is the friendship with the doctor's wife, Katherine, who is only a figment of the writer's imagination.

A high-school prank set in a Maine cemetery can't end well. In David M. Fitzpatrick's telling, the young characters' lives, filled with hopes and desires, go skidding off the rails. The quiet blue wheel is unmoved, unchanged as it observes the events unfold. But don't think you've got it all figured out; the story's narrator holds his pain close and reveals it slowly.

— Greg Westrich

The Curse of
John Trafford's Grave

David M. Fitzpatrick

I remember every detail of that terrible night in 1981 like it happened yesterday. Thirty years later, I still don't go anywhere near that cemetery — not even during the day, when the sun makes the grass appear the happiest green, and the gravestones seem like bright and cheerful monuments. That is, except for one day out of the year: my birthday. Every year, when I should be celebrating making it through another trip around the sun alive, I steel my nerves and I go there long after the sun has gone down, when it's dark and foreboding and utterly haunting, and try to find peace with what happened that night so long ago.

We were in high school, too old to be kids and too young to be adults. Jimmy Ellerby was my best friend, as he had been since kindergarten. And we were friends with Darcie Keegan, although we both wanted more than friendship with her.

While Darcie wasn't one of those popular preppies, she was definitely above our social status; we'd always been the kids nobody liked much. But she hung out with us anyway. She was that kind of friend.

And she was beautiful. I can still see her face that way when I close my eyes. Hers was a soft beauty framed by quiet elegance, innocent and overpowering, and so pure it made my heart ache. I first met her when her family came to town while I was in the third grade, in 1974. They'd moved in right across the street from me, in the old Fenton place. I remember the whispered rumors about that house, because Old Man Fenton had supposedly smothered his wife with a pillow. Years later I found out she'd actually died of a heart attack in bed, and he'd gone crazy with grief. But kids keep crazy rumors alive, so of course we believed the Keegans were moving into an evil-ghost house, and that something in there would eventually drive them all mad and smother each other with pillows.

Those silly stories flew right out of my mind the moment I saw Darcie, pretty as a princess in her green-and-red plaid dress, with yellow ribbons in her auburn-colored pigtails. We grew to be great pals over the years, but eventually puberty grabbed hold of me and I started thinking of her in other ways. Her mane of silky auburn hair, her widening hips, and the bulging lumps we'd been teasing her about that had become full-fledged breasts suddenly seemed attractive. And she smelled nice, too — of melon-scented shampoo, of coconut lotion, and sometimes of flowery perfume. It was intoxicating.

Jimmy had it for her, too, but he was just horny. It was far more than that to me. On my twelfth birthday, I told her I loved her; she just laughed and called me silly and gave me a quick birthday kiss on the cheek. I told her again on my thirteenth birthday; once again, she laughed and called me silly, but this time the quick kiss was on my lips.

When I told her on my fourteenth birthday, there was no laughing. She locked her lips to mine for many long seconds, and it was exciting and wonderful and neither of us had any clue what to do. But when it was over, she wished me a happy birthday and called me a good friend, and headed home. We didn't talk about it again.

Since my birthday kiss had been getting more special every year, on my fifteenth I got myself alone with her and we actually made out. She let me touch her in places I thought I'd never get to touch a girl, but when it was over she breathlessly told me that we couldn't do this again, because we'd end up ruining our friendship. I agreed, because I thought I was supposed to agree and didn't want to make things difficult by going against her. But secretly, I was willing to wait another year. I was sure we weren't just being careless friends; I loved her, and I knew she loved me.

The day before I turned sixteen, Jimmy came up with the idea to scare the pants off Darcie's little brother, Lenny. He was ten and quite naïve, so when Jimmy told Darcie and me about his plan, we knew we could pull it off. It would involve the grave of the long-dead Captain John Trafford.

Like the Old Man Fenton story of Darcie's house, there had been tales told about Longview Cemetery — but people had told them as far back as anyone could remember. Nobody had been buried in its back half of Longview since the mid-1800s, and the headstones dated to the 1770s. It was spooky even in broad daylight; kids never went there even close to sunset. Even our parents and grandparents had told the stories of the faint, but unearthly, wailing that had occasionally been heard over the centuries. We'd never heard it — not one single wailing note — but we all told the story as if we had, and we stayed away from the place at night.

On the sunny afternoon the day before my birthday, the four of us had cut through the cemetery after throwing around a yellow Skyro flying ring in the park. We walked four abreast, Jimmy and Lenny to my left and Darcie to my right. I was already thinking of what my birthday might bring this year —

heck, I'd been thinking of it every day for the past year. And I knew she was thinking about it, too, the way she'd turn her eyes away and blush a little when I caught her looking at me.

As Darcie and I bounced looks back and forth, Jimmy was telling Lenny he'd been out near the graveyard the night before and had heard the wailing.

"I wonder what it is," Lenny said. He was a little slow, but an innocent, nice kid. Darcie always looked out for him, but had a weakness when it came to Jimmy messing with him. Jimmy did it a lot, and it was always funny.

"It's the ghost of a man who can't rest in peace," Jimmy said, reciting his prepared script as he spun the Skyro on his wrist. "He wails because his lover abandoned him for another man."

Lenny's eyes were wide. "Why'd she do that?"

"I dunno — guess she didn't love him anymore," Jimmy said. "He died of sadness, so he haunts the cemetery. Here, check it out."

He led us to the farthest corner of the cemetery, where the giant headstone stood. It began as a massive, octagonal block of granite in the middle of the plot. Atop that was a towering obelisk standing fifteen feet high. The giant monument was tilted slightly, the result of centuries of the ground beneath it settling. Beneath it all, we knew, was a dead man who had slumbered for two centuries. In big letters on the facing side of the octagon base, mostly obscured by countless decades of dead lichen never scraped off, was the name TRAFFORD.

But the cool thing wasn't the octagon and obelisk. The massive headstone was surrounded by a strange circle of blue granite stones. They were big, and they butted against each other like some crowded Stonehenge. The blocks were a foot high, containing a circular plot of land a foot higher than the surrounding landscape. At a dozen points around the stone wheel were blocks twice as wide as the others, jutting out like the handles on a ship's wheel. It was unlike anything in the graveyard — or in any other graveyard. Jimmy and I had been entranced by how cool that stone wheel looked since we'd been old enough to venture alone into the cemetery. There were neater, bigger, and older headstones in the graveyard, but that wheel had drawn us to it ever since we'd discovered it. It's what led to everything that happened to us afterward.

So we stood then, surveying the bizarre little Stonehenge, watching Lenny's wide eyes and gaping mouth. "Wow," he finally breathed. "That's really cool! But why are those rocks blue?"

"They say he had the granite quarried in another country and brought here," I said, and this was true. The rocks were predominantly very dark, but were filled with shiny blue crystals that made it look as if it were burning with blue fire in a bright, noontime sun. "He built it himself, before he died."

"Who was he?" Lenny asked.

"Captain John Trafford, one of the oldest residents of this graveyard," Jimmy said, he voice as solemn as a minister delivering a eulogy. "He was a sea captain who traveled all over the world, exporting granite out of Maine and importing it from other countries. He built the ring in honor of his ship's wheel. He was buried here in 1781."

Lenny squinted at the hard-to-read engraving. "He died on June seventeenth," he announced, and then he spun to us, eyes big. "That's two hundred years ago tomorrow!"

"Hey — that's Marty's birthday," Darcie said, feigning surprise as part of our plan. Our eyes met again, and she looked away with a slight smile, her freckles climbing her high cheekbones. She was so absolutely beautiful.

Of course, Jimmy and I knew all about Captain Trafford's grave and its coincidental death date. We'd discovered it several summers before, and it had been a source of minor amusement for us. But with Lenny unaware, Jimmy's tale would hook him. "You've heard about the wailing here, right?" he pressed Lenny.

"Yeah." Lenny was visibly nervous. "Everyone says it's really faint, and nobody can hear where it comes from."

"Oh, they know where it comes from, all right," Jimmy said with a grave expression befitting of a cemetery. "They say that every year, as the anniversary of his death approaches, Captain Trafford wails because he misses his beloved. The wailing comes from right here — from right inside this ring of stones. It comes from his grave, Len."

"No way," Lenny said, and his bright eyes were big blue wheels as well.

"Yes way. But on that night, he can be put to proper rest — if someone dares."

"How?" Lenny said, incredulous.

"Supposedly, he needs only to see his love again, but she's dead. If only she could appear to him at midnight and tell him she loves him, he'll move on to the next world. Otherwise, he'll haunt the graveyard forever."

"Wow," Lenny said.

"Come to think of it," Jimmy said, scrunching his brow like a master scam artist and tapping his chin with a finger, "Darcie looks a lot like her."

"She *does?*"

"Yeah — I saw a painting of her in an old book at the library. She was pretty, with auburn hair and green eyes and freckles. Just like your sister."

She was pretty, all right, in all her Irish glory, pursing her lips as she tried to stop a smile from spreading across her face in the wake of Jimmy's ridiculous story. She and those beautiful lips were all I could think about. I'd be kissing them the following night, and maybe more, and I could barely contain myself enough to stick with the joke.

"Hey, you know what?" Jimmy said, eyes brightening. "We should do it."

"Do what?" Lenny said.

"We come here tomorrow at midnight, with Darcie

dressed up to look like John Trafford's beloved. She tells him she loves him, and the poor guy can finally rest in peace."

I could tell from the look Darcie shot at me that she felt the same way I did. There was no way we were coming to this graveyard at midnight. Lenny didn't seem to like the idea, either, turning pale and stammering more than usual. Jimmy kept messing with Lenny's head during the walk home, until Lenny met up with some of his friends and parted company, giving us a chance to hear Jimmy's plan. It involved a white dress for Darcie and me hiding in the woods in the dark behind Trafford's grave, dressed in old clothes and fake blood and white makeup. When we realized he was serious, Darcie put a stop to it.

"I'm all for messing with my little brother, but there's no way I'm coming here at midnight," she told Jimmy. "And anyway, I've never heard about putting his spirit to rest."

"Well, of course not—I made it up," Jimmy said, flipping the Skyro over his head and resting it on his shoulders like some futuristic necklace. "But Lenny swallowed it, hook, line, and sinker! That's why we've got to do this. We may literally scare the crap out of him. How cool would it be to make him actually shit himself? There's no way we can pass this up."

We argued about it for a while, the deciding factor was that Lenny might actually soil himself and give us something to laugh about forever. The only loose end was how Jimmy and Darcie would explain to Lenny why I wasn't going with them—seeing as how I would be secretly waiting there, dressed as the dead guy.

"That's the beauty of it," Jimmy said. "It's your birthday. We'll tell him your parents are taking you to see *Superman II* again, and you'll join us as soon as you can."

"He'll never buy it," I said. "He already knows I'm going to see *Raiders of the Lost Ark* tomorrow afternoon."

"So it's a double feature. Your parents love you. This is Lenny we're talking about here. You could tell him you were seeing a triple feature of Disney cartoons with your grand-mother and he'd fall for it."

It was hard to argue with that logic. Jimmy parted com-pany from us then, but not before making Darcie promise to keep a straight face and talk her brother into doing this. There was no doubt she'd succeed; Lenny ultimately would do any-thing his sister told him to do.

I walked Darcie home, like I'd done a thousand times be-fore. We walked in silence for a while down suburban streets shaded by the lush canopy of elms and oaks before I said, "You don't have a boyfriend."

"So?" she said. "You don't have a girlfriend."

"Sounds like a match." It seemed so simple. I don't even know where the courage came from, but it didn't feel weird at all. No nervous feelings, no shaking, no fear.

We walked a little while longer before she said, "I just like being friends with you, that's all."

We left it at that and walked in silence. Soon we rounded the corner onto our street. We finally made it to her house and said good-bye.

I went down her steps to head for my house, but she called me back. I stood there, looking up her steps at her, and she said, "You're the only boy I've ever kissed."

The way the sunlight hit her freckled face and gleaming eyes made her look more beautiful than ever. All I could do was just stare at her.

"Except for Corey Higgins in fourth grade, but that hardly counts," she said, and I laughed.

"Well, you're the only girl I've ever kissed," I said.

I don't know what I thought was going to happen next, but she smiled and waved and said good-bye again, and off she went into her house.

Jimmy came to my house the next day with an ancient suit that had belonged to his great-grandfather, who had been a tailor before the turn of the century. It was moth-eaten and tattered after years in Jimmy's attic — just like, Jimmy said, a dead man's suit would look. We figured a sea captain likely would have been buried in his captain's uniform, but we couldn't come up with anything like that and decided Lenny wouldn't figure that out anyway. Jimmy was really into the prank, and I guess I was, too. That's what makes it so damn hard to think about, all these years later.

It fit me, more or less. Jimmy had gotten some white face paint at Woolco and had some fake blood left over from when he was a vampire the previous Halloween. And Darcie had found a white dress at a local thrift shop.

"Wait until you see it," he said, the hormones bulging his eyes and widening his smile. "It's really thin, man. I bet we'll be able to see her underwear."

He repulsed me with that statement for some reason — probably jealousy. I couldn't say I was annoyed that he wanted to see her underwear, because I did, too. But he didn't know what she and I had shared in our ever-increasing annual dance of excitement. We headed to her house, where she was home alone, and he tried to get her to put it on.

"It needs a slip, and I don't have one that fits," she said, her pale face reddening. "You can see through it."

"Oh, please, Darcie — it's us!" Jimmy said with widespread hands. "We're your best buddies. It's hardly any different than seeing you in a bikini, you know. So come on."

"Give it up, Jimmy," she said, and she meant it.

He tried arguing anyway, but once Darcie made up her mind, there was no changing it. Finally, Jimmy said he had to get home and eat before the night's antics, and left us.

He was no sooner gone than she said, "I'll try the dress on now."

I felt my eyes widen a bit. "But I thought you'd be too embarrassed."

"Only with Jimmy."

She grabbed the dress and headed into her bedroom, and I was left standing in her living room with my heart pounding. There was all the nervousness and fear I hadn't had the previous day. What if her parents came home? What if Lenny showed up? What if I couldn't handle it?

All those thoughts flew out of my head as soon as she came out of her bedroom, and I think my heart stopped beating for a moment. She was tall and slim, with full breasts and flaring hips that made her look like a centerfold model. She wore white underpants and bra, both of which I could easily see. And I could see her nipples jutting out, and the way her cotton panties hugged the cleft between her legs.

"It fits," she said, almost in a whisper. "What do you think?"

"I think... it's perfect," I said, not able to look her in her eyes but trying like hell not to look at anything else.

"Marty," she said in a soft voice, "look at me."

I did, and she looked back. And when she locked eyes with me, I knew we both wanted to explore each other beyond this. And there was an unspoken agreement in that exchanged look—an agreement that, after our graveyard shenanigans that night, we'd do just that.

But I didn't want to wait. I moved toward her, and she toward me, and we reached for each other... and then her parents' car pulled into the driveway, and she rushed into her bedroom to change in a flash. I sat in the living room, trying to conceal my raging physical response to their nearly naked daughter with a sofa pillow in my lap and an innocent look on my face.

At my house, it was after eleven by the time Jimmy got me made up like a corpse. I looked dead, all right, with a coating of cigarette ashes graying my face and trickles of fake blood to give me a bit of gore. We headed off to the cemetery, and Jimmy outlined everything.

"I came up here this afternoon and hid a blanket in the woods behind the Trafford wheel," he said. "So you go hide behind the headstone, and I'll go get Darcie and Lenny. They'll be waiting for me at the east entrance."

"You want me to wait here alone?" Icy bugs swarmed up my spine. I didn't like that idea.

"Sure, why not?" he said, and then he laughed loud. "You're not afraid, are you?"

Hell, yeah—I was terrified. But I wasn't about to admit it. "No, I'm cool. So you go get them. Then what happens?"

"We'll get back here, and Darcie will stand in front of the grave. I'll call on Trafford's spirit, and make a big production out of it. When I say the line, 'I command thee, John Trafford, to show yourself,' you come out. You grab Darcie and drag her toward the grave. Lenny will freak out, and I'll act like I am. You two get out of sight behind the headstone, then crawl into the woods, wrap up in the blanket, and keep quiet. He'll think Trafford dragged her into the grave. After he's completely lost his mind, we'll come clean, and then we'll find out if he really does shit himself. We're going to laugh our asses off about this for years to come."

It sounded good—especially the part where I got to roll up in a blanket with Darcie in the woods, with her wearing that dress.

"I know what you're thinking, you know," Jimmy said.

I blinked back from my fantasy. "Huh?"

"About Darcie." He smiled that crooked, wry grin he was always famous for, and he slapped me on the shoulder. "I'm not stupid, man. You've been in love with her since we were kids. So I'll get you guys wrapped up in a blanket together— and don't forget who made it happen."

I blushed, and he laughed.

"I've got your back, buddy," he said. "You two are a perfect match, anyway. Two peas in a pod. Darcie just hasn't seen it yet."

She had, of course, but I didn't tell him that. But it was nice to have my friend looking out for me. And for her.

I could clearly see the hundreds of cold headstones in the light of the full moon. I knew they stood watch over dead bodies, just a few feet beneath the earth, and I couldn't help but think their buried zombies would claw their ways to the surface and come for me at any moment.

I found the Trafford headstone, encircled by its ship's-wheel ring of stones. The stones' blue flecks were eerily dazzling in the moonlight. I gave the wheel-shaped plot a wide berth, to the trees just beyond. I stumbled around the bushes in the dark, my heart pounding so hard my chest hurt, until I found the spot where Jimmy had stashed the blanket. It was a green wool Army blanket, big enough for us to wrap up in together. This would all be worth it soon.

As I unfolded the blanket, my heart still thudded madly, skipping a beat every time I heard a twig snap in the black woods beyond. It's amazing how attuned you are to little sounds you wouldn't normally notice unless you're crawling around the bushes in a graveyard at night.

I headed for the plot, stepping up over the stone circle and making my way to the headstone. I crouched low behind the octagon base, listening for the others. It was a good walk to the east entrance and back, so I had a bit of a wait.

A tiny twig snapped somewhere far behind me.

The light rustling of bushes somewhere in the dark distance.

Just animals. That's all. There was no wailing, anyway. The night was actually as silent as one could expect, without even the sound of a car from the distant road.

Presently, I heard them talking, close by and getting closer. My terrors flew away like a cloud of bats frightened from a cave—the game was afoot! We'd pull off this legendary prank, and then I'd get to be alone with Darcie, and look into her eyes and tell her how I felt about her—how I'd always felt about her. And then we'd have the rest of our lives together.

I dared to peek around the headstone as they approached. I could see them clearly in the moonlight, which lit Darcie in her white dress as if the moon were a spotlight. She'd draped a white shawl over her shoulders to keep her warm. I wondered if she'd gotten a slip.

Jimmy and Lenny, in dark clothes, were just shadows flanking her. They had all stopped facing the headstone, about five feet away from the edge of the blue-stone ring.

"I don't think we should do this," I heard Lenny say.

"Are you chickening out?" Jimmy said.

"Well... no," Lenny said. "I mean, I want to help John Trafford rest in peace, but..."

"Then let's do it!"

I ducked my head out of sight, so I was fully concealed behind the headstone, as Jimmy began speaking. I couldn't see him, but I envisioned him with his arms thrown up in the air, ever the showman.

"Spirit of John Trafford!" he hollered. "Come before us now, for we are here to set you free!"

An owl hooted nearby, and the leaves of the trees spoke in a million whispered voices in the nighttime breeze. If only the wind had been really blowing, maybe a few thunderclaps and lightning flashes, the mood would have been perfect. I remember fleetingly thinking that at the time, but my mind kept coming back to being with Darcie in that blanket, and who knew what else beyond for the days and months and years to come.

"Your suffering is at its end, John Trafford!" Jimmy called out. "We have brought your beloved to you. Show yourself, so that we may help you move to the next world!"

John Trafford made no effort to respond. My legs were starting to cramp from crouching. I knew Jimmy was just milking this, but I wished he'd hurry up.

"This isn't right," Jimmy said. "Lenny, come to this side,

with me. Darcie, maybe you should move closer to the grave."

"Closer?"

"Yeah, inside the stone ring. Get up there, and I'll invoke him again."

I heard her shuffling through the grass, and I dared to peek around the left side of the headstone. She'd lost the shawl, and was holding her skirts up with both hands as she stepped up onto one of the twelve oversized stones. She stopped just inside of the ring, which glinted blue in the moonlight. She was a beautiful Gaelic Venus in an ethereal bridal gown. She caught my movement then and looked right at me, and she tried to suppress a smile. It didn't work; her cute cheeks puffed up, and she looked away. Jimmy and Lenny were off to her left and out of sight.

"That's good, right there," Jimmy said. "Okay, let's try this again."

Now he raised his voice and was yelling at the top of his lungs, as melodramatically as he could. "John Trafford! Hear me! We come before you now, two hundred years after your death! We seek to free you from your earthly confines! We bring you your beloved, here before your grave, for we mean to set you free! Come before us now, John Trafford!"

I tensed and readied myself, and then the line came:

"I command thee, John Trafford, to show yourself!"

And that was it. I stood, obscured by the obelisk, and took a deep breath. I put on my best sagging-jaw, rotting-corpse expression, and lurched out from behind the headstone.

Darcie should have started screaming first, but she was trying not to laugh. But when Lenny saw me, he made up for it. He screamed like a little girl and staggered back, trying to get away, but Jimmy grabbed him and hollered at him to stay put.

"Yes, John Trafford, your beloved is here!" he screamed. "Go to her, and find your eternal rest!"

I staggered toward her like a zombie, and now Darcie got

into the act. She screamed, high-pitched and piercing, throwing her hands to her face, grinning all the while.

"Stay there, Darcie!" Jimmy cried out. "We have to help him! Just hold your ground, and it will be over soon!"

"Don't let him touch her!" Lenny screamed.

Somehow, I kept from laughing and staggered forward, reaching out for her with my dead hands, and I let loose with a ghoulish "Unnnngggghhh!" Darcie screeched like a true horror -movie scream queen as I wrapped my arms around her. Even in all the acting, it felt marvelous. I pulled her close, and she screamed again right next to my ear, almost loud enough to deafen me, and then she stifled a giggle.

"Tell him you love him, and it will end!" Jimmy howled.

And in my ear, she whispered, "I love you."

And I whispered back, "I love you, too."

I dragged her back toward the headstone, completely in character, and she started screaming as if I really were taking her to the grave.

But suddenly, Jimmy was crying out my name.

"Marty!" he screamed. "Enough! Enough!"

I let go of Darcie and we both spun around. Why was he ruining our big plan?

Jimmy was on his knees. Lenny was on the ground before him, his body quivering uncontrollably. His limbs seized and relaxed, arms flopping and legs kicking out in irregular spasms.

"Something's wrong!" Jimmy yelled.

Darcie and I bolted for them. I tripped over one of the wheel stones and sprawled onto the grass, recovered quickly, got to my feet. Lenny's eyes were rolled back in his head, and he flopped on the grass like a fish, clawing at his chest with his hands.

"Get help!" Jimmy screamed.

I took off without another thought, running through the cemetery in the dark, running through the trees and the headstones and the dead bodies, running through the panic, and then running through all the years that would follow…

Turned out Lenny had a weak heart. A previously unknown congenital defect, they said. He died at the hospital that night. We'd set out to make the poor kid crap his pants, so we could all have a good laugh and keep laughing about it forever after; instead, we literally scared him to death.

Jimmy never forgave himself. He dropped out of school after our sophomore year, and his life quickly degenerated into drugs, alcohol, and crime. He died in prison twenty years after that night.

Darcie's family came completely apart. Her parents always said they didn't blame her, but of course they did. They blamed us all. Jimmy and I weren't allowed near her, and her parents divorced before we graduated high school. Darcie and I saw each other anyway, but all hope of romance was lost. She was a bland soul after that night, as dead inside as John Trafford was in the ground. You could see it in her eyes.

She'd always been a straight-A student who was college-bound, but she never went. She worked at a laundry right out of high school, and spent the next thirty years jumping from one shit job to the next, not even caring, and always using welfare as a lifestyle. She lived in one dumpy apartment after another, ultimately failing to pay her rent and moving on to another unsuspecting landlord. She never ran out of landlords, but I think she often paid them with special favors to keep from being evicted. She went through countless boyfriends, three of whom she married. Each was the type of person Jimmy had become. She had five children by five different men.

I was never one of those men. I wanted to be, but Lenny's death put that on eternal hold. I did better than her, I suppose, finding a good factory job while I attended community college. I earned a business degree and went on to run that factory.

I'd bump into Darcie every now and then, and we'd exchange pleasantries and have what's-new-with-you conversations, but we never once talked about the old days. That was probably best, because I knew she blamed me for her brother's death as much as she blamed Jimmy and herself. That's why we could never be together.

I stayed away from the cemetery, except for that one day a year. I'd do my usual routine, which was typically visiting my parents, who always insisted on a cake and presents no matter how old I got. Then I'd head out for a few beers with the few good buddies I had and close out the evening at midnight. I'd ignore the fear and anger and sorrow as I walked through that dark, foreboding place, until I found John Trafford's grave. I'd step inside the stone ring and stand before the headstone, and I'd call out in my mind to a sea captain, dead over two hundred years, begging him to bring Lenny back. I always knew it never made any sense, but it was all I could do. Maybe there was a magic there. Maybe, if John Trafford could be put to rest, he could send me back in time to June seventeenth in 1981, so I could undo what we'd done.

I wanted Lenny back, and I wanted Jimmy alive, and I wanted Darcie to be mine. But every year I'd stand there, pretending to believe I could somehow make it happen. I'd listen to the faint wailing everyone had always talked about, but every year I'd stand in that stone circle and hear nothing. Some years, there was rain or blowing wind; some years there were noisy owls screeching in the darkness or squeaking bats fluttering about. But usually there was nothing but the sounds of still silence there with that wheel of blue stones, with nothing answering my midnight sobs.

It was the afternoon of my forty-sixth birthday, thirty years since Lenny had died, when Darcie called me. She'd never done that. I was pleased to hear from her, and after some small talk, she reminded me of the date.

"We need to go back to John Trafford's grave," she told me.

My heart began pounding like it had that night. "I go there every year on my birthday," I said. "Trust me, going there won't bring Lenny back."

"My kids are all grown," she said, as if unhearing. "It's time for me to face what I did. And it's time you did, too."

I didn't know what to say to that. She was probably right. We'd never really faced what we'd done; time had moved on, and we all just did what it took to dull the pain the best we could. I'd gone there every year and cried like a baby and wished for dreams that would never come true, but I'd never really faced it. I'd been there every year for twenty-nine years, and it only caused more pain, anguish, and guilt. I couldn't bear the idea of Darcie going through that. She'd already suffered enough living a life that shouldn't have been.

There was a long silence before she said, "So midnight, then, at Trafford's grave."

"Darcie—"

"We owe this to Lenny," she said, calm and serene. "And you owe this to me, Marty."

The back part of the cemetery, full of ancient graves, looked exactly the same as it had every year. I hadn't given it much thought, coming there every year and all, but when I saw Darcie standing within the stone wheel, before the tilting headstone, I realized that the stone was perhaps leaning a bit more than it had thirty years before.

She was wearing the same white dress as that night. It still fit her because she was a thin shade of the woman she had been blossoming into in 1981: skinny, with bony calves and sagging breasts, haggard and old, bags under her sunken eyes, her teeth yellow and crooked. Fittingly, she looked like some skeletal zombie. But even as she turned to me in the light of a moon just barely waning away from full, she was still so wonderfully beautiful to me.

"It still fits," I tried.

"Yeah," she said.

"I'm so sorry about what happened to Lenny. None of us meant for it to happen. Nothing will change the mistake we made."

"I know."

"If any of us had known he had a heart condition, we never would have done that. Jimmy felt terrible about it. It really screwed him up. He paid for that for the rest of his life."

She nodded in silent answer.

"You're still beautiful," I said.

She shook her head and sighed. "I'm a disgusting woman, Marty. Don't play games with me."

"You're beautiful to me."

She met my gaze. "Have you ever wondered what would have happened to us, you and me, if that night hadn't gone the way it did?"

"Every single day of my life," I said, and the pain of it lanced through my soul like a cold knife. I didn't want to cry.

She stepped closer, until we were a hand's width apart. She seemed so old and so tired, but that wondrous Irish goddess was still in there. I could feel the heat of her body, and I wanted to reach out for her, touch her, hold her.

"I was going to give my virginity to you that night," she whispered. "It was going to my birthday present to you. I was in love with you."

"I loved you too," I said.

She moved even closer, until her breasts pressed against my chest, and I could feel her breath on my chin. "But we blew it, Marty — we blew everything. Lenny was innocent and sweet and the best kid anyone ever knew, and we killed him. It was our fault."

"I know," I said, and I stifled a sob, because the tears were trying to flow. She saw this, and sniffled, and tears streamed down her face, too.

"I'm glad you're crying, because it means you're truly sorry," she said. "I always hoped you were."

"Of course I'm sorry. God, I've regretted that night every day of my life since then. I wish it had never happened."

I felt her hand on my stomach, lightly touching me. "Now answer my next question honestly, no matter what. Do you regret it because Lenny died, or because you and I never happened?"

"Both," I sobbed.

"More for Lenny, or for us?"

Her dead eyes dived through mine and sank deep into my soul.

"Be honest," she whispered softly, her hand still touching my stomach.

And, God help me, I had to be honest. "For us," I said, and broke into loud, racking sobs. "I'm sorry, Darcie. I've thought about what we could have been ever since."

She nodded, crying. "Me too. And when I think of how I feel worse about us than Lenny, I'm so terribly ashamed. I can't live with it anymore. And neither can you."

There was a sound like a thunderclap.

I was temporarily deafened, and my ears rang. At first I thought she'd poked me hard in the stomach, but as I reeled backward and fought for my balance, I realized that hadn't been her hand on me. She was holding a revolver, and smoke snaked up from its barrel in the silvery light of the moon. I looked down in horror at the blood soaking the front of my shirt.

"My God!" I cried, my voice hoarse, and met her calm eyes. I grabbed for my belly, clamping my hands tight, afraid my guts would spill out the hole. Blood surged through my fingers. It was everywhere.

"I'm sorry, Marty—I love you!" she said, her face wet with tears. "I always have."

And I never had the chance to say it back to her, because

she put that gun up under her chin and pulled the trigger.

*   *   *

I lived. She didn't. I wish I hadn't.

And I know someday I'll have to finish the job. I just have to work up the balls to do it. I've decided that I've always owed it to Lenny, but now I know I absolutely owe it to her.

The kids still claim to hear the faint wailing in the cemetery, and maybe it's a trick of the way the wind blows through the trees and the headstones. Or maybe there just isn't any sound. Or maybe—just maybe—there really are restless spirits in there. I'm certain there's at least one. If it takes my death to put her to rest, so be it.

I go back all the time now, every week or so at least. It's always night, and I always cry and talk to her, but regardless of the woodland sounds around me, despite the howls of wind or dance of raindrops, I never hear from her. The inside of that blue wheel never answers me; it's always quiet, her voice forever silenced.

Lenny's death, and what happened with Darcie and me thirty years later, has the kids all the more scared of the place. Nobody goes near John Trafford's grave—at least, they don't go inside that blue stone wheel that surrounds it. They say the ground is sacred, like an Indian burial ground, and if you go inside, you'll be sucked into the curse of John Trafford's grave.

But while the kids will always live in fear of it, talking in hushed tones about it, nobody who grows up really believes there's a curse. I know better.

I f you're looking for a literal quiet blue wheel here, you won't find it, but Paula Burnett's story does center on a blue wheel of sorts. And what's quiet about it? It might seem like very little, but with the bottled-up emotions and festering pain both Megan and her new-found friend are trying fiercely to handle, you'll soon see that what's truly important on Blue Wheel Drive is sadly quiet, and desperately in need of being voiced. This is a story of loss and redemption for two unlikely friends who, when they most need it, find each other.

Until We Meet Again

Paula Burnett

Sitting alone on the sunlight-speckled porch in the early afternoon, Megan's mind was racing. The agonizing thought of making new friends due to yet another of her dad's relocations for his employment with various university engineering programs drained her of any momentum. For a couple of weeks, she had been sleeping late into the morning and dreading this summer vacation. At sixteen, Megan was already tired of the many starts and stops in her life. However, this time was different. Her mother was gone, having been killed earlier that year in a head-on collision with a truck whose driver had fallen asleep at the wheel. One day they were all giggling and preparing a dinner together to celebrate their move to Maine; the next day, on the way to a dentist appointment, she was killed.

Her mother's special ways of connecting Megan and the family socially whenever and wherever they moved from state to state would be missed, especially for someone as shy as Megan. Her dad rarely talked of his grief and just kept telling her to cry whenever she needed, as if that would be the remedy. Since the move to Orono to accept a job her mother had persuaded him to take, her dad seemed to just want to be left alone with his computer and only deal with people at the engineering department. Now Megan felt abandoned in her new surroundings.

Subconsciously, she knew that her dad was genuinely doing the best he could to smooth things for her. He allowed Megan to finish softball season at her last school prior to moving. Also, until school started in September, he would be working from home on one of his various university research projects. Today's conversation over breakfast centered on how he believed she should get involved with a summer church or recreation program.

"You don't get it," Megan replied to her Dad's suggestion. "I'm not going to sing hallelujahs to a god that took Mom away and make stupid little crafts no one really wants."

"Well Megan, I don't want you moping around the house all summer in hopes friends simply fall out of the sky," he said. "You've got to make an effort to meet people halfway. I want you to be safe, happy, and connected with *good* people. So just give it a try."

After conversing at the table with her dad, Megan sprinted with her jellied toast in hand to her thinking spot on the porch stoop. Here she could watch the world go by without her participation. Images of her mother crept into her head and tears raced down her pink cheeks as Megan wrapped her arms around her knees and rocked side to side.

In the summertime, Megan and her mom would hit the road early in the morning for a bike ride around the neighborhood and would come back to a leisurely breakfast with the music blaring. Sometimes they would take turns spinning her mom's records from the 1970s or singing karaoke, pretending to perform like rock-and-rollers as their lithe bodies twisted and gyrated to the sounds from the Beach Boys' *Surf's Up* album and hit songs from the Rolling Stones. Often, they would lose track of time and reality as their air guitars moved and rolled to the music. The performance would conclude with them bowing to an imaginary mass of screaming fans below them.

Megan had not touched any of the record albums since her mother's death. The turntable, once prominent in the living room of their previously rented house, now sat tucked in a corner covered with a dull, grey dust next to the unpacked box of records.

Two days later Megan woke to the sounds of a squeaky garage door being opened. A few minutes later Don Higgins yelled to his daughter, "Get up, Megan, get up! Your ride awaits you!"

Megan raised the shade slightly and peered out her bedroom window with one eye open a slit to discover her dad was polishing her bicycle in the front yard. The last thing her mom had bought for her was that ten-speed bike in her favorite color, royal blue. The bike had been hung from the garage rafters alongside her mother's Schwinn, as her father hadn't been able to part with his wife's prized possession.

"I know you love riding this bike and dream of taking a bicycle trip across country some day," her dad said when a dressed Megan finally reached the front yard. "This is a good day to remember that dream and work on getting in shape for your eventual trip. Plus, biking is a wonderful way to explore the neighborhood and check out summer programs. Hint, hint, hint..."

"Fine, I'll do it," Megan said while shuffling her feet and rolling her eyes. "I'll ride the damn bike. But I don't promise to stop at a church."

Megan meandered back and forth on her bicycle down her long street, College Avenue, with its mixture of older homes with carriage houses that had been turned into apartments and university buildings housing sororities and fraternities. Then she decided to check out a street with what she thought was a queer name, Blue Wheel Drive. Some kids were out playing in one house's front yard, which was strewn with toys, but they were little ones. "Oh great, the streets around here are lined with snotty brats and mothers pushing babies in strollers," Megan muttered.

At the end of the street was a grand, Victorian-style, perfectly landscaped home overlooking the Stillwater River. The house had two turrets with a few missing shutters and was painted brick red with yellow trim. This house fascinated her, especially the turrets with their pointed roofs and tall bay windows bordered with stained glass. It was similar to the sole bay-windowed turret in their previous house in Minnesota. She'd loved the upstairs turret room. Her mother had promised her it would eventually become Megan's bedroom and writing room. But they'd moved to Maine, so that had never happened.

She could picture herself inside one of this house's turrets writing a bestselling mystery novel, which was a dream of hers. Megan inched her bike toward a closer view of the vine-draped house with its fancy latticework veranda lined with hanging planters of sweet alyssum and geraniums.

From behind a tall bush, an older woman with a straw visor and denim shorts hollered to her, "Come over here, I need another pair of hands, now!"

Megan was immediately suspicious of this frantic woman, so she spun her bike quickly around and booked it home.

But, like a bungee cord, curiosity kept pulling her back to Blue Wheel Drive. The bike ride to Blue Wheel Drive became a daily jaunt for Megan. Maybe her dad was right about being more open and meeting people halfway. He kept insisting she needed to improve her attitude. Having someone to hang out with instead of merely chatting online with out-of-state friends, who were slowly disappearing as they knew she was never coming back to Minnesota, was suddenly a desirable goal.

Megan's next trip to Blue Wheel Drive found her staring at the FOR SALE sign on the turreted house. The woman with the straw visor was getting her mail from the box near the sign. She smiled and waved a gloved hand towards Megan.

"Hi there, I'm Grace Larson," the woman said with a slightly forced smile as she looked up at Megan on her bike. "I bet you thought I was a crazy old woman when I yelled and madly waved my arms at you the other day," Grace said, her smile widening.

Megan looked at Grace closely. She had wild, wavy gray hair and tan limbs with a very pale face. She wore a man's denim shirt over a summer jersey that had been tie-dyed to reveal a peace sign. She squinted fiercely in the sunlight at Megan, as though she had X-ray vision.

"Hi, I'm Megan Higgins," she finally replied. "It's nice to meet you."

"I apologize if I frightened you." Grace said as she fingered a tarnished gold pendant around her wrinkled neck. "I was at my wit's end trying to secure a window shutter and needed someone to hold the ladder for me. Never anyone around here when I need them, it seems. So I don't blame you for taking off, Megan."

Megan no longer feared Grace. Here was a chance to meet someone halfway, even though Grace was definitely not her age. When Grace suddenly interrupted their conversation to snap at a neighbor about his dog in her yard, Grace appeared to have what her mother referred to as a feisty personality. Megan felt the need to test that theory.

"I just moved to Orono from Minnesota," she said. "I see you're about to move, so where are you headed?"

"Not sure, but I'll know when I get there," Grace responded. Megan got the sense that she didn't want to reveal personal information. Maybe she was still torn inside about the move.

"I've lived in five states in sixteen years," Megan said trying to push the conversation along and feed her curiosity. "I'm used to moving."

"Then I could sure use some help packing," said Grace. "I'll even pay you. Are you interested, Megan? With all your moving experience, I'm sure you're an expert at packing by now."

If there was anything Megan knew how to do well, it was packing. Her mother had always made a game out of packing various objects. Maybe Grace would play the game, too.

"Great, I'd like to do that," Megan said.

They agreed Megan would come over for the next couple of weeks to help Grace finish packing up several rooms before the moving company arrived. Megan said nothing to her dad about this; he was too absorbed in his work anyway.

On her first day, framed photographs and various gem-colored glass pieces were among the living-room items for Megan to bubble wrap. They chatted easily about a variety of subjects from wildlife to the Penobscot Indians, whose basketry Grace collected and displayed on her marble mantle. Then Megan asked, as she pointed out a photograph of a young girl on a sailboat, "Who is this? She's pretty."

"My daughter," Grace said as she quickly seized the framed picture from Megan's hands and shoved it into a box of miscellaneous items. "Do you want a snack? It's my tea time anyway. Come this way," she said directing Megan to the kitchen, "and don't touch anything until you've washed your hands."

Megan wondered if Grace had barked commands at her daughter. She also wondered why Grace packed her daughter's picture so abruptly.

"I hope you like apples," Grace said. She cut up an apple,

sprinkled cinnamon and ground allspice on it, and zapped it in the microwave. Then she topped the treat with a dollop of cream. "I don't bake, so you won't get any fancy desserts here."

In hopes of lightening up Grace a bit, Megan asked, "Would you like to play a packing game with me? My mom taught me the game, and we had great fun stretching our imaginations before each move."

"Hmmm… a game, you say?" Grace said. "I'm not one for games, but the old imagination could use a workout. Did you and your mom play the game before moving here?"

"No," Megan said and hung her head. Now they both had things the other would not discuss, Megan thought. Maybe she and Grace were two-of-a-kind.

"We can play the game tomorrow if you want me to come back," Megan said.

"All right," Grace agreed. "We'll play the game tomorrow, and maybe I'll tell you about my daughter."

At home after supper, Megan scurried upstairs to type up the rules of the game and some examples on her bedroom computer. She hoped Grace would at least try the game, as Megan loved being imaginative and playing with words.

"Hey, remember we clean up the kitchen together, Megan," her dad shouted from the bottom of the stairs.

Then she heard him dash to the top of the stairway. Megan had yet to get comfortable with him in her bedroom. In her memory of the past few years, he only ventured in whenever she had been sick or something needed to be fixed. This room was her sanctuary and crying place these days. She often wondered if her dad was disappointed that he did not have a son instead of an emotionally sensitive girl.

"Let's talk, Megan," her dad said as he gingerly pushed her slightly open door wider. "It feels like we're drifting further apart. I *really* want us to be closer," he said as he tentatively inched into the room to sit beside her. "Maybe doing chores together doesn't seem like me trying to get closer to you, but it's a start."

Megan wanted to cry and crumble into his arms. Instead she fought off the urge. She realized he was reaching out to her, but she instinctively knew that tears made him more uncomfortable.

"Maybe we can start a habit of sharing what we learned or saw each day before you go to bed, like you used to do with your mother," her dad suggested. "You go first, kiddo. Anything you want to talk about is fine with me."

"Well, I've made a new friend," Megan said without looking him in the eyes. "She lives on a dead-end street not far from the rec center. We hang out there sometimes." She knew this was lying, but she was not ready to talk about Grace; it was better to let him think the new friend was around her age. She just needed to get this conversation over so she could put on some music and eventually cry herself to sleep like she did most nights.

Her father asked a few more questions and quickly realized that Megan apparently was still in no mood to share. He was beginning to feel like a failure as a dad to his grieving teenage daughter who kept so much to herself and who often seemed older than her age, even as a little girl. He had noticed a stack of papers on her desk that she quickly tucked into a drawer when he entered. Perhaps she had the writing bug like he'd had in his youth. Somehow he had become a grant writer for university engineering programs instead of the journalist he had dreamed of becoming. Having not grown up with a sister, and being somewhat reclusive, he figured Megan would be fine once school started in September, especially with this new friend in the picture. At least Megan gave him a "Good night, Daddy" as he left her room.

* * *

The next day Megan showed up at Grace's house with a printed copy of the rules for the game; she was excited to do something familiar and fun with someone at last. When she arrived, Grace waved to her from one of the turret windows and shouted, "Come on up, Megan."

Megan raced up the stairs and Grace greeted her in a bright, cheery room whose walls were painted cotton-candy pink and which was filled with white wicker furniture and throw pillows of varying sizes. A huge, brightly painted, well-worn rocking horse was the centerpiece. Stained glass lined the upper portion of the turret windows and contained small birds, fairies, and dragonflies in its design. Books, stuffed animals, games, and record albums overflowed in a bookcase near a bright-yellow bean-bag chair. Window seats had been built underneath three tall windows overlooking the Stillwater River. The room seemed to be frozen in time, and Grace seemed wistful. On the other hand, Megan felt right at home in this space.

"This was her room... my daughter, Suzanne," Grace said as she anxiously darted about the room touching various objects and gently blowing dust off others. "I'd not been in here for several years until I decided to sell the house. So whatever you see that you like, Megan, you can have. Suzanne never came back here after running away with a boyfriend before she was to start college."

Megan replied, "I'm sorry, Grace," as she started to wander about the room to avoid contact with Grace's sorrowful eyes.

Grace, forgetting she was talking to a teenager, suddenly found herself divulging the rest of her misery.

"Her running away further broke an already broken marriage. So her dad and I parted. Now you know my story," Grace said letting out a huge sigh. It had been ages since Grace had revealed those excruciating events in her life. Keeping her emotions in check around others was her credo.

However, as Grace observed Megan's twitchy pacing around the room, she abruptly concluded the conversation, silently chastising herself for blurting out so much information. "I must finish dusting in here before it's packed up, so let's go down to the den," she said. "Besides, it's time to play your game."

"Here are the rules," Megan began. "One: We take turns. Two: Hold an object and imagine how it came into being. Three: Describe it in ways without using numbers and primary colors. Mom would encourage me to use a variety of adjectives to develop my vocabulary. Four: Give the object a name different from what it really is. Five: Pack it and say, 'Until we meet again.'"

"In other words, it's like painting a picture and telling a story at the same time, only with words, not with brushes and a palette," Grace said. She grabbed for the first thing that caught her attention and held it up. "Okay, let's start with this snow globe."

Megan closed her eyes and handled the object like a psychic going into a trance, and then she shook it wildly with her eyes open. "I'm thinking this came into being 'cause a little girl loved to skate on a pond near where she lived, and she loved to catch the snowflakes with her tongue while doing figure-eights on the ice. The snow in the globe is like sparkling confetti, and the ice is a silvery shade of steel. The skater's heart races as wind and snow tickle like quick kisses on her chapped face."

Megan paused for awhile, with her head tilted to the side to think, and eventually said, "So, I'll call this globe *Kiss of Winter in a Bottle*. Now, together we say 'Until we meet again, *Kiss of Winter in a Bottle*.'"

Megan took it upon herself to go back to the pink room in

the turret after a few rounds of the game while Grace dozed off after her tea time. Grace had said Megan could take anything she wanted from Suzanne's room. Now was her chance to poke around in the room. From all appearances, Grace had made an effort to dust and shine the objects in the room. Megan found herself drawn to the first of three window seats. "What a perfect spot to sit, think, and dream," Megan thought aloud.

She glanced around the room and finally got the courage to explore by opening a couple of drawers in a chest and lifting the window seat covers. The contents of the window seats had been emptied. The closet was filled with hangers and old shoe boxes. On one side wall, at the deep end of the closet, was a pair of skates hanging on an old rusty nail. The sun was softly shining in this room, and one ray fell upon the cabinet below some shelves. Megan decided to explore its contents.

Like an antique trunk in someone's attic, the cabinet was filled with scrapbooks, family albums, and love letters. Just as she was about to open a photo album, Grace suddenly appeared from behind her, yanked the album out of her hands, and slammed the cabinet door.

"I told you anything you saw that you liked you could have," said Grace in a loud, angry voice. "That doesn't include snooping around in closed spaces. Now, I need you downstairs," she said with an emotionless face as she ushered Megan from the room into the hallway. "Let's get to work. Then you can have the rest of the afternoon to yourself."

Megan was very rattled by Grace's reaction, and upset that she had apparently blown Grace's trust in her, so she figured this would be her last day on Blue Wheel Drive. She busied herself with packing teacups and saucers from one of two large glass dining-room cabinets and decided not to speak to Grace. There was less chance of another outburst if she kept quiet. She even pushed back a few tears and wondered how her mother would advise handling this woman.

Megan had overheard Grace on the phone to the movers earlier. They would arrive at the end of next week, so Megan figured a few more days, if Grace's current mood changed, and some pay would ultimately be worth it. Megan knew very well how to keep her feelings to herself and still keep on functioning.

When she finished emptying the glass cabinet, Megan inquired with her face scrunched up as though she could cry at any moment, "Do you want me to come tomorrow, or is this my last day?"

"If you want to continue to help me, I'd appreciate it," Grace responded without looking directly at Megan. "The last room to pack up besides my bedroom, bathroom, and kitchen will be my studio in the other turret. If you liked Suzanne's room, you'll probably love that room. We'll tackle the contents of that tomorrow — if you *want* to come back here."

After Megan left for the day, Grace poured herself a glass of wine to relax while fixing supper. For some reason, her mind kept returning to Megan's little game. Suddenly, she remembered the connection. Her father had grown up during the Depression and taught her to treasure any possession as they moved from farm to farm in northern Maine as he sought work as a foreman. He used to preach, "Take care of what you have while you have it, and it will take care of you in ways you may not realize at the moment. And if you have to let it go or leave something or someone behind, simply say 'until we meet again.'" This made Grace wonder about Megan's appearance in her life, as Grace had never been able to tolerate children other than her own Suzanne. Her behavior with Megan earlier that day had clearly illustrated that.

Between packing up her world and having that red-haired Megan with her inquiring, jet-blue eyes in the house, Grace realized this evening she was about ready to explode. No husband, no children, no grandchildren, and best friends who had died or moved to be with their family members had left Grace beyond being alone. Grace felt as though she had no purpose in life; she merely existed, flowing from one day to the next to an unknown destination. Her heart had hardened to the point where she dared not make any new attachments. Her art and her landscaping efforts here had been her life since Suzanne ran away from Blue Wheel Drive.

Around the holidays, Grace would pore over an album of her daughter's pictures and weep profusely. During the last few months, she could no longer feel her daughter's presence, which prompted Grace to move out of the house which, despite its spaciousness, had become her prison.

"So, how's it going with your new friend?" Megan's dad asked as she bounded into his home office.

"What friend?" Megan said as she flopped into a recliner. "I only have people who pass through my life. No one stays. She'll be moving soon, and it's back to just me!"

"Well, you must have met some potential friends at the rec center where the two of you were hanging out, right?" her dad asked.

"Come on Dad, I'm the new kid," Megan blurted. "I'm the oddball with red hair who doesn't tan and who's klutzy even in softball. I hate being me!"

"Megan, I'm sure it isn't that bad," her dad tried, but she interrupted him.

"Like you or anyone else cares how I feel!" Megan cried. "I just want to go back to the way it was, and I can't, so why should I bother getting up each day? Life sucks!"

Before slamming the door and running off to her sanctuary, she hollered, "By the way, Dad, I don't go the rec center! I spend my days reading, writing, riding my bike, and helping an old lady pack her junk. *There's no friend!*"

Don Higgins knew the explosion of feelings from inside

his daughter would come eventually. Whatever he said lately would set off more emotional rants from Megan. He'd have to make her school counselor aware of her depression and anger before school started. He didn't know how to deal with it and was contemplating getting grief counseling for himself; Megan's former school counselor had encouraged them to get counseling together. He just kept putting it off—the good old "denial and procrastination method" was at work in Don Higgins once again.

Don could not bear to touch upon his wife's death, so he often ignored the majority of Megan's references to her mother, all the while noting how much Megan physically resembled his wife. He was still unable to accept the passing of his beloved Anne. Anne's smile, warmth, her penchant for life, and her open-armed acceptance of those around her were sorely missed. Many times, he would be overcome with a flood of emotion, and tears would come to his eyes, all of which he hid from Megan.

Then he recalled Megan's outburst. *What old lady?* Don thought.

He needed to check out this person further. Megan was vulnerable now, and who knew what this woman really was exposing her to in that house. If only there was a female relative with whom Megan could find some support—but his mother was busy with her younger grandchildren, and besides Megan was too high-spirited for her anyway. Cards, holiday gifts, and a few calls came Megan's way when his mother remembered them. They simply were not a priority to his mother. And Anne had fled from an abusive home after high school and never looked back, so there was no connection to be had with her family. He would have to find a way to fix this situation; maybe he could hire a live-in housekeeper or nanny.

Megan dreaded the approaching end of summer and the beginning of a new school year. This summer had been a bust.

Not even a stray kitten or dog had wandered into their yard for her to play with as when she had lived in Minnesota and Indiana. Come to think of it, her mother had always been the magnet for stray animals, whether they were healthy or wounded.

She wondered what her dad would say now after her screaming, woe-is-me spell from yesterday. He was big on lecturing about consequences and attitude these days. Occasionally, he would say, "How would your mother feel about this behavior of yours?" That line really grated on her nerves.

Megan's diary was filled with attempts to recall her mother's advice, beliefs about people, and how to do various things. Megan wanted to get as much in writing while it was still fresh in her mind. She was afraid the voice inside her would stop one day forever. She could still hear her mother's words, *I love you with all my heart and soul,* whispered in her ears every night before she tearfully fell asleep.

The diary was buried in a folder in her computer to be shared with no one except her mother, wherever she was now. Megan was not sure dead people could hear the earthly ones or read the thoughts of loved ones, but she deeply hoped it was so. Without her mother's encouragement, Megan felt like a lost soul or a zombie merely wandering the streets of a strange town.

As Megan slowly rode her ten-speed to Blue Wheel Drive, she wondered what Grace's mood would be today. Megan just wanted to finish the work and get paid, although she had no plans for the money. She had no plans in general. It didn't seem to make a bit of difference; in her world, hopes and dreams and plans never came true anyway.

When Megan arrived at the house, she found Grace sitting on the porch, teacup and saucer in hand, gazing towards the river. "Good morning, Ms. Higgins," Grace said. She was smiling, which was rare, and this made Megan wonder which version of Grace had shown up today.

"Megan, I want you to enter a vibrant world of color and texture today. Upstairs to my studio, now," Grace commanded as she moved swiftly to the other turret. "You are the only person outside my once-upon-a-time family to ever see this room."

Grace opened the oak door and light poured from the room into the doorway. Megan felt as though she were being sucked into a huge kaleidoscope. Her mother had taken her to art galleries, but this was beyond the typical gallery experience. Every inch of the room reverberated in bold, striking colors with paintings on easels, wall panels, parts of the floor, and a section of the ceiling. The few pieces of furniture in the room possessed hand-painted appliqués. There were portraits, landscapes, and bold mosaic designs everywhere. Canvases were spread haphazardly. An old hewn picnic table served as a repository for her brushes, palettes, and miscellaneous drawing pencils, which were scattered on the top and seats. As Megan wandered about the studio, she discovered that the initials SL, accompanied by a smiley face, had been carved on each seat. This appeared to be the only room in the house in which chaos and whim ruled. Apparently, Grace preferred oils, but also dabbled in watercolors and acrylics. It seemed to Megan that Grace had managed to use all the colors one would find in a 64 -count Crayola box in this one room. Grace was right; Megan loved this room. All Megan could utter was, "Wow, unbelievable!"

As Megan toured the room, she peered inquisitively into each portrait as though she were an art critic. Always one to notice details, Megan's keen eyes detected an object that appeared in every painting, just in different locations. Sometimes the object came before Grace's signature, and other times it was embedded somewhere in the scene. The object was an icon that looked like a blue wheel.

"Why did you put a blue wheel in each picture?" Megan

asked Grace.

Then it struck Megan; the portraits had the same eyes, mouth, and hair in each painting, only the person aged in each frame. This was Suzanne, Grace's daughter.

"Yes, Detective Higgins, these are paintings of my daughter," Grace said as she pressed her hands to her chest momentarily. "I have one that is incomplete on that easel. I'll finish it just before I move."

Grace pointed to the only canvas in the room covered with a paint-spattered sheet. "Now, to answer your question, the blue wheel represents Suzanne living here in those years," she explained as her chin dropped toward her heart. "My last painting of her won't have the symbol, as I've no clue where she went. When I leave here, I'll find that missing piece of my daughter's life somehow, some way."

Grace's daughter fascinated Megan. Suzanne had a huge smile in one painting; however, the way she held her mouth belied a certain degree of sadness. The young girl was barefooted in each portrait, and her hair seemed to be tucked up under various straw or cowgirl hats. Megan wanted to peek at the unfinished painting of Suzanne, but she knew that could potentially set Grace off again.

Together, Megan and Grace carefully wrapped, taped, and labeled each painting. There was a synchronicity to their busyness that day. Neither talked and the game was never played. However, each seemed to be at peace with the other's desire to remain reticent about her past. With all the portraits packed except the sheeted one, Megan and Grace simultaneously said aloud, "Until we meet again" as they stacked the paintings for the movers.

Two more days and the movers would arrive. Blue Wheel Drive would be history for Megan and Grace.

Many times as she traipsed through the large, lonely house over the years, Grace had talked aloud to herself. Occasionally, she would even debate with herself on various topics for mere amusement. But Megan had touched Grace's long-buried, playful-little-girl side. So why not pretend Megan was here and play the game aloud one more time before the movers were to arrive.

"My turn!" Grace said aloud in a giggly voice.

Grace reached for her favorite mug, one of the few surviving pieces of her young daughter's attempt at pottery while attending a summer camp. She carefully washed and dried the slightly chipped mug which was ideal for hot chocolate on chilly winter evenings in Maine. This was the final kitchen item to be packed. Grace cradled the mug in her hands as she pulled it tightly to her chest, squeezing her eyes shut like Megan would do. With her eyes still closed, Grace traced the rim and decorative indentations on the mug with a tanned, gnarled finger.

"The day you were conceived, mug, was a day my daughter felt homesick for Blue Wheel Drive," Grace said recalling the first time her daughter went away to camp and how it had rained throughout her stay. At the end of Suzanne's first week, Grace had called and listened to her daughter's sobbing pleas to come home despite just one more week for her session. Suzanne had attended the camp for swimming and sailing lessons, as she loved being in nature, but she had merely tolerated indoor activities like pottery classes.

Settling into her recliner, Grace pondered ways to describe the mug as though Megan was sitting in the chair beside her.

Grace said, "On the outside, a crudely painted bicycle with cobalt fenders and spokes is featured against a pewter background. The misshapen handle and rim are lined with needle-point-sized magenta polka dots from Suzanne's shades-of-pink phase that year. The interior of the mug is iridescent at the top, with soft hues of coral and aqua swirled together like the inside of a seashell. The bottom half is stained with ever-darkening chestnut rings from years of sipping cocoa and coffee."

Suzanne's initials, which she carved into anything she could as a kid, were still visible at the bottom of the mug. Grace remembered asking Suzanne why she put the initial on the inside rather than on the outer bottom. Chuckling to herself, she recalled Suzanne's simple yet wise-beyond-her-years response: "Because what's inside is always more important than what's on the outside."

Grace was getting drowsy. It was time for her afternoon nap. In that floating haze of consciousness, Grace gave a name to the mug and tucked it into the box on the floor.

"Until we meet again... *Suzanne's Gift* is the name. Yes, that's it," Grace mumbled as her head bobbed until she drifted off to sleep.

A few days later, while Megan was out, Don decided to snoop in her room. The privacy issue was no longer important to him; he had a need to know right away what was really going on in his daughter's life away from home. Too many bizarre things happened to young people nowadays. He opened a few desk drawers and found nothing of major concern. If there was information of the relationship with the older woman, it would exist on Megan's computer. He quickly checked to see if her bike was leaning up against the porch railing. It wasn't; he was safe to search her computer.

After a few minutes, he found it: her diary and pages buried within, labeled *Conversations with Mom*. The first entry was the day after his wife's funeral. Don did not have the stomach to read her notations, so he skipped ahead to a date from last week. Several days simply had the words *Blue Wheel Drive* and *The Game* on them.

Don was desperate. The feeling of something bad about to happen was creeping through him. He had lost the love of his life; he wasn't about to lose Megan. As he was shutting down her computer, he noticed a file entitled *The House of Turrets*.

Here it was, the beginning of a story about a grumpy, lonely artist named Grace Larson and Blue Wheel Drive. After reading this, he knew exactly what to do next.

Don checked the phone book for a Grace Larson; there was no listing. He was not too familiar with all the little side streets around Orono, but he trusted Megan to have not meandered too far from home.

The next day, he knew that Megan's habit of watching certain shows on Saturday morning while lounging late in bed, sometimes until noon, afforded him the opportunity to play detective.

"Hey, Megan," he called as he knocked on her closed bedroom door. "I'm off to the post office and a few errands. I'll be back soon, and we'll have brunch or do something together, okay?"

"Whatever," Megan replied opening her bedroom door a crack and then promptly shutting it.

Instead of driving his Subaru, Don decided to walk to Blue Wheel Drive. He had researched its location ahead of time. The street was not far from a church that had caught his eye on a drive-about before he settled on renting the house on College Avenue.

The house in Megan's story was the last one on this street and appeared to be quite dilapidated. The minute he saw the turrets, he could see why Megan would be attracted to it. Their previous home in Minnesota had had a single turret with bay windows. Anne had promised Megan that one day, if they stayed, it could become Megan's bedroom and writing room. It had been a storage room, and Anne had meant to clean it out in preparation for Megan to decorate in her own unique style.

Don rang the door bell. He could hear no ringing noise. He pounded on the front door several times and waited for someone to answer it. No one appeared to be home, so he checked out the garage. It was empty. Now, Don was getting nervous.

He headed back to the front door. This time, instead of knocking, he tried the door knob. It turned easily.

He yelled, "Grace, anyone here?" No answer. He saw no furniture, and a thin coat of dust covered built-in cabinets and bookcases. He felt compelled to explore the house further. Don carefully strode to the top of the stairs and entered one of the turret rooms. An easel covered with a sheet captured his attention immediately. He peeled back the sheet and gasped.

It was an unfinished painting of a female dressed like the young women who attended outdoor rock concerts in the late 1970s from his youth. In the portrait, the woman was barefooted with beads around her neck and both wrists wearing a gauzy, ankle-length skirt. From a distance, the woman, with her long tresses blown by the wind covering half of her face, was staring at the backs of a young girl and an older woman on the beach as they collected sea shells in a basket at low tide. The woman was his wife Anne; there was no doubt about it.

Tacked to the easel was a slit envelope. It was addressed to Ms. Grace Larson, 3 Blue Wheel Drive, Orono, ME 04473 with no return address, but it had been date stamped in 2006. Don opened the envelope and found two sheets of paper with one entitled *The Game*. Five rules were typed on a crisp sheet of paper in Comic Sans font, the style Megan often used. The words *Until We Meet Again* were circled on that paper. The other sheet was a letter on fancy stationery that matched the envelope handwritten to Grace and signed "Suzanne." The letter had clearly been unfolded and folded many times, with small tears along the fold lines. Don dropped to the floor as he read the short letter.

Dear Mom,

I hope this letter reaches you.

You have a beautiful granddaughter and an honorable son-in-law. Both have given me joys that I never thought possible. My husband encouraged me to get a college degree as you

often did. Life has been good to us. We are the three wander-
ing amigos!

I saw one of your paintings in a gallery on a trip last sum-
mer to Camden, Maine. When we arrived back home from our
vacation, I promised to write you and tell you why I left with-
out saying good-bye. You deserve to know that much.

Here it goes. It's an ugly truth.

When I turned 16, the night of my birthday was the begin-
ning of many nightmares to come. Dad's drinking was out of
control as usual, but this time he needed comfort. He came to
my bed and fondled me. Then he pressed his lips to mine and
forced himself with all his might into me. Afterwards, he
threatened to hurt you if I told on him. I had witnessed him
hitting you when he was drunk before and knew he was capa-
ble of more violent actions. So I kept quiet. The scene repeated
itself for many months. After high school graduation, I knew I
had to leave, never return to Blue Wheel Drive. Everything
and everyone there had become dead to me, except you. I held
onto you, ever so tightly in my heart, never wanting to let
you go. I prayed every day for your safety. I just could not
come back to that house.

But I do believe, when the time is right, you and I will be
reunited.

By the way, my daughter has your feisty demeanor and an
artistic flair — only with words, not paintings — and your ea-
gle eyes for detail. Some day you will meet her. This is a
promise I intend to keep, no matter what happens.

Mother, I love you with all my heart and soul.

Suzanne

The voice inside Megan's head was subsiding. No matter
how hard she strained, she could no longer connect with it;
this is what she feared would happen. Also, images of the
house were fading... everything was going dark in her mental
turret. And now Grace was gone from her world, too. She
knew her dad would not believe her hearing the voice. Maybe

it was time for her to go away as well. Her dad didn't seem to care about her, and she knew, even at sixteen, that people only give genuine attention to what and to whom they love. She knew her dad had loved his wife, but Megan had always felt like an intruder in his world ever since she was born. The pain was overwhelming for Megan, and she longed to be hugged tightly by her mother.

Don had put the pieces of the puzzle together, and he wondered if Megan had already figured it out: Suzanne and her mom were the same person. Had Megan seen this portrait and read the contents of the letter? Now, Don knew why his wife was so shut down when it came to talking about her parents. At one point in their marriage, while in the midst of a move, his curiosity about his wife's past drove him to riffle through a hatbox of letters and miscellaneous papers. However, he learned nothing from the endeavor. Although he did recall Anne stating, after their family vacation in Maine, that she *needed* to come back one day. No wonder she was so delighted with his University of Maine job offer.

He felt compelled to find Grace and to comfort his daughter's tortured soul that he had neglected for too long. At last, he allowed himself to cry outwardly as his stomach heaved. No more choking back the tears, he told himself. And no more would he lock himself in his head and work to the point of not knowing what was going on in the heart of the daughter he loved. He sobbed, trying to recall the last time he had said "I love you" to Megan or held her close since the committal service. Anne would be so disappointed by his lack of emotional support for Megan.

Financially, Grace was fortunate enough to be able to move into a lovely retirement community near Orono called Dirigo Pines. The cottage setting was cramped in contrast to her huge house, but the smallness felt cozier and the loft with skylights made a perfect studio for her.

For some reason, she missed having Megan around. Grace never liked saying good-byes, and had ended their relationship with a card displaying one of her prints that Megan liked, along with the pay for her packing assistance. Grace decided not to tell Megan her new address, assuming that a teen heading back to high school soon would not wish to hang with an old lady. Grace had brought several paintings with her to the cottage including the ones of her daughter, except for one. In case Suzanne came back, she left the last one she painted in the house with the letter attached so her daughter would know she had received it. Grace was simply listening to her gut on this one; some inner voice commanded her to leave these items behind, even though the house was for sale.

"I have a special gift for you, Megan," Don said one evening. He headed into a closet and came out with a large, wrapped, rectangular object. "No peeking until our guest for the evening arrives," he warned.

"Guest?" Megan asked. "We don't have guests. Dad, you hate having people in the house. It's like *we* hide in this house,"

"It's about time we started having guests," Don said. "Besides, this is someone your mother knew very well at one time. It's time we all met. Now, see if you can find that picture of the house we rented in Minnesota. Our guest will be fascinated by it, I'm sure."

Megan rolled her eyes and spun around towards the living room to seek out an album of miscellaneous photos, one of the few albums that had been unpacked recently. Something was quirky about her dad lately. Megan couldn't put her finger on what. And now they were having company all of a sudden. She was in no mood to meet new people and go down memory lane with old photos. Oh, well; at least she'd be getting a present out of it.

*   *   *

"Our guest has arrived!" Don hollered to Megan.

Megan lingered in the living room while her dad met the guest at the door. Then she heard a familiar voice.

"I bet you thought you'd never see me again," Grace said as she entered the living room. "Your dad and I had a wonderful conversation recently, and we agreed that we wanted you to have more of an opportunity to know your grandmother — me! Now I know why you and I were meant to strike up a conversation. I had no idea at the time that we're related. I feel privileged to be your grandmother, if you'll have me. We really are two of a kind." Her eyes brimmed with tears despite a huge smile as she pulled the snow globe that Megan had named *Kiss of Winter in a Bottle* out of her purse and handed it to a speechless Megan.

After a few wobbly moments of conversation, Don sat them both down and shared the story of Suzanne, who had shortened her name to Anne for her new life beyond Blue Wheel Drive. He revealed his recent discovery of Grace's house, but not the envelope contents, and how he learned of Grace's existence in Megan's world.

"You see, Megan, your mother is still with us... taking care of the ones in her life that she loved... taking care of you and her mother — and teaching me how to show you how much I love you and always have," he said. "She talks to each of us in different ways, across time and place, and she always will." And he pointed to Megan's heart. "Her spirit brought the three of us together. See, my dear Megan, there are no dead ends. Every ending leads to a new beginning.

"So open your gift," Don said as he leaned over to hug his daughter.

"I know you'll like it, Megan," Grace said.

At long last, in this moment with her son-in-law and granddaughter, Grace felt the presence of Suzanne once again—and with it a renewed sense of purpose in her life. Leaving Blue Wheel Drive had brought her the family she always wanted.

As Megan ripped the wrapping paper off her present, revealing a portrait of her mother, she could hear the echoes of her mother's soothing words once again as the heavy black cloud of abandonment lifted from her mind.

*T*here's nothing like a murder mystery, but they're usually told from the point of view of the investigator trying to solve the case. This one sort of is, but Nora isn't a typical detective. Rather, she's a woman caught up in the midst of circumstances, with connections to the suspects, a blooming romance with the police detective, and a big wheel of blue cheese that isn't talking... because nobody knows where it went. Kelly Jean Richardson's first published story takes her love of a good mystery and puts it to good use.

Pungent Death

Kelly Jean Richardson

I could see the steam-clouded window panes of the commercial-quality kitchen, and I could already smell the fragrance of potent and exotic spices. The warmth of the spices contrasted sharply with the crisp fall air outside the house, tinged with the faint smell of burning wood and the muffled crunch of the decaying fall leaves under my feet. On West Broadway, grand old houses sat on either side of the wide, tree -lined street. I'd finally reached my destination. The stately house loomed in the dark, conjuring up ghostly tales. Garbage cans cast spooky shadows into the street. I shivered despite my warm, down-filled coat. I walked partly to stave off the indignities of age, though I admit I mostly did it for the pleasure. Walking makes me feel strong and vigorous — an increasingly delightful feeling the older one gets.

The housekeeper led me into the kitchen, announced me to Regina, and just as quickly disappeared. I'd started the gourmet club several years ago with members chosen from people I had met while taking night classes. Some were teachers, others students, but all had an avid interest in good food. None of the members were close friends, although some I had known many years—like Regina, who was cooking tonight's meal.

I tossed furtive glances around the kitchen, making sure everything ran smoothly. On several occasions, disaster loomed large, but I always stepped in calmly to assist. Everything ran like clockwork as Regina chatted while working with practiced steps. Her parents had raised her with old-world values, despite their enormous wealth, and expected her to give back generously to the community. She had devoted her adult life to working tirelessly as a patron of the arts.

Regina said, "Nora, Victor is in the conservatory setting up the wine and cheese course. Anthony just dropped off a wonderful selection of cheese. I'm sure he'd enjoy some help setting them out, and you two can quibble over the proper wines to serve."

I said, "I'd love to, and I can see you have everything well in hand here." She smiled at the compliment, and I went in search of Victor.

Victor stopped arranging the mounds of crumbled and cut cheeses on a delicate crystal platter to greet me. Smaller china platters held crackers and a variety of breads. The platters displayed garnishes of fresh fruits, vegetables, nuts, and fresh herbs. The room overflowed with fresh flowers, a faint smell of exotic incense, and soft music from India playing in the background. I smiled in absolute delight, and, of course, Victor saw and smiled at my pleasure. He always noticed every detail, including when you were genuinely pleased or merely pretending; not much got by him.

We had met in a wine-tasting class about four years before when Victor first moved to Bangor. Quite an elegant man, he had recently opened his own art gallery with his wife Regina's financial backing. When I invited him to join the gourmet club, he asked if his assistant, Anthony, could join us, as he felt the young man could use some refinement. I assured him Anthony was welcome, as was Regina, if she wished.

Lew Walters arrived first; he wrote grim tales of horror and the macabre. He was world famous, yet down to earth. Witty and energetic, he was not at all the dark, brooding type you'd expect if you read his material. He adored eating gourmet food, but he'd be the first to admit that his cooking skills were rudimentary at best. I routinely paired him with another cook, and he pitched in however he could. He was followed in by Anthony, and then Susan Montgomery. A thoroughly delightful woman, I took an immediate liking to her when we met in a photography course. She hesitantly asked if she could join the gourmet club after she had heard other students talking about it.

Susan's smile lit up the place and, after seeing the way Anthony flirted with her, I suspected why. I sensed that, bound by convention and slightly uptight, Victor disapproved of Anthony's playful and lighthearted banter. I think he disapproved of Susan rather more strongly at all times. The wariness on Victor's part puzzled me. Susan treated everyone in a warm, friendly manner, including him. Perhaps she reminded him of someone that he disliked. That did sometimes happen.

I put several delectable pieces of cheese and bread on my plate to eat as we mingled and talked, fueled by excellent wine and anticipation of the meal to come. I noticed Anthony walk over and hand Susan a small plate. She turned a bright smile his way and laid a light hand on his arm. "Thanks, Anthony," she said. "Did you know that I happen to adore blue cheese?"

"I have insider information," he replied. "I picked out the cheeses myself and I wanted your opinion of the Cashel. Did you know that it's an Irish farmhouse cheese?"

Susan savored the cheese slowly and cooed over it in delight.

I was disappointed that Victor had left the blue cheese in the pantry and I'd missed my chance to try it. As I knew others would be eager to sample it as well, I asked Victor to bring out the cheese wheel. I was momentarily distracted by a late arrival, Rosemary Henderson, a librarian and my dear friend. She was reserved until she knew someone well; then her warmth and intelligence made her a real pleasure to have around. We chatted briefly and then I looked around for Victor. Just as I moved towards him, he announced that we should seat ourselves for dinner.

We found seats and admired the exquisite Indian linens, and the fine china with intricate patterns in saffron, paprika, and sage colors. We ate curried soup, followed by Tandoori lamb, several side dishes, and numerous condiments. We drank spiced tea, ate stacks of naan bread, and finished the meal with homemade mango ice cream. Lively conversation flowed, and the meal was the star. We questioned Regina at length about the history of the dishes, the recipes, and even the exotic spices she used. Susan, unusually subdued and listless, moved the food around on her plate but ate little. She looked paler and far less animated than when she first arrived. Perhaps she felt ill; I understood that she had a serious heart condition.

Moments later, she crumpled and slid to the floor beside me. The hum of conversation in the room instantly hushed. I reached down to touched her wrist and felt her pulse race erratically. I thought that perhaps she had fainted, but she did not respond to my voice or my touch.

"Victor, I think she needs an ambulance," I said. He was sitting closest to me, right on the other side of Susan.

He didn't answer me, but instead opened his cell phone to dial.

"Nora, is she breathing? Do you think we need to try CPR or something?" Rosemary said as she sat wringing her hands.

"She's breathing fine and her heart is beating, although it seems erratic and jumpy. But it worries me that she's not responding."

I looked round the room at the anxious faces. The silence

was palpable as we all willed the ambulance to hurry. Victor had told Regina to start clearing up the dinner service. Though most of us were only half-done eating, dinner was clearly over. Just as she finished picking up the last plates we heard the sirens wailing in the distance. Anthony had gone outside to show them the closest door to enter. Lew paced back and forth like a caged rabbit. Moments later, the ambulance wailed into the driveway.

The paramedics worked frantically to revive her, and prepared to transport her to the medical center. I could see their frustration mount as she failed to respond in any way. They asked us a few questions, and took her purse which contained her identification and her medication.

After they wheeled the stretcher out the front door that Anthony held open for them, we talked while cleaning up. It was frustrating to have no idea how things were going in the ambulance, and I knew that if we tried calling the hospital, they wouldn't release any information without her consent. So we worked quietly together, speaking only when necessary. We were all left alone with our thoughts.

The elderly housekeeper would not be in until morning. We always tried to spare her any extra work on our account. When everything was spotless, Victor emptied the trash and carried it outside to the curb. Regina graciously thanked us all for cleaning up—especially tonight, as we all had so much on our minds.

We all knew, but nobody said, that it looked like Susan might not make it. Her heart condition must have been very serious indeed. Lew asked Rosemary and me if we'd like him to walk us home. We agreed, though it was a little out of his way, as his presence comforted us. We walked home in almost complete silence, as words would have felt intrusive. Lew waited until I was safely inside the building and then continued on with Rosemary. Feeling distraught and not quite ready to be on my own, I stopped to see Owen, my closest friend, who lived one door down from me on the second floor.

As soon as he saw me, he said "Something's wrong, Nora. What's happened?"

After I filled him in on my evening, he poured me a snifter of brandy. We sat in front of the fireplace and let the fire and the brandy warm the cold spot inside me. The elegant, hand-crafted woodwork and the ornate fireplaces gave our apartments character that new buildings would never have. The building grew shabbier over the years, and that too lent an air of gentility and charm.

Later, I went home to bed, still wondering if Susan would make it through the night.

I slept fitfully until the sun rose. A hot shower and a good breakfast improved my mood. The people they managed to save these days at a modern trauma center amazed me. I hoped that Susan's condition was not as dire as I imagined.

Jed Grayson, detective for the Bangor Police Department, knocked at my front door. I had taken numerous classes with him over the years, beginning with one on crime-prevention tips. Owen had suggested that I take the class shortly after Charles' death. He could tell that living alone for the first time in my life frightened me a bit. Jed's classes were always filled with pretty women, both widowed and married. Like me, he treasured his long and happy marriage, yet for some reason he had chosen not to remarry after his wife died. Sometimes I wondered if it was simply fear, for both of us. We'd been friends for years, and sometimes I wished that Jed would take things to the next level. I was quite attracted to him but I'd never been much of a flirter, and I was afraid of looking ridiculous by throwing myself at him, so I did nothing.

"Nora, may I come in?" Jed said. "There are some things we need to talk about."

I invited him in and offered him a seat at the kitchen table. I pulled out one of my blue pottery mugs and filled it with coffee, adding a big splash of heavy cream and two heaping sugars.

"Susan Montgomery died shortly after arriving at the hospital," he said. "We need to determine the cause of death. I'll need to reconstruct her last few days."

"I thought the cause of death was her heart condition," I said. "We all thought that. What would make you think it could be something else?"

"Her cardiologist said her heart condition was not life-threatening. So, what did cause her death? Right now, it appears to be suspicious. She had a large amount of digitalis in her bloodstream."

I sat back, horrified. It was sad contemplating a natural death, but unthinkable to believe that she had killed herself or that someone murdered her.

I composed myself before speaking. "It's difficult for me to believe it's anything other than a natural death, but I'll help any way I can. I understand her heart worked inefficiently. Isn't digitalis a heart medicine?"

"Her cardiologist didn't prescribe it, because it's dangerous with her particular condition. She had a lethal amount in her system."

I felt sick to my stomach. It felt surreal to be sitting here calmly discussing what had happened last night when my mind was reeling with the fact that Susan may have been murdered—and by someone I knew, and that I may have even been there as it happened.

Jed took notes as I described last evening's meal: who ate what, the dinner guests, the cook, the ingredients, the conversations I heard, and my own personal observations. I admired his attention to detail. He listened carefully, asked pertinent follow-up questions, and noted everything.

He said, "Thanks, Nora. I know you liked Susan, and I'm sorry to bring you bad news." He stood up, stretched his long legs, and smiled. "That's it for my official spiel. Now as a friend, are you okay?"

I nodded as he pulled me into a warm embrace and kissed the top of my forehead. Sometimes, as a widow, I missed the touch of a man, the comfort of a strong shoulder to lean on when things were difficult. Jed was a handsome man, but we'd been friends for years, and I think both of us would have hated to ruin a great friendship by having a little fling that might have fizzled and left us both feeling awkward.

After he left I sat down to think. Jed would spend the day interviewing everyone involved and the police would scour the house looking for any forensic evidence. We'd unwittingly destroyed potential evidence at the crime scene by cleaning up after dinner, because her death didn't raise any suspicion at the time. Still, none of us likely killed her, but I saw no reason for her to commit suicide either. Oh, well. Let Jed sort out all the police business, and I'd handle the memorial arrangements.

I knocked on Owen's door. He answered a little quicker than usual and smiled at my surprise.

He said, "Jed predicted you'd be stopping by soon to pick my brains." He chuckled with amusement and I grinned.

"Yep, Jed knows my number all right. No secrets here."

I followed Owen as he limped to the living room. I always felt so comfortable in his home because it stayed the same for decades with a heavy, tobacco-colored leather love seat and arm chair and row after row of sturdy shelves, fitted specially for paperback crime novels, from floor to ceiling on every wall. The brass lamps with amber-colored shades, a massive oak desk with an old-fashioned wooden office chair that swiveled on brass casters, and a heavy four-drawer file cabinet made it a room Hemingway would have felt at home in.

We batted ideas back and forth in a rapid-fire motion until we'd exhausted the subject. I left to pick up groceries, stop at the drug store, and go to the post office. I'd wait until that evening to contact the other group members about a memorial service, so Jed could question them all first. I stopped at the downtown post office on Harlow Street. I mailed some letters for Owens and one of my own to my cousin before noticing Regina huddled on a bench. She clutched a large, thick manila envelope to her chest. I asked if she needed anything, and she shook her head vigorously but didn't speak.

"Did you receive some bad news, Regina?" I asked.

"No, I didn't!" she practically shouted. "Just leave me in peace, would you?" She trembled and pulled her coat around her thin body, while still cradling her mail, and scurried out the door.

Her abrupt and odd behavior puzzled me. I'd never seen her be anything but cordial to anyone, ever. She seemed to have infinite reserves of patience as well as complete control over her behavior and emotions at all times. This could not be the same person; something had to be dreadfully wrong. As I walked to the nearby drugstore, I wondered what could have caused such a marked change in her personality.

At the small drugstore I greeted Warren Taylor, the pharmacist. I'd known Warren for several years; he was an intelligent but bland sort of man who appeared to be a good twenty years older than his wife, Eva. Rumors indicated that she played around with wild and indiscriminate love affairs; folks said she'd passed through the hands of several of the town's leading men already, but those were just rumors.

Eva greeted me and went back to tidying the shelves. If she were unfaithful, her husband must have been unaware, because I'd never heard a cross word or angry look pass between them. Warren handed me Owen's refills and inquired about my health. I carried a few too many pounds as a result of my passion for good food and sitting on my butt, reading for long hours every day, but I tried to walk as often as possible to balance things out.

After a quick stop at the grocery store I headed back home. Having seen Owen's pitiful array of bread, cheese, and canned soup induced me to cook him a good meal. He liked good food but found cooking wore him out, and he would rather spend his energy doing other things.

I practically ran home to avoid the bitter weather, but still felt icy by the time I arrived; perhaps the temperature had dropped below freezing already. I left my bags at home on the counter before I stopped by Owen's place with his meager groceries, several bottles of medications, and a large batch of personal letters. This time he moved more slowly getting to the door; this was more like his usual speed. He looked tired but quite interested when he asked about my day.

"Nothing major to report, I'm afraid," I said. "But I feel like going home and cooking. Good therapy for me; it helps me to think. Come over at six, and we'll have some Italian food and talk shop?"

He agreed, perhaps a bit too easily, which meant that the excitement that morning had worn him out. I bustled on home to chop garlic, red onions, and bell peppers. I lightly sautéed the vegetables, browned spicy Italian sausage, and then added marinara sauce. I added oregano, basil, and a bit of red pepper flakes, and lowered the heat to a slow simmer and put on a lid. I set the kitchen table for two with a colorful set of Italian dishware on bright Provencal linens. I made a simple salad of a peppery blend of mesclun greens that I would dress just before serving with simple vinaigrette. I showered and put on a pretty dress for dinner. Whenever I cooked for him, Owen dressed for dinner.

He rang the doorbell precisely at six and handed me a good bottle of red Italian wine. I ritually added the first splash of wine to the sauce before pouring us each a glass. I sliced a loaf of crusty Italian bread and dressed the salad. I drained the vermicelli and splashed in a little olive oil before filling our plates.

Owen ate with relish while I told him about my trip to the drugstore. His eyes twinkled when he told me that he heard rumors that Eva ran a bit on the kinky side. He laughed at my shocked face until the doorbell rang.

Jed Grayson smiled when I opened the door. He said, "Sorry for interrupting your dinner, but…" I saw him smell the air appreciatively with anticipation, and I laughed.

"Bachelors!" I said. "Sit down, Jed; I can't stand to see a hungry man."

Jed sat down and said, "Okay, Owen, What the devil made you laugh so? I heard you from outside."

Owen leaned over and pretended to whisper, "The look on Nora's face when I told her that I heard about Eva Taylor's kinky sexcapades."

Jed burst out with a laugh at my red face. I shoved a big plate of food at him and said, "Here, eat. I wanted to tell Owen something that happened today."

I cleaned up the kitchen as I spoke and Jed ate. I mentioned Regina's strange behavior in the post office earlier. Both of them agreed that it was uncharacteristic for her to speak and act that way.

We retired to my living room and Jed perched comfortably on the aqua love seat, so Owen could have the big flowered armchair to himself. Owen sat down, grateful for the comfort. I was grateful for Jed's diplomatic treatment of Owen. He'd cared for his own father at home until his father had died a couple of years ago. Jed's father had been a Bangor cop, and had been close friends with Owen.

Jed filled us in on the investigation. When Jed had gone to the scene of the crime early in the day, Regina had appeared serene and composed, but Victor had acted nervous. He claimed to have met Susan only recently, but they had both attended the Portland School of Art during the same years. Her college roommate mentioned that Susan and Victor had dated briefly. They had quite the passionate affair until he dumped Susan, with scarcely a thought, for a rich society girl from Philadelphia.

The coroner had ruled Susan's death a murder. The police

searched her house on Patten Street and found documentation backing the roommate's story up. Susan had been obsessed with documenting every sleazy move Victor had ever made after dumping her. Pinned on her bulletin board were surveillance photos, diary entries with dates and times, and newspaper clippings. The search uncovered photographs of Victor in graphic and compromising positions with Eva Taylor, as well as a blackmail note threatening to send them to Regina if he didn't fork over two thousand dollars immediately. When confronted with the evidence, Victor admitted that he'd lied about knowing her, and that she blackmailed him about his affair with Eva Taylor. He refused to speak when questioned about the murder. Regina phoned a lawyer, who advised him to remain silent.

Jed paused, and I blurted out, "But his, um, mistress has access to digitalis—she's married to a pharmacist." I swear these two enjoyed seeing me all embarrassed and red-faced every time something sexual came up in the conversation. It's just I was not used to such frankness about these matters.

"Absolutely," Jed said. "She could easily have accessed drugs for him." He winked at me and I blushed.

Jed pointed out that most of us could access the drug fairly easily, which was true. I routinely picked up Owen's prescription for him. Regina knew numerous elderly socialites who probably took the stuff. And, of course, Warren and Eva were surrounded by prescription drugs. So digitalis was not particularly difficult to procure, but not everyone had a motive.

I liked Susan and thought I knew her well. I never suspected she carried dark secrets, not at all. Regina had a motive: jealousy. Victor needed to hide his double life, and protect his marriage and career. Even Eva's husband, Warren, might not be as clueless as he seemed. I could come up with no reasonable motives for the rest of the people in attendance that night: the housekeeper; Lew Walters, the horror writer; Anthony, Victor's gallery assistant; or Rosemary Harris, the librarian.

Eventually, Jed noticed that Owens' eyelids were closing and his head bobbing forward as he sat. "Owen, I'll walk you back to your apartment," he said. "There's another case I wanted to check on tonight." Jed kissed me on the cheek, and thanked me for dinner before he and Owen left. Then I heard the door in the hallway close quietly, and then the downstairs door on the street as Jed left the building.

The doorbell rang early the next morning, just as I got up and put on the coffee. I looked through the peephole, to see Jed with a bag from Frank's Bakery. Jed and I shared a secret addiction to anything from Frank's, so he brought it by often. Jed glanced at me as he walked in.

"You are awfully pretty so early in the morning, Nora," he said.

I handed him the usual large blue pottery mug of coffee. He inhaled the scent of the coffee and said quietly, "I could get used to this. There are some things a man misses about being married."

Before I could even blush, he said "I arrested Victor this morning on a charge of felony murder."

I said, "Wow… what changed since last night?"

"I visited Eva Taylor, and she admitted supplying Victor with the drugs. She said Susan blackmailed him, so she got what she deserved. Eva loves Warren, but he knew from the beginning that she needed frequent erotic adventures. She'll likely be charged as an accessory; no doubt Warren will stick by her."

"Wow," I said again. "So just like that, it's all wrapped up. I see motive and means, but what about opportunity? So how did he give the drugs to Susan and when?"

Jed said that Victor had asked Anthony to supply the cheese plate for dinner, an excellent blue cheese because Susan could never resist blue cheese. Anthony did, but was irritated Victor never bothered to put the blue cheese out. When he mentioned it, Victor took him into the pantry and handed him a small plate he prepared for Susan, and ordered him to deliver it. Anthony delivered it with a bit of flirtation, which he made sure Victor noticed, and before Anthony could ask if anyone else wanted to try it, Victor announced that we had to find our seats for dinner. Anthony detoured to the pantry where he noticed the entire wheel of blue cheese had vanished. It irritated him that Victor had probably hidden it to eat alone with his lover later.

Victor confirmed everything—except he claimed he never poisoned the blue cheese, and he had no idea where it went after dinner, but he supposed the trash. No one else tasted the blue cheese, except Susan, so the poison must have been in it. She didn't eat much else; the coroner said her stomach been nearly empty. Not to mention that everyone saw Victor take the trash out to the curb, and it just happened to be on trash night. Trash removal had been early in that neighborhood—five in the morning—which Victor knew. The police had been unable to find the remaining blue cheese, the empty prescription vial, or the negatives of Susan's photographs.

"It sounds good, Jed, but something's not quite right," I said. "I can't put my finger on it, though. Maybe it's all too easy, too neat."

"Well, it bothered me that we don't have any physical evidence, but we know Victor put the trash out. He admitted it—plus we have loads of witnesses. It felt like something was missing at first, but now it all adds up."

I nodded as he bent down to give me a kiss on the forehead before he let himself out. Jed might have been hoping for a pat on the back for a job well done, but something bothered me and I needed to sort it out first. I dressed, feeling distracted, and decided to talk it over with Owen and see if he could pinpoint the problem.

Jed had already been to Owen's and filled Owen in. But Owen had something else he wanted to talk about; I could tell by the twinkle in his eyes.

"Jed said when this case ended, he hoped you two might be more than friends," he said with a smile. "I told him you were my closest friend, and that you were just figuring out how strong you were. Jed assured me that after years of taking care of his wife, and taking care of his dad before he died, that he was now ready to properly appreciate a strong, independent woman."

My heart melted to know Owen considered me his closest friend, not merely my husband Charles' friend now. Jed wanted to take our relationship further, and I realized that it's what I wanted too.

I knew the people at that dinner party and understood what made them tick better than the police did, no matter how expert they were at their jobs. I thought we didn't know everything yet, that it somehow went deeper than blackmail. If we hadn't all been so eager to clean up after dinner, we might have at least some of the evidence in hand. The housekeeper had already left for the night, so the trash might not have gone out until morning, and possibly traces of poison might have been left for forensics.

If Charles were still alive, he'd tell me to leave it to the experts, and that I was naïve in the ways of the world. He'd say not to worry, that he'd look out for me, and no one would hurt me. I'd been absolutely sure he was right for many years, and even now I felt a little disloyal thinking otherwise.

Not that I thought that Victor incapable of murder; in fact, I think that most of us could commit murder if pushed far enough. Yet when it came down to it, the blackmail money just kept his life from getting messy. Victor did what he needed to do to get where he wanted in life. If this town, this job, and this wife didn't work out, he'd leave and conjure up a similar situation elsewhere. After all, he'd already proven he could do it once; he could certainly do it again

I needed to devise a way to get everyone who was there

the night Susan died to confide in me. I could talk to them all about some sort of memorial service. I called Regina and asked if I could come over to discuss this with her. She said she felt it was our obligation under the circumstances, as Susan had no living relatives. I decided to walk there despite the chill and the gray, murky sky.

I pulled on my hat, mittens, and paisley down jacket and set out at a brisk pace to walk the few miles. The walk involved several steep hills and lots of deeply cracked sidewalks. I walked often because it let me sort out my thoughts, and right now I had a lot of thinking to do. For starters, how was I going to get people to confide in me? Anything they thought was important they would surely convey to the authorities—at least, the innocent ones would. Still, they would be more apt to tell me small, seemingly insignificant details.

Chimneys spewed black smoke, squirrels raced back and forth in a hurry to get ready for winter, and people rushed about, bundled up in thick clothes as their breaths came out in little clouds of warmth in the freezing air. I finally arrived, and the housekeeper showed me into a small sitting room where Regina sat. The recent strain clouded her eyes and tightened her mouth. She served tea and finger sandwiches in front of the small, grey-marble fireplace. After we ate, I complimented the coziness of the room, perfect for an intimate tea like we were having. I hoped with some encouragement she would show me around the less public areas of the house. I'm not sure what I was looking for—maybe a tangible clue, or maybe just a feel for the world these two inhabited.

"Victor thought it not grand enough, as it gave people the wrong impression of us," she said in a soft voice. "But since he's not here..." Her voice trailed off. "Well, I played in this room as a child. The grand one upstairs made me feel lonely, so I always gravitated to this one."

"I never knew this room existed," I said. "It's a gem. Of course, I've only seen the public rooms until now. Thank you so much for sharing it with me."

Regina stood up and almost shyly asked, "Would you like to see the house, Nora — the private areas where I played as a girl?"

At the far end of the house, her father had played billiards, drunk whiskey, and smoked cigars with his cronies in the massive room Regina showed me first. Then she took me into the playroom at the other end, the one that she rarely used as a child. The immense size of it alone was intimidating; it was big enough for several nursery-school classes, rather than one tiny girl. It was a room lost in time, with toys from fifty years before displayed neatly along the shelves, very expensive toys that sat as if waiting to be played with. Next she showed me the ample guest bedrooms, and finally her and Victor's spacious and very elegant separate bedrooms.

Victor's room, like the man himself, revealed little about him personally, despite its impeccable taste. Regina's room oozed femininity, soft and so utterly unlike the public woman I knew. Clearly, in Regina beat the heart of a full-blown romantic. I took in the telling little details, and savored each one: the little dressing table filled with perfumes, the delicate fabrics, and the books of love poetry on her bedside table. As I looked at the lacy bed skirt, I saw the edge of something sticking out from beneath. I reached under the edge of the bed and Regina gasped as I pulled out graphic sexual pictures of Victor and Eva.

I looked up in bewilderment as Regina crumpled on the bed sobbing in shame and embarrassment. I sat down gently beside her. She said, "Oh, please, please leave me alone." Her voice shook.

I rubbed her trembling back and said, "No, this time I'm not leaving until we talk about this. I know it's shocking; I've never seen photos like those. But you weren't in them."

When the crying subsided she sat up and said, "Yes, you're right. I felt humiliated and mortified when I saw these. I apologize for the way I spoke to you."

"I understand," I said "Who do you think mailed them to you? Who would want you to know?"

Regina confessed that she knew about his problem years ago. Until now, she'd managed to keep Victor's ungentlemanly behavior from becoming public knowledge. She also feared that the police might suspect either of them of the murder. "Eva admitted to the police that she gave Victor some digitalis," she said. "That, and her readily admitting the affair, clinched the case as far as the police are concerned."

"Yes, Eva's utterly without a conscience, and as sexually compulsive as Victor," I said. "Still, I don't believe she had anything to do with Susan's murder. Do you?"

"No—I don't know why anyone would kill her. Victor told me he met her in college and he thought her an easy conquest—that she was so naïve that she didn't understand his game."

We planned a small memorial service just for the members of the gourmet club. I agreed to call everyone and Regina would take care of everything else. It stood to reason that one of us was responsible for her death or at least knew something valuable, even if unaware of it. I was thrilled that Regina had taken me into her confidence, now if I could just get everyone else to be as forthcoming. Maybe Victor did it and that was the whole story. I just wasn't convinced yet.

I stopped by the gallery to talk to Anthony, Victor's assistant, on my way home from Regina's. The vibrant colors inside contrasted vividly with the dismal day outside.

Anthony said, "To what do I owe the pleasure, Nora? Are you here on a personal matter, or have you come to see the new exhibit?"

"Both, but art comes first. Do you have time to walk with me today?" I wanted to get a feel for Anthony's state of mind before I talked about Susan or the murder. Perhaps if he saw me as non-threatening he'd be more apt to confide in me.

He nodded with pleasure and led me around, pointing out interesting details and sharing tidbits of relevant history. Anthony's response to the art, as well as my reaction to it, impressed me as genuine. In comparison, Victor's slightly flat recitation of facts, history, and importance of each piece always seemed too rehearsed.

The tour completed, Anthony invited me into his office. I noticed he still used his own office, not Victor's. We sat down and he said, "So how can I help you today?"

I told him about the service and he managed a sad smile. "Of course, I'll be there to pay my respects. I didn't know her well, but I'd hoped that would change."

"I thought I noticed a bit of chemistry that night. Something new, perhaps?"

"Ah, that. I wanted to irritate Victor, so I flirted outrageously with Susan. Childish, I know."

"So you weren't romantically interested?"

"My real love is art," he said. "Susan didn't interest me on a personal level. I had hoped to do a showing of her work here. Her photography touched a nerve with me; it's raw sense of honesty."

I mentioned displaying some of her work at the memorial service, which he promised to take care of personally, and soon I left for the short walk home.

It grew quickly colder and darker, and for some reason the dark seemed unfriendly that night. Rarely had I felt such a sense of foreboding and menace, and I had no idea what caused it. The small hairs on the back of my neck stood straight up. I'd walked these downtown streets at all times of the day and night for years without ever worrying. I kept turning in my tracks, to see if anyone was lurking in the shadows. By the time I got home, I was completely spooked. I pulled all the shades down, switched on every light in the house, and turned the volume on TV up as high as it would go.

A knock on the door startled me, but when I saw Jed I

relaxed. My nervousness must have been obvious, because as soon as he came in, he asked me what was wrong.

I shook my head and shrugged my shoulders. "Nothing. I don't know."

He sat down on the love seat and held out his arms. I nestled inside them and spilled out my story. He looked serious and a bit worried. He made me promise to be careful and to let him know if I felt uneasy or nervous again. I nodded mutely. I felt like someone still watched me now, but it sounded ridiculously melodramatic to say so. Instead, I snuggled up closer and let the warmth of his body and the safety of his arms lull me into sleep.

I woke up when Jed gently tried to extricate himself from my sleeping body. The bright morning light in my eyes made me squint. I felt shy and awkward this morning in the light of day, though I hadn't been uncomfortable with things last night. We had officially spent our first night together, though in a completely innocent way. My neighbors might not think so, but no regrets flooded my mind; I'd needed him that night. I sat up on the sofa, still wearing yesterday's rumpled clothes, as Jed brought me coffee.

I drank my coffee and savored the gentle pleasure of waking up in a man's arms.

He finished his coffee and put on his heavy overcoat. "I'm sorry if this causes you any embarrassment with your neighbors," he said. "The long day just caught up with me, and it felt so nice holding you that I relaxed. Maybe a little too much

"No, thanks for being here for me, Jed. Nosy neighbors are a small price to pay."

After I got dressed, Lew Walters called. He sounded nervous and hesitant, not at all his usual playful and ironic self. He asked me to meet him in the Bangor Room of the public library as soon as I could. His voice worried me, so I left right away and walked downtown. Something felt wrong, dreadfully wrong. When I got to the library, I found Lew pacing back and forth like a lion in a cage.

I took a seat and waited. After a minute he sat, looking all around first to make sure no one could overhear us in this spot.

"I saw you leave the gallery last night," he finally said. "I wanted to tell you something, but I realized that we weren't alone. A man in a black overcoat and black hat followed you. I couldn't see his face, but it worried me, so I followed him until you got to your house. I saw Jed go in right after you, so I didn't see any reason to call the police. It's not like he'd let anything happen to you, and it probably doesn't have anything to do with Susan's murder."

I said, "What did you need to tell me, before you noticed someone following me?"

"The night of the dinner, I saw Anthony leaving the back entrance of the house when I arrived. At the time, it didn't seem important, but now that someone has been killed, it makes me uneasy. I was going to call the police—but when you're in the public eye as much as I am, you have to decide if it's worth having your name dragged through the mud."

I told him that Victor said Anthony came by earlier to drop off all the cheeses, and the butler's pantry is at the back of the house.

"That makes sense," he said, "but if you still think I should call the police, of course, I will."

I thanked him for his concern, mentioned the memorial service, and told him to call me if anything else worried him. He seemed relieved to get that information off his chest.

My suspicions were clearly not unfounded. So who was the man who watched me, and why? Of course, it could have been a woman in a man's overcoat. Plenty of women are tall enough to be mistaken for men—Regina, for instance. Why were they watching me? Did they think that I knew something? If someone thought I knew what happened, what would they be prepared to do to keep me quiet? Perhaps Charles had been right. Maybe I did need to be protected and sheltered from life.

Jed called to ask me to meet him at a local Mexican restaurant for the lunch buffet. I was excited about a real date with him, but I also wanted to tell him what happened. I brushed my hair, changed into a pretty turquoise top, and bundled up before heading over to the restaurant. When I arrived, he stood waiting outside. He bent down and lightly kissed me, not on the cheek as I expected but on the lips, and then he quickly took my hand and led me into the restaurant. It flustered me, and made me feel a bit giddy — and at my age! He picked out a table far from the other diners.

I said, "Let's get our food, and then we'll talk."

"As long as you don't tell me I'm a terrible kisser," he said with a grin. "I'm a bit out of practice, you know."

We got back to the table, our plates piled high with spicy food. While we ate, I told him everything: my meetings with Regina and Anthony, about meeting Lew, about being followed, and about the plans for the memorial service tomorrow. Jed's face darkened with concern.

"I don't like it," he said. "I truly believe we have the killer behind bars, but if I'm wrong... then you could be in danger. I'm not infallible."

I told him I understood, and that I'd be extra-careful until this case was wrapped up.

"You're important to me, Nora," he said. "I couldn't bear it if anything happened to you. I'm not professional or objective when it comes to you. I hoped to stop by tonight... well, to spend more time with you."

"I'd like you to," I said. I wasn't sure whether this murder investigation was helping or hurting our fledgling romance at this point. But I knew what I wanted.

*   *   *

I stopped by Owen's and filled him in on the past few days. He didn't mention my overnight guest, but he did compliment the new bloom in my cheeks. I finally admitted to my dear old friend that I liked Jed, a lot. We visited for a while and I told him that Jed planned to stop by for dinner and he beamed. "Ah, taking a chance on love then, dear," he said. "It's a rare and wonderful thing."

I went home to get ready for dinner with Jed when Rosemary called. She mentioned that perhaps she ought to call the police but first she wanted my opinion as to whether something she had seen, or thought she had seen, was significant. I told her to take her time, and to tell me whatever was on her mind.

"I worked late the night before Susan died," she said. "I saw a man parked in that empty lot across from her house. It was hard to tell in the dark, but it could have been Anthony. I also noticed Victor walking down the street towards her house as I drove by. Maybe it's not even important; I certainly don't want to waste the police's time. They have already arrested Victor, so I'm not even sure if it matters now."

I thanked Rosemary for the information and told her I'd let Jed know just in case it proved to be important later.

When Jed arrived I asked him to tell me about his visit to Anthony's house the morning after Susan's death. He said the police had questioned Anthony as they had me, but they made no formal search.

"He offered us a drink, and I noticed his fridge contained fast-food remnants and lots of low-quality processed food — not exactly a gourmand's refrigerator," he said. "When I asked why he'd joined the gourmet club, he said bitterly, 'The boss tried to polish me to perfection. He just didn't get that I'd no interest in being like him.'"

It all made sense to me now, and I explained my theory to Jed. Anthony had killed Susan merely to set up Victor, and doing it at the gourmet club because he thought the club pretentious, and he hated it. Somehow, he'd stumbled onto the fact that Susan and Victor knew each other and that she was blackmailing him. Victor gave her the money but told her he wouldn't pay her again. Anthony flipped because Regina had bankrolled Victor and introduced him to all the right people, and yet that wasn't enough. Victor devoured everything and always wanted more—more than others, and more than he had a right to.

Victor planned to use the digitalis to kill Susan but couldn't go through with it. He invited Eva to meet him at the gallery that night to return it. When he discovered the medication missing, she laughingly told him not to worry about it, because her husband handed the pills out like candy to his old-fart patients. This happened late the night before the gourmet-club dinner.

Anthony discovered the bottle of medication earlier when he went back to find the photographs and blackmail note from Susan. He hid there while Victor called Eva and waited until she arrived. Anthony hid until they left and then he decided to seize the opportunity that suddenly presented itself. Now he could watch Victor squirm, and maybe he could take over the gallery. He'd always liked Regina; perhaps she could do for him what she had done for Victor. But he was different—he would appreciate it. He took some of the medicine, the envelope of dirty pictures, and the blackmail note home to use in framing Victor for the death of Susan at dinner the next night.

When I finished laying it out, Jed looked at me, amazed, and said, "Very plausible, but all circumstantial."

"Hey, you're the cop—*you* prove it. But make it tomorrow," I said, knowing that Anthony, secure in knowing the police thought it was Victor, wasn't going anywhere. "I'm more interested in the romance you promised. And the dinner you were going to cook for me."

*　*　*

The next morning I wandered around my apartment as Jed lay sprawled out on my sofa, asleep. He'd returned an hour before, utterly exhausted. I'd cooked him breakfast, which he devoured as he told me how they had gotten a search warrant and found enough evidence to connect Anthony to the murder. He'd arrogantly tossed the empty pill bottle in the trash can along with the blue cheese because he thought the pungent cheese was vile. Fortunately, *his* trash didn't get collected until Friday morning, or the evidence would have been destroyed.

Jed complimented my fine detective skills right before falling asleep on my sofa. I liked the look of the huge man filling up my house and maybe my life.

*T*ourists think that Maine is all about lobsters and Bar Harbor, but there's something about rural Maine that goes far beyond those things. There's the tenacity and perseverance of Mainers, and the strong work ethic you'll find in them. There's the deep sense of pride those folks have. And there's the time-hardened Maine concept of what it means to be "from away" — a concept often adhered to with the fiercest resolution. In his story, Greg Westrich — who is, in fact, "from away" — shows us how keenly he understands those things, and he weaves them together into a tragic mystery where one quiet blue wheel tells a terrible story. What happens in the lonely woods of this fictional Maine community could happen in any of the real towns you'll find once you venture even a short way off Interstate 95.

Greenland, ME

Greg Westrich

I coasted to a stop at the top of the rise and leaned forward onto my ski poles. An echo of the dry rasp of snow spread out from me, up into the bleached blue of the sky like ripples on a pond. With each breath I could feel the bitter cold burn my throat and cool my chest. The moisture in each exhale froze into a fog that hung about my head in the still air. A raven glided silently over me, turning to peer down at me as it banked off toward the woods to my right. In front of me the snowmobile trail dropped down through the hay meadow, across a small alder-lined stream, and into a smaller hay meadow along the Station Road. The trail disappeared where it turned sharply to the right — avoiding actually going into the meadow — and hugged the edge of the alders until it entered the woods.

On the side of the meadow sat a hay baler, little more than a giant lump in the deep snow. Its faded green shell around blue metal machinery and wheels were hidden; the grass stubble, grease, and bloodstains were all frozen beneath a deep blanket of snow. The baler had been sitting there since early October.

~~~~~

It had happened on a Monday; I remember because I was eating lunch before heading into Bangor to the bookstore when the first ambulance roared down the road, past the house, across the bog in a cloud of dust, and down to the Kimballs' dairy farm. A few moments later a State Trooper and two of the town's fire trucks followed into the farm's dusty front yard.

Polly and I went to the kitchen window. "What do you think it is?"

As we stood watching from our kitchen window, the ambulance backed out of the yard and drove slowly farther down the road.

"Doesn't look good."

"Yeah—jeez, and I'm gonna be late for work. I'll call at dinnertime."

As I drove into town, I was wondering what had happened, and thinking that even though we weren't close with the Kimballs, Polly would have us involved. Helping someone. We'd lived in Greenland for ten years, but I still felt like an outsider. I was very much from away. Hell, my daughter had been born in our house, but she was from away. That's the way it was. Greenland had once been a thriving community of well-off vegetable and dairy farmers with its own train station, grist mill, and downtown. All that was left of the mill was a broken dam on Dead Stream that was great fun to run in a canoe during the spring; downtown was a clapboard general store, a gas station, a tiny brick library, the Baptist church, and a concrete slab where the pizza place had been before it burned down. We lived on the Station Road, which used to go from town to the railroad station. The town didn't even maintain the road all the way to the tracks anymore. One retired neighbor, who we would meet occasionally on our family walks, told us that when she was a girl you could see from her house all the way to town hall. All the land on both sides of the road was in crops or hay; now it's almost all woods.

The town was down to a handful of dairy farms: Every barn fire, retirement, or long winter meant fewer families willing or able to stick with it. Everyone said that there were more people growing pot for a living than farming something legal; given the number of drug busts every year, I tended to believe them. There were more rusty mobile homes than farm houses, and most of farm houses—like ours—weren't farms anymore. Somehow the Kimballs had held on. It took everyone in three generations to do it. Even so, they were barely getting by. I wondered if they had been on the land for more than two hundred years because they were too ornery to quit or if they had been at it so long that they couldn't imagine anything else. The previous Christmas, Dawson—who was in second grade like my son Ben—and his older brother had come over to the house to show off their new winter coats. They were satin jackets, like baseball players wear with a Holstein embroidered on the back and said: "Sixth generation Kimball farmer." The boys' names were over the pockets on the front. Straight out of Norman Rockwell.

At dinner I called Polly; she was crying. "It was Edwin. Something with the hay baler—I don't know. They have three kids. We—we—gotta do something." She didn't say he'd been killed. She didn't need to.

"Can you make something for me to take down tomorrow? Maybe I should see if Masha needs help with Dawson. Jerry?" A covered dish: a bit of a cliché. I knew better than to say so.

"Yeah, I'll have time before work." And besides, if I make it, Polly will deliver it. I really didn't want to go down to the farm; I didn't know what to say to them on a good day.

"Thanks, Jerry. Those poor kids..." I'd have to talk to Wayne; he was the biggest gossip I knew. Even though he moved in across the street only a couple of years ago, he managed to know everyone in town and their business as well. I never saw him in the general store, and I don't think he went to church in town. Maybe his secret was his Southern charm.

On the road in front of Wayne's house is a bad frost heave that never completely goes away. I downshifted to go over it slowly and noticed Wayne standing on his front porch. I stopped in the road even with his mailbox. He waved, so I got out and walked up the gravel drive.

"I guess you heard."

"Sorta. Polly didn't have any details." I waved my hand in front of me rather than say anything derogatory.

"She called. Talked to Susan. They just want to worry about the kids."

"Covered dishes. I'm sure I'll be spending time with Dawson." None of the kids at school seemed to like him; he was a little different. Behind the family's back, people claimed it was because he'd fallen out of the hayloft when he was four. I figured he was just being himself. Ben would be friends with anybody who wanted to be his--and besides, Dawson had a trampoline.

"Hang on a second." Wayne followed his old, half-blind Lab into the house. Across the street the lights were on both upstairs and down at my house. Polly was putting the kids to bed. Ben didn't like going to bed alone, and was no doubt fighting harder than usual tonight. Polly, Ben, and Anna were probably all in our bed reading a book. Polly would want to fall asleep before either of the kids; I had to go help.

Wayne came back out onto the porch with two bottles of beer. He handed me one. I nodded thanks. It was getting cold. The stars were almost bright enough to see by; there'd be another freeze tonight for sure. I took a swig of beer — Miller; at least it was a bottle.

"Delmont found him. Edwin was out baling one of the small meadows 'bout a mile down the road. When he didn't come back for lunch, his dad went down to get him." It had been a cold, wet fall and the Kimballs were no doubt behind getting hay up for the cows. I'd seen Edwin out on the tractor after dark several times in the last two weeks. Man works twenty-four/seven and can still barely feed his kids. Not for the first time, I decided there was something profoundly wrong with this country.

"The rig was sitting there idling with Edwin leaning up against it, not moving." Wayne took a drink of his beer; he was drawing the story out. I was used to his Southern ways, or maybe this time he didn't really want to think about it again.

"Polly said he stuck his hand in the baler or something."

"Yeah, the EMTs said that the drive wheel must have gotten jammed, and Edwin tried to pull the jam out with his hand."

I could see it now. "He left the motor engaged because he was in a hurry."

"It's easier to tell if you got it that way. When the baler started back up it pulled him in by the arm. He got pulled up tight to the body of it."

"Which is the way Delmont found him. Was he already dead?"

"Yeah." Wayne drained his beer. "Funny thing is, Edwin told me that he chewed his little brother Otis out for stickin' his hand in the baler earlier this summer. You want another?"

I waved at my house. "I better get home. Polly'll want to talk. If you hear anything, let me know. You know — what they need or..." I turned and started for my truck, wondering how much of the haying was done. There were plenty of farmers in town who weren't farming anymore and could help the family. I wouldn't want to be the one to bring that baler back to the barn.

~~~~~

The sound of a snowmobile coming up behind me brought me back. I looked over my shoulder; the hay meadow dropped gradually down to a now-frozen swampy area along Dead

Stream which was hidden by an extensive alder thicket. The snowmobile had just come out of the woods on the trail near where the alders gave way to fir and maples. I needed to get moving to warm up, but was curious who was out riding on a weekday. And besides, snowmobiles were pack animals; I rarely saw anyone out riding alone. The machine seemed to push the quiet of the world into the trees and under the frozen ground as it whined its way toward me. The sound seemed to stay near the ground; the pale-blue arc of the sky was impervious to its insignificance.

I stepped to the side of the trail as the rider eased his machine up next to me. He turned and looked at me through the mirrored visor of his helmet. He lifted the visor.

"Don't you know it's fucking ten below out here?" It was Bill McGriff, Ben's soccer coach. We had mutual friends, and often ran into the McGriffs at birthday parties. Bill was always the one holding fort on the couch telling hunting stories you could follow from the other room. If you really wanted to. He was from away—Boston. Sometimes it felt like there was a club in town for folks from away who hung out not because we had anything in common, but because we were all outsiders. Bill had pretty much gone native.

"How you doing, Bill?"

"Brenda's making me crazy. Had to get out of the house."

"Or you made her crazy, and she kicked you out."

He looked hurt, then laughed. "Same thing."

"Too cold for work today?" Bill repaired hydraulic systems of 'dozers, diggers, and the like.

"Nothing's moving today."

Without realizing it, I looked back toward the snow-covered baler.

Bill followed my gaze, got a serious look in his eyes and asked: "So, Sherlock, did you ever catch the killer?"

~~~~~

After Edwin's death, Dawson practically moved into our

house. I wouldn't have wanted to be at home either, constantly reminded that my dad was never coming back. Nobody expected him to be in school that week, so he hung quietly around our house, playing with Ben's toys or just sitting in front of the kitchen window. We had a big bay window that looked out over our pond and the bog beyond it. With the leaves mostly off the trees, you could see the Kimballs' farm off to the right, and directly across the bog on a pine-covered rise sat the town cemetery where Edwin would be buried Friday. Some of the White Pines were a hundred feet tall; they must have been there almost as long as the cemetery. There were almost as many graves from before the Civil War as since, many of them Dawson's family. I doubted that's what he was thinking about.

My three-year-old daughter Anna walked in from the living room. "I'm hungry."

"Hey, Dawson, is pizza okay for lunch?" No response. I went and squatted next to him, looking at him out of the corner of my eye. "You hungry, Dawson?"

I watched the chickadees take turns going to the feeder. Fall was a slow time for birds.

"Last night I heard my mama talking on the phone. She said it wasn't an accident." Dawson turned and looked straight at me. "My dad wouldn't get hurt like that. He was a better farmer. Somebody else did it."

I didn't know what to say, so I just tried to look sympathetic. He looked away, trying to work it out for himself. I thought about putting my hand on his shoulder, letting him know it would be okay. But I didn't know. Six or seven goldfinches dropped out of the sky onto the feeder. "Nobody knew how to work like your dad."

"Jerry. Can you find out who killed my dad?"

Now what was I supposed to say? "Yeah. I'll see what I can find out." What could it hurt to talk to a few people? Polly wanted me to find out how the family was doing anyway.

We stayed like that for a few moments, as the birds hopped around on the feeder nervously collecting sunflower seeds.

"Pizza's fine."

And just like that, I was in the middle of it. I'd barely known Edwin; whenever I'd seen him, I waved. He usually just looked at me with no expression at all. That was our relationship. Each time I saw him, he was working; I was usually doing something with the kids. He was a farmer, not Superman, but the world owed Dawson, and I could pay him back a little by pretending I thought his dad hadn't had an accident.

As I kneaded the pizza dough, I thought about what Dawson had said. Even I knew not to stick my hand into a baler while it was running. Maybe I should go talk to Masha or Delmont, Edwin's dad. Yeah, that'd go over real well: *So, Masha, Dawson says you said that someone killed Edwin.* I decided I could go down and take a look at the baler. I didn't know what that'd prove, but when in doubt, take a hike. I turned the oven on and set the dough on top to rise for a few minutes. Anna dragged one of the kitchen chairs across the room from the table to the counter where I stood.

"Can I stir the dough?"

"Sorry, Squirt; I forgot and did it already. After lunch we can go for a walk."

"Can I throw rocks in the water?"

"Sure."

I pulled the pizza pan out of the cabinet and set it in front of Anna, then got the rest of the fixings out of the fridge. If I took Anna down to the Kimballs' with me, it might go better. Nothing like a cute three-year-old to hide behind.

After lunch I got out the Kelty pack to carry Anna and collected our coats. I bundled Anna up and put my hat and coat on. I never knew how to dress for October: it'd be cold in the shade or wind, but hot in the sun. Dawson was at the kitchen table picking at his pizza.

"Hey, Dawson, Anna and I are going for a walk. If you need anything, Polly's in the den working."

He nodded without looking at me. What would I do if Edwin's death really wasn't an accident? I put Anna in the pack. She was getting too big for carrying, but still too little to really hike on her own. I lifted the pack to my left knee, slipped my right arm through the strap, and swung Anna up onto my shoulders. Dawson was staring at his pizza.

"You can watch a movie if you want. You know where the DVDs are."

"Let's go, Daddy. I wanna throw rocks."

We went out the back door and the birds all scattered from around the feeder up into the nearby trees and bushes. A chickadee scolded us from the lilac behind the feeder. Instead of going out the driveway to the road, we went past the feeder and down to the pond. There were high clouds rippling across the gray-blue sky. It was going to rain tomorrow or Friday. We followed the path around the pond and past the abandoned beaver lodge.

"Any frogs?" Anna was standing in the pack and leaning way over to the right to look down into the cattails for frogs.

"There're all sleeping in the mud under the pond, honey."

"Why?"

"Too cold for them out here. They're gonna sleep right through the winter."

We ducked under the big White Pine and stepped out onto the road. As we walked past the bog, the cattails rattled in the breeze. I really didn't want to stop at the Kimballs'. I never knew what to say. Edwin's death had gotten under my skin, but it was more political than personal. Sure, I felt for the kids, but it was the futility of all their hard work that really got me going. They were losing five bucks on every hundredweight of milk they got from the cows. And why? Because Congress thought it was important to rewrite the dairy subsidies to favor the giant corporate farms in California. It seemed like nobody valued actual work anymore. Edwin could work himself to death and have nothing to show for it, but that didn't mean I knew how to get past his mistrust of my education and being from away.

Their farm was across the road from my house, just past the bog. As I approached the house, I could see all kinds of broken or forgotten equipment parked in the weeds along the road. The two-story house was mostly painted white with red shutters. They had begun painting this summer, but hadn't finished the job yet. There was scaffolding set up next to the first attached barn where the white left off. The barns were badly weathered; their roofs sagged in the middle. The drive that led past the house and back past the milking parlor was rutted and muddy, even though it hadn't rained in over a week. Behind the barn I could see Holsteins standing up to their knees in mud. Beyond was a fifty-acre field of dry, brown corn waiting to be harvested.

The trampoline was in the small front yard, surrounded by several bikes. That probably meant the whole family was home. On the far side of the house, a gravel drive led past the side door to the barn. The big barn doors were open; I could hear someone working on the tractor. Delmont was sitting in a chair by the side door to the house with Buddy at his feet. He usually had a ready smile, but not today. He sat glumly, with his arms folded across his chest. As I walked into the drive, Buddy got up and ran to me.

"Buddy. Come. Buddy." Like most Huskies, Buddy pretty much did what he wanted. He knew how to avoid getting kicked in the ribs, but that didn't mean he obeyed. I scratched his ears.

"Hey, Del."

He nodded.

"Anna want down."

"Not now, honey; when we get to the creek. Okay?"

"I hope Dawson's not being a bother. You just send him on

home, if you need to," Del nodded as he spoke.

"You got enough to worry about without worrying about Dawson. It's fine." Buddy sniffed at me and circled around me a few times. I stopped about ten feet from Delmont. The banging continued in the barn. I could hear a radio playing country music.

"Work goes on."

"Yeah. Uh... Del, man, I'm real sorry. I can't imagine how you must feel."

He looked from the barn to me, then past me, across Dead Stream and the hay meadows beyond. "Folks been helping. Cows can't milk their damned selves."

I nodded. Buddy trotted around the front of the house and out of sight. Anna squirmed in the pack, trying to see where he was going. I looked at my feet. "We'll be there tomorrow." At the funeral. I couldn't even say the word; Delmont might just shrivel up and float away like the dry leaves blowing around and collecting against the side of the barn.

"I do appreciate it."

"Well..."

A young guy came out of the barn, wiping his greasy hands on a dirty rag. I think he was a cousin or something. At any rate, he seemed to work for the Kimballs.

"Del, I need to run up to Dover. The bearing's shot." He walked over to a beat-up Ford F-150 and opened the creaking driver's door. "I'll be an hour or so." He got in the truck and backed out of the drive.

"It's always something," Del said.

"Hell of a thing. If you need anything, just ask." I turned and walked down the driveway.

"Daddy? We gonna throw rocks now?"

"Sure thing." The road dropped down to the bridge over Dead Stream. Actually, it was a ten-foot-high culvert, not a bridge. The last bridge had washed out twenty years ago. Below the road, the stream dropped off a shale ledge, curved past the Kimballs' barn, and disappeared around a bend to the left and into the woods. Through the woods, it ran roughly parallel to the road for several miles, although you'd never know it unless you spent time exploring the fields and woods down to the train tracks. The gravel bank below the ledge was a good place to find skipping stones. On the far side of the bridge, we followed a rough path down the steep slope to the stream. I swung the pack off my shoulders and onto the ground. Anna held up her hands so I could lift her out.

"Thanks, Daddy." She squatted down and began collecting rocks to throw. I sat down on the gravel and scanned the far bank for birds. Fall was a good time to see plovers here. I was probably the only one in Greenland who knew that.

"Don't get your feet wet."

"I won't." Anna threw a rock the size of her fist into the stream, and laughed when it made a ker-plunk. I preferred sifting through the rocks to find skippers. Each spring's flooding replenished the supply for me.

I hadn't told Delmont what Dawson had said. I hadn't even asked if anyone else was home. I wondered if maybe I should walk down the road and take a look at the baler.

Anna walked up to me and took my hand. "Daddy, can you help me find rocks?"

"Sure. How about these?" I scooped up a handful and held them out to her. She took them one by one from my hand and threw them toward the water. Only about half made it that far.

"How 'bout we walk down and see the horses? Maybe we can find some apples for them."

"Not yet." Anna threw another rock. I sat back and looked at the barn on the high bluff above the far bank. This side hadn't seen any paint in a decade or more. The section that connected to the house had no siding at all — was just white Tyvek. Yeah, it's always something. The cows were beginning to noisily congregate behind the barn; it probably was about time for milking.

Edwin wasn't the friendliest person, but I couldn't imagine anyone wanting him dead. The Kimballs didn't seem the type to be involved in anything drug related, but with all the land they owned, someone else could have been growing on a secluded corner somewhere. I was always being warned not to spend so much time wandering around in the woods.

"One more rock, Anna. Then we'll go see the horses." It was always work to get the kids away from the stream.

I let her throw four more then went over and picked her up. She started to protest, so I pulled up her jacket and blew on her tummy. She relaxed enough so I could get her back in the pack. We walked back up the path to the road, and then continued down to where the horses were. Anna spent the walk explaining how to feed an apple to a horse without getting bitten.

Beyond the stream, the road passed between two large hay meadows. The one on the right had an island of trees in the middle that the Kimballs used as a blind for hunting coyotes. Past the meadow the road rose slightly and turned toward the south. On the right were some woods; on the left was the rocky field where the horses usually were. There were several apple trees between the road and the fence. We walked over to the first tree.

"Sorry, Anna; look, no horses."

"Where'd they go?" I could feel Anna shrug.

"I don't know. Let's just keep walking."

The hay meadow where the "accident" — I was trying to think of it in quotes — happened was about another half-mile down the road on the right. Along the way we passed one beat -to-hell trailer surrounded by equally beat cars and toys. Across from the trailer, the snowmobile trail went into the woods toward a swampy field down near the stream. One of the Kimballs' biggest hay meadows went from there all the way back to within sight of the road — behind the meadow where the baler sat. Up the next rise and beyond a few hunting camps was where the road went past the field. Anna seemed to have fallen asleep with her head forward on the back of my left shoulder.

The baler sat all the way in the back of the meadow, maybe two hundred yards from the road. Behind it was an alder thicket that ran along the back of the meadow and came almost all the way to the road where a culvert passed under. There were several large round bales in the meadow, but most of the grass was still raked into rows waiting to be baled. The grass was packed down with lots of tire tracks, leading from the road back toward the baler. I left the road and walked straight toward it. It was a faded, green New Holland. The tractor was gone; I think it was the one being worked on back in the barn. How did it get broken if Edwin had just been using it here three days ago?

I stopped a few feet from the baler. My eyes started tearing up, so I took a deep breath. I tilted my head back. The water in my eyes made the sky look like a pale blue wheel ringed by trees gently moving with the wind. It was quiet enough that I could hear Anna breathing. My own breathing slowed to match hers. I lowered my head and re-entered the terrestrial world. The baler was just sitting there.

Wayne said that Edwin had died standing up. On the near side of the baler was a round hole about a foot across. As I stepped up to look more closely, I noticed blood around and below it. Inside the opening was a blue wheel about the size of a bike tire. Near the ground, below the hole, was a dent in the outside of the baler—like someone had kicked it. Without really wanting to, I imagined Edwin sticking his hand in the hole to loosen something off the blue wheel. When whatever it was—a tree branch, a length of twine—came free, the wheel grabbed his arm and pulled with enough force that his knee dented the outer shell of the baler when he hit it. Then the baler didn't let go.

I shook my head, trying to lose the image. Anna grumbled

and shifted to the other side. A dozen steps to my right and beyond the baler was an opening in the alders where the snowmobile trail came out. There were fresh, muddy four-wheeler tracks in the trickle of water that ran through the alders. I walked over to take a look; up close, they looked a few days old. In the confusion of tracks around the baler, I couldn't tell where the four-wheeler had gone. The only thing to do was follow the tracks away from the baler and see where they came from. I looked up to check the time. The sun was still above the treetops; it was about three o'clock.

The land rose up to where the woods on either side almost came together, then dropped slowly to the alders along Dead Stream, a quarter-mile away. The snowmobile stayed to the right near the trees almost all the way to the stream, then turned into the woods and went out to the road. About a hundred yards from the highest point, the trail went through a swampy area. There were no tracks in it. If the four-wheeler had been someone out trail riding, they would have had to go through it. As I skirted around the left of the wet area, trying to keep my feet dry, I realized the grass was pushed down in parallel lines. The four-wheeler had gone around the wet area, too.

I tried to stay in the tracks as I walked, but in the long, dry grass it was more a matter of feel than sight. Every once in a while I would see tire tracks in a small muddy spot or where the wind hadn't yet rearranged the grass and hidden the four-wheeler's passing. Just before I got to where the trail went into the woods, I passed an old, broken-down piano. I've discovered any number of these hints of the more settled past of Greenland.

Past the piano was another wet area. Again the four-wheeler had avoided it, this time looping way to the left away from the woods and toward the alders along Dead Stream. I had always assumed that the area between the trail and the stream was all swampy, but the four-wheeler had found a way, which I followed, from the trail in the woods to the piano without leaving a single clear track. The trail in the woods was a lot of rocks, stumps, and mud; since it was cut for snowmobiles, anything that stuck up less than six inches was left. I just followed the muddy rocks.

About a quarter-mile before the road, the trail dropped down and crossed a small stream — really just a trickle. There were no tracks in it. I backtracked to the last place that there was an obvious sign of the four-wheeler's passing: a large, flat rock with a smear of mud across it. I went carefully forward from there. About halfway to the trickling stream, a fallen tree had been moved alongside the trail; I could see wet, yellow wood where some bark had recently fallen off. Behind the tree, four-wheeler tracks went through the woods on what looked like an old, overgrown skidder trail. It was slow going following through all the young trees, but I could clearly see where they had been bent over and then snapped back up. Like most skidder trails I'd followed on bushwhacks, it went straight.

After ten minutes or so, I came to an open area surrounded by beech trees. The overhanging branches full of bright fall leaves made the air in the clearing glow bright yellow. The leaves that had already fallen crunched under my feet. A family of chickadees was feeding in the branches around and above me. I cocked my head and listened; in the colder months, chickadees formed loose flocks with other small birds that stayed all year. I listened for the distinctively high pishing of a kinglet. It was much easier to identify a kinglet by sound than to actually see one. You just had to trust your ears and intuition; often it was more about sensing the bird's identity from a glimpse, or a few notes heard from the treetops, than actually seeing a bird that matched the picture in a guide book. I didn't hear one, but there was a pair of nuthatches in the flock.

I hadn't brought a compass, but I felt that I was going roughly parallel to the road. That should mean I would come to the stream near a large beaver flowage. Just upstream from the flowage, the stream passed through a stand of large hem-locks where someone had illegally cut right down to the streambank on both sides and skidded the logs across the stream when it was frozen. Maybe the four-wheeler had an-gled through the woods from that skidder track to the one I was following. They'd have to know the woods pretty well.

Another fifteen minutes of walking brought me to Dead Stream. It was just as I predicted; I could see where the four-wheeler slipped as it tried to go slowly down the far bank. The only problem was that I wasn't willing to wade through the knee-deep water, not after the cold nights we'd had recently. And not with Anna on my back. I didn't know exactly where the skidder track on the far bank went, but it had to come out on Muddy Lane somewhere. Muddy Lane came off the Station Road about halfway between my house and the town hall. The first mile was paved and lined with nice houses; then it became a gravel road that petered out into a couple of muddy drive-ways and a gravel pit. The folks who lived down at the end of the road were more than a little rough around the edges and unfriendly, even by Greenland standards. On a walk one day, Polly and I had almost gotten shot at by one guy while we were still on the road near his property.

Even if I could cross the stream, I wasn't sure I really wanted to. What did the four-wheeler tracks really prove? So someone rode a four-wheeler in to where Edwin was killed about the day it happened. They didn't use the trail. It didn't prove anything, except that I would rather walk around out-side than talk to my neighbors, and some people aren't law-abiding four-wheelers.

"Let's get home, Anna."

On the way to work the next morning, I stopped at the Shell station in town to fill up. Buck, the owner, came out of one of the bays. I stuck my head out the window: "How's business?"

He scowled at me. "Regular?"

"Fill it." Buck was getting on in years, but could neither find anyone to buy the business nor good help to run it in the meantime.

"I hear young Dawson's been spending time at your place." Buck started pumping the gas.

"He doesn't seem to feel like he belongs anywhere."

Buck nodded.

"I guess he'll have to go home eventually."

Buck nodded again. These lifelong Greenlanders didn't give much. We listened to the gas pump for a while.

"Dawson thinks his dad was too good a farmer to die in an accident."

"I've heard folks say as much. I just mind my own business."

"It's not like he got killed defending his pot patch or something." It came out harder than I wanted. Last evening's bushwhack up the stream to the Station Road from where I stopped following the four-wheeler had been tough. It was after dark before I had made it home; I was wet, scratched up, and tired. Then having Dawson look at me with his sad eyes and ask me if I found out who killed his dad wouldn't help my mood any.

"Kimballs aren't that type."

"No, no. I'm just saying. Anyone can get tired and make a mistake."

Buck nodded. The gas pump stopped. He put the cap back on and came to the window. I handed him my credit card. Buck took it without a word and went inside to ring it up. I watched him through the dirty window. The funeral tonight was going to be real fun. And it looked like rain.

Buck came out of the station to return my card with the receipt. As I took them, he looked me in the eye. "Dawson's just a confused kid. Don't take what he says too seriously." The coldness of Buck's voice and the hardness in his eyes made it more of a threat than an observation.

Greenland only had one church, next to the library and across from the general store. It was an old-fashioned, Bible-thumping, Baptist church with four points on its steeple. Everyone in town was on their mailing list; we were always getting invitations to see some visiting preacher speak about the evils of evolution or watch the latest *Left Behind* movie. Polly and I went to the UU church in Bangor; its official name was the Unitarian Universalist Society of Bangor—not "church"; that was too religious, too judgmental. Personally, I got religion beat out of me by the nuns in parochial school. It got my dander up the way the Greenland Baptist Church had the air of the town's official religion. Thanks to Ben explaining how I felt to his kindergarten class, it was common knowledge around town that *we* didn't believe *that*. Anna still called churches "castles." I liked that, but I wasn't looking forward to walking in to the Baptist church for the viewing and funeral this evening. Part of me wondered if they'd let me in the door, or if alarms would go off and lights would flash when I crossed the threshold. Then some deacon who used to be middle line-backer for the Maine Black Bears would physically remove me. Or maybe I just was dreading walking to the front of the church and looking down at Edwin's lifeless body. His face peaceful, calmer than in life; his destroyed left arm subtly hidden beneath the velvet lining of the coffin. His family silently crying through my lame attempts at comfort, and Dawson's pleading eyes.

When we pulled up to the church, there was already a line outside in the cold rain. We joined the line behind a guy in a worn Carhartt jacket and steel-toed work boots who was talking to someone in jeans and a T-shirt. People weren't dressed for a funeral—at least not one I'd ever been to; it looked more like the beer line at a football game. I turned the collar up on my fleece jacket, wishing I'd worn my rain shell like Polly. Rhett and Julie from up the road joined the line behind us. Rhett clapped me on the back. "How you doing?"

"Lovely weather." The women began quietly discussing Dawson.

"I guess you're not enjoying this any more than me." Rhett had gone to school with Edwin, but I didn't think they were friends. Rhett had gone away to New Jersey for college, which in and of itself set him apart from his peers; he came back sounding like he grew up in Newark.

Julie touched my arm. "It's nice that you've been helping with Dawson. I really worry about him." I nodded, and she continued. "Does he really think that it wasn't an accident?"

I took off my glasses and tried to find something I was wearing that was dry to wipe them off on. "I don't know. Maybe he needs to believe it."

"Are you really trying to find a murderer?" I really wish Rhett hadn't said it so loud. I felt the eyes of those in the line around us converge on my back. Mr. Carhartt didn't turn, but he did stop talking. I put my glasses back on.

I leaned in close to Rhett: "Yeah. At first it was just because I didn't know how to say no to Dawson. But now I really think he's onto something." We all took a few steps toward the church doors as the line moved. I felt hot.

"Seriously? Who?" Rhett never was very subtle. I told them about the four-wheeler tracks. Mr. Carhartt leaned over to his friend in the T-shirt and said something. They both laughed; I don't think Mr. Carhartt had told a joke.

"You know, that cutting was done by Cal," Rhett said.

"Isn't he the same guy who cut the woodlot next to Wayne's and went thirty feet over the line?" I asked, leaning in toward Rhett to quiet him. "Wayne was hot about it for a while."

"The same," Rhett spoke loudly, ignoring my body language.

"Cal's friends with Edwin," Julie said. "Er — was." She was right; I'd seen his truck in their drive more than once.

"I'm not saying Cal had anything to do with it, even if he

is a butcher in the woods." The line moved forward again. The wet was starting to leak into my bones. I let the conversation get away from me, and stood in the rain, thinking. Did I really believe Dawson? He just wanted his dad back. Who wouldn't?

Polly took my hand and squeezed it. The rain had let up; now it was just misting. A logging truck downshifted as it slowed to make a turn at the general store. The tiny raindrops seemed to be suspended in the pools of pale yellow light beneath the streetlights. Eventually, we passed through the church door. No alarms went off; no deacon threw me back out into the wet night. The line inched beyond the doors and up a ramp to the church itself. At the top of the ramp was an easel with a large posterboard on it. It was covered with photos of Edwin, many with his family. I was drawn to one of Edwin with his two boys at the summit of Mt. Katahdin. It seemed completely out of character. He causally leaned against the summit sign, an easy smile on his face. As far as I knew, Edwin never did anything except work. And the looks Polly and I got as we walked down the road with the kids made me think that the Kimballs thought there was something wrong with adults having fun.

I stepped past the posterboard and looked down the aisle where the coffin sat in front of the pulpit. Masha and Delmont stood greeting people as they approached Edwin's body. I started rehearsing what I would say. The pews were about half -full. The church was neat and tidy but, like the Greenlanders, couldn't quite rise above its circumstances. The church had been remodeled a few years before; to pay for it they had cut the wood lot the church owned, a strip of land that contained a beautiful stand of big hemlocks that the deer used as a yard every winter. All that was left now was rutted skidder tracks, slash piles, and stumps. The deer were gone, and so were the coyotes that serenaded us most nights. Destroyed to put tacky white paneling and new carpets in the church.

When Polly and I got to the family, the women hugged

and Delmont took both my hands firmly in his. His eyes were red and swollen. "Thank you for coming." The words were strong and sincere. "Thank you for Dawson. We haven't had to worry about him at all."

I shook my head. "I'm so sorry, Delmont." I felt my voice catch; I couldn't hold his gaze. To my right, Edwin lay, staring straight up at the ceiling. His face was relaxed in a way that I never saw in life—the way it was in the photo on Katahdin. "Dawson's no trouble. As long as you need the help..."

I stepped up to the casket and looked down at Edwin's face. I addressed him under my breath: "Man, I'm sorry. We didn't really know each other, but I respect you. I hope they can get by without you." Polly stood next to me and shifted her weight so she was leaning against my left side. After a moment she pulled me away. We found seats near the back and off to the side, befitting our status as outsiders.

Polly leaned in toward me. "Did you notice his arm? It looked pretty bad."

"No." I didn't remember anything but his face.

"Masha is a mess. What can we do?"

Another covered dish? Hand them Edwin's killer like Dawson wanted? "They're gonna need help with the farm."

"Masha said that they're getting all their feed free for the winter."

The service was short and forgettable. The minister spoke of Edwin's soul having moved on to a better place; at first it made me angry, then it made me think of Katahdin. It was funny, but, now that he was dead, I felt closer to Edwin than I ever had when he was alive. We had always seen each other as stereotypes, but his death forced me to see his humanity.

While we had been in the church, the temperature had fallen, and the wet mist had changed to big fat snowflakes that drifted silently down out of the darkness.

"That was hard, Jerry." Polly leaned against me, as we walked.

I lifted my head and stuck out my tongue to catch a flake. Somehow I had forgotten that Edwin was human, was more than the scowling face I'd see drive past on the tractor. And humans make mistakes. Edwin's death was an accident. I had spent all that time chasing no one. "I needed that."

Polly bumped me with her hip. "Let's go get the kids."

It was still snowing as I undressed later for bed. It was the first real snow of the year, and the kids hadn't wanted to go to bed. But it was a school night, so Polly tucked them in and read to them—usually my job. She seemed to need the connection; she lay on her side of the bed facing away from me. I stood in my underwear watching the snow, listening to her breathe. A pick-up I didn't recognize drove by; it needed a new muffler. I climbed into bed and set my glasses on the bed stand. I lay back, with the lamp still on and listened to the snow falling.

Half asleep, I heard the same truck coming back up the road. It slowed in front of the house; suddenly I was awake, listening. There were two loud blasts and a lot of breaking glass. The truck accelerated away; Polly screamed something as she came awake. I jumped up and grabbed my pants and shirt off the top of my dresser, putting them on as I stumbled down the stairs to the living room, my heart in my throat. They'd shot out our two front windows. There was glass and buckshot all over the floor. Polly and Ben were both yelling, wanting to know what happened.

I looked out through the window frames and saw Wayne running down his driveway, cell phone in hand. "It's okay, Polly, but don't come down. There's glass everywhere." After checking for glass in my sneakers, I slipped them on and went out to meet Wayne.

"I already called 9-1-1. Is everybody okay?" Wayne asked, reaching out to hold my arm.

"Yeah. We were in bed." We were standing in the middle of the road.

"Did you see who it was?"

Surprisingly, I didn't really care. Maybe it was Mr. Carhartt and his buddy, angry that I was sticking my nose where it didn't belong. Being from away and all.

"Naw. It was a truck. A Ford." Whoever it was didn't know what that picture of Edwin on Katahdin had shown me: He was just a man. It really was an accident, even if we all wanted to believe that Edwin was above that. I had already gone back to minding my own business.

"I got some plastic in the garage. I'll go get it."

~~~~~

The cold was creeping into my joints and stiffening them. I flexed my knees and put my weight on my ski poles. I looked over at Bill; he was as lost in thought as I'd been. I heard a raven quork, and looked up. It was rocketing across the sky with its wings half-closed. Another was above it, dropping down toward the first its feet held out playfully. When the two were a few feet apart, the first raven flipped over onto its back and stuck its feet up to meet the others. As their feet locked, they wheeled, quorking through the pale blue sky. They dropped for several yards that way, down toward the baler, then separated and flew off together.

I knew Bill was just pulling my chain, asking if I found the killer. His wife dumped on him, so he dumped on me. I could imagine Masha telling someone—everyone—that Edwin was too good a farmer to make the mistake he did. What she really meant was he was too important to her to be gone, too good to die. No one wanted it to be true, but we're all human. We all get tired. Edwin grabbed the blue wheel and it pulled him in.

I looked back to Bill and nodded. "Yeah; I found the killer, all right."

Before he could respond, I pushed off and poled down the slope, picking up speed. I crossed through the alders, turned in the packed-down trail, and skied past the buried baler.

M arsha Libby had two distinct story ideas for her contribu-
tion to this anthology. Unable to decide which she most
wanted to write, she decided to do them both. The result is
an intertwined pair of tales about coming to terms with difficult circumstances and finding the power to go forward. One story happens
in our world, in the here and now; the other takes place in a world of
fantasy, where magic prevails, but where the challenges of the human
condition are just as prevalent as they are in ours. Libby gives us two
subtle quiet blue wheels, both wrought with power — one literally, the
other metaphorically. What follows is an expert blending of two stories, two protagonists, and two quiet blue wheels into a tale you
won't soon forget.

Reclaiming Candace

Marsha Libby

The moment had come.

Ilyana swallowed, willing her nerves to calm. "Are you ready?" she asked the two mages standing with her at the top of the hill. They nodded, eyes dark, faces somber.

"All right, then, let's do this." She bowed her head, concentrating, readying herself to embrace her power.

She hesitated. The magic lay just beyond her reach, her ambivalence and misgivings forming a barrier between her and the sparkling river that she saw in her mind's eye. She took a deep breath, steeling herself, and pushed past the invisible wall. She was inundated with magic; it filled her with a quiet confidence and peace as its power washed over her.

Something was missing, however. Once, she had been a fire mage, a powerful one. A small corner of her mind ached with emptiness, yearning to be filled with the recklessness, the feeling of barely contained power, which always accompanied fire magic. Its loss had opened up a wound that could never heal. Water magic was a poor substitute, a consolation prize that only served to remind her of what she had lost.

Anger sparked within her, causing the peace induced by the water magic to shatter, the mental barrier to slam down once more. Victory in the battle against the rebels depended on her using her magic, yet she abruptly turned her mind away from its glittering stream. She knew she should be grateful that she had it, that she should welcome water the way she had once welcomed fire, but she could not bring herself to do so.

Her desire to once again touch fire magic overcame her reason. She reached deep within herself, striving to grasp that which had once been so readily accessible to her. She encountered a void; nothing remained where once a magical fire burned except the cold ashes of extinguished hope. She could just as easily capture sunshine in her hands as seize fire.

Fury flared up in magic's stead, and she fell to her knees, fists pounding the dry earth, frustrated sobs racking her body. All around her, battle raged, a losing battle, for water magic was the key to winning, and in her agitated state she was unable to use it. She had failed.

~~~~~

Candace woke, disoriented and shaking. She gripped the arms of the rocking chair so tightly her fingers ached. Feelings of anger and helplessness threatened to overwhelm her. She had had this dream before, she knew, and always woke up feeling this way. She tried to capture the details of it in her mind, but they flitted away like a butterfly avoiding a toddler's clumsy hands.

She forced her fingers to loosen, and shook them to relieve their aching. She stood and took a deep breath, willing the frantic beating of her heart to slow. She stretched, fists pushed into the small of her back in an attempt to ease the pain that, along with her swollen belly, was becoming her constant companion. She felt a kick; her rising had awakened the baby. A wave of resentment washed over her; she knew it was wrong, but she could not get over the feeling that this little creature sought to take Gabriel's place in her heart.

The kicks became stronger and more insistent. She sighed and resigned herself to a beating from within. The baby was getting stronger, and sometimes its kicks hit with enough force to make her gasp.

She moved to the window and drew the blinds, blocking the reddish rays of the setting sun and plunging the room into darkness. Passing the crib, she ran her fingers along its rail, pausing to straighten the ribbon on the little brown stuffed bear sitting on the nearby dresser. Its contented expression only amplified Candace's sorrow. She slipped out of the room and drew the door shut behind her. She leaned against the closed door a moment, hastily wiping away a tear as she attempted to get her emotions under control; Owen would be returning home soon and he would not appreciate seeing her like this.

He missed his son as well, Candace knew. After Gabriel's death, they had grieved together, seeking comfort in one another. But lately, he had shown impatience with her tears; once, he lost his temper, saying, "Just let it go, Candace!" as he stormed out of the room. That had hurt her deeply, and as she could not let go of her grief, she did her best to hide it from him. Deep down, she felt that he blamed her for Gabriel's illness. How could she fault him for that, when in her darkest moments she felt overwhelmed with guilt? She couldn't help thinking that if she had just monitored her diet more carefully or paid closer attention to her obstetrician's advice, it may have somehow prevented Gabriel from developing his fatal heart defect. She and her husband had been drifting apart these past few months, and she suspected that her feelings of guilt over their baby's death were part of the reason why.

Her friends from work, too, had long since distanced themselves from her. Most did not call her anymore, and the few who did usually kept their conversation brief and made no mention of her loss. She remembered well how she would talk nearly nonstop with them about her pregnancy, about her hopes and dreams for her son and her family. She had known that her chattering was keeping her coworkers from getting their work done, and leaving hers undone as well, but she hadn't been able to stop herself. Now, nine months after Gabriel's death, she needed someone to talk to more than ever, but there was no one left to turn to.

When Candace reached the stairs, she was met by Butch, her little Yorkshire terrier. He ran to her, yapping and wagging his tail frantically. Candace smiled at him as he jumped up on her. She picked him up and held him against her chest. He squirmed in her arms, trying his best to lick every square inch of her face. She stroked him, the simple act calming her a bit. Here, at least, was one creature who didn't judge her; Butch didn't mind in the least if she cried, soaking his silky coat with her tears. After a few moments, she put the dog back on the floor. He looked at her expectantly and then raced downstairs. Candace followed him.

Once in the kitchen, she glanced at the clock above the sink. With as jolt she realized that Owen would be home in fifteen minutes, and she hadn't even started dinner. Guilt washed over her as her eyes darted around the kitchen. Clutter covered the countertops and dishes remained unwashed in the sink. This would not put her husband in a good mood, she knew, but there was no helping it now. She was just hurrying to the freezer to see if there was something she could cook at a moment's notice when she heard a car door slam in the yard.

Her heart sank. Owen was home early.

Keys jingled at the door, and it opened, admitting a tall man clad in a business suit that had once fit him perfectly but now hung loosely on his spare frame. He surveyed the kitchen from the entryway and closed his eyes briefly, running a hand through his curly blond hair. He removed his sport coat as he walked into the kitchen and said, "Hi, Candace."

Candace attempted a smile; it felt stiff and foreign on her

face. "Hello, dear. How was work today?"

"Oh, the usual. What's for dinner?"

"Uh..." her mind raced. "I was thinking, how about we go out for pizza?"

Owen sighed. "I just got home. I don't feel like going out again."

"Oh... well, okay. I guess I could have something ready in about an hour, then."

He raised an eyebrow, causing creases that up until a few months ago had not been on his forehead to deepen. "Pizza it is. Let's go."

Candace tried hard to keep her tears in check as she got her jacket out of the closet, silently berating herself for being incapable of pulling herself out of self-pity long enough to accomplish even the most basic housekeeping. Owen, after all, managed to work all day without breaking down, so why couldn't she even hold a job, let alone do a little work around the house? Biting her lip against her dejection, she followed her husband out the door, disappointment in herself weighing on her heart.

~~~~~

The sun rose, blood-red on the eastern horizon. *With any luck, that will the closest thing to bloodshed that we have to deal with today,* Ilyana thought. Although, she ruefully admitted to herself, drowning was certainly no pleasanter a way to die. She reminded herself that the rebels brought this on themselves, and that she was merely performing her duty.

Hers was the final stroke of a two-pronged attack on the enemy. First, the fire mages were to summon an enormous drake to terrify the enemy, pushing them away from the front line and toward the sea. Ilyana, working with two other water mages, would then create a massive wave to swallow them, drowning them and carrying them out to sea, where the ocean creatures could feast on their remains.

Ilyana longed to be with the fire mages, to summon the

dragon alongside them, but such was not her fate. Once, she had been certain she would be a fire mage, and she had spent a good part of her childhood playing at being one, much to the annoyance of her sister, who was often mercilessly recruited into her fantastic adventures. Jena would have rather been hosting a tea party with her dolls; indeed, it was usually that sort of play that Ilyana interrupted. She smiled at the memory. Her sister had since grown to be a young woman, and had recently married a nobleman. Jena's dream of one day becoming one of the nobility had come true. She could now host all the tea parties she wanted without fear of them being cut short by her domineering sibling.

And what of my dream? She thought of the future that would likely be hers after this battle. While fire mages had adventurous careers, engaging in heroic battles and protecting their country, water mages generally spent their days roaming the countryside, aiding farmers by coaxing the groundwater that lay far below their crops up to a level where the roots of the thirsty plants could reach it. It was an important job in this arid land, but by no means glamorous. Ilyana sighed.

"What bothers you, little sister? I would have thought you'd be excited for this moment. Or have you second thoughts?"

Ilyana looked up at the speaker, though she would have rather ignored her. Only Takyra would speak to her in that sneering, condescending way. Ilyana tried for the same tone. "No, Takyra. I am quite looking forward to defeating the rebels and reclaiming peace for our country. My mind was elsewhere, that's all."

"Well, I have been sent to inform you that we will be leaving for our post soon." Her voice conveyed her annoyance at having been sent on such an errand. "Really, I would have thought you the first to be ready to go."

"Thank you for the message, Takyra. I'll be ready in a few minutes. You may go." Ilyana stayed seated and, waving her hand dismissively, said nothing further to her messenger, concentrating instead on eating her breakfast. Takyra huffed in disgust and stalked off. Ilyana smiled. Takyra was one of the three water mages who made up her group. Though she was talented and fully entitled to her post, Ilyana disliked her intensely, and had since the day they had met. She enjoyed irritating the prickly mage.

That day had started full of excitement and promise. Ilyana's mother, herself a fire mage, had walked with her to the gates of the Academy. Her face was solemn, but fierce pride and love shone in her eyes. "Good-bye, my daughter," she said as she clasped Ilyana's hands in her own. Then, without another word, she left. Ilyana had been tempted to call after her, to tell her she loved her and would miss her, but pushed down the impulse. Her mother would not have appreciated the gesture; she valued dignity and self-control, and would not like to see their lack in her daughter. Ilyana turned and followed the servant to her new quarters.

The girl, who must have been no more than eleven, had guided her down a maze of halls, all paneled in dark wood, to a set of double doors. Opening one of them, she said, "Here is your room, Miss." Ilyana nodded her thanks to the servant and entered.

She stepped into a long room with a low ceiling, lit dimly from a lone window by the setting sun. The walls were lined on either side with a row of beds, each with a small bookshelf to one side and a wardrobe to the other. A quick count showed there were fourteen beds in all. Ilyana sighed. She had never had to share a room in her life; now she had to share this one with thirteen others. She walked down the narrow walkway between footboards, noting that attached to each was a card with a name written on it. It was at the end of the right-hand row that she found her bed. She was grateful for this; having a wall to one side gave her some sense of personal space, however illusory. She opened the wardrobe next to the bed. It was empty even of dust.

A sconce on the wall held a candle. Ilyana concentrated, reaching for her fledgling magic to light the taper. A bright fireball flashed suddenly, threatening to set the entire wall on fire, before settling onto the wick as a steady yellow flame. Taking deep breaths, she willed her thundering heart to slow. Her magic was capricious; no matter how hard she tried to control it, sometimes it nearly exploded when she used it, and at other times it barely produced an ember. She knew time and practice would give her more control.

She heard the hum of conversation in the hallway, becoming louder and more intelligible as it came closer. One voice was sharp and indignant, the other pleading and apologetic. She stood beside her bed and watched as one of the double doors opened.

"And to think they keep such as you for a servant! You are little better than the meanest beggar on the street!"

"My apologies, Miss. I beg your forgiveness." It was the same servant girl who had shown Ilyana to this room just minutes earlier.

"How dare you keep me waiting! I may have become ill standing in the rain. My family would hold you personally responsible if anything were to happen to me." The girl speaking was tall and slender, with dark hair and fair skin; Ilyana would have considered her beautiful, but the spite and arrogance in her delicate features rendered her anything but.

The servant's face became pale at her charge's words. "Oh, Miss, I am so sorry!" She looked as though she would collapse where she stood; tears trickled down her cheeks.

It was more than Ilyana could stand. "Excuse me," she said. "I believe she was late in reaching you because she was showing me to this room. I detained her a moment, so the fault lies with me, not her." The lie slipped easily from her lips; she could not stand to see the servant girl upbraided so.

The tall girl shot a venomous look Ilyana's way. Then she

turned back to the servant, who was inching her way to the door. "What? Are you still here? You've done your duty, however badly. Now leave." The servant turned and ran out the door.

Ilyana overcame her distaste for the girl to go over and introduce herself. She would be sharing a room with her, after all, and it would be wise to be civil. She held out her hand and said, "Hello, my name is Ilyana Deverel."

The girl looked at Ilyana's hand as though it carried the plague. "I'm Takyra Thanir." She turned away and sought her bed; finding it, she lay down and said no more.

Takyra, Ilyana mused, had changed little since that day. She had no friends, nor did she seem to want them. But she was an extraordinarily good water mage and, as such, she had Ilyana's grudging respect. Today, Ilyana would do her best to cooperate with her. They were working toward the same goal, after all, and afterward, they would likely go their separate ways.

She gathered up the remains of her breakfast, swallowing down the last bite only through force of will. She hadn't been hungry, but she would need every bit of strength she had, and skipping breakfast would certainly not help her any. Washing the bread down with a swig from her flask, she wiped her mouth and hurried to the commander's tent, where everyone was waiting.

She pulled aside the flap and was greeted by Commander Briggs. Her two fellow water mages stood off to one side. Takyra gave her a sour glance before resuming the study of her fingernails. Emira was wringing her hands, shifting from foot to foot and biting her lip. She smiled wanly at Ilyana and said, "You ready?"

Ilyana nodded and replied, "As ready as I'll ever be." She tried a reassuring smile at Emira but managed only a weak grin.

After the commander issued his orders, they filed out of

the tent and made their way slowly up the hill, the rising sun casting long shadows behind them. The top of the hill glowed a bright gold, sun reflecting off dew, and the tall grasses waved in the wind. Ilyana looked over at Emira, who was trudging up the hill beside her. She stared straight ahead, her lips trembling so much she nearly looked like she was talking to herself. Ilyana walked closer to her and gently touched her shoulder. Emira jumped and looked at her with green eyes grown round with fear. Ilyana felt guilty for startling the little mage, who had always been the nervous type. There was something about her that made Ilyana feel a certain responsibility toward her; it had been that way ever since the day they had met in the Academy's dining hall.

She had noticed the lone figure in the hall on several occasions. That particular day, as always, the girl sat alone, writing on some paper, books open all around her. Ilyana was usually too caught up in her own studies to pay her much attention, but that day, she noticed a group of older boys walk over to the girl and start to harass her. The young mage's cheeks became red and tears stood in her eyes as the boys grabbed books off her table, mockingly pretending to read them before throwing them down carelessly, places lost. At first, Ilyana was not inclined to go over and help. She had just come out of a meeting with Professor Alderin about the instability of her magic.

"But, Professor," she had said. "Surely this will all work out in time. Maybe I just need more rest."

"No, Ilyana. I've taught at the Academy for some time, longer than most of the other professors here, and I've seen this before, more times than I like to think about. Sometimes a mage may seem very strong at first, but, well, the very strength of the magic seems to make it unstable."

He passed a hand over her forehead, his own brow wrinkled in concentration. "I sense great power. It glows brightly within you. Think of your magic as if it were a real fire. For most mages, the power is like an oil lamp. The wick burns slow and steady, a ready supply of fuel meaning they never have to work at maintaining the fire. For you, though, your power is more like a wildfire. It starts out as a spark, but quickly becomes difficult to control, and after its fuel has burned, the fire can go out. It's your job to keep feeding that fire, by practicing and studying hard. I can teach you how. But," he said, gazing into her eyes, "Should that fire ever go out, nothing you or I can do will ever help you relight it."

Ilyana's heart had thudded in her chest at the thought of losing her magic. "What do I have to do, then?"

They had spent the next two hours working out a program for her to follow. It was demanding and more than a little overwhelming. Ilyana was determined to follow it, but the knowledge that she had to work so hard to do something that came so easily to everyone else grated on her.

And so she sat at her table, feeling bad enough for herself without adding the burden of someone else's troubles. But as the hazing of the poor girl escalated, Ilyana felt she could stay out of the situation no longer. She slammed her book closed and stalked over where the boys surrounded the girl's table. As she walked, her irritation with the boys burned within, and she felt her magic gather in response.

She concentrated, shaping the power into a small spark. She aimed it toward the nearest bully's back. Just before it landed on his shirt, it flared into a small fireball. Ilyana panicked and worked to quiet the flame; she wanted to teach the boy a lesson, after all, not immolate him. With great effort, she managed to bring the spark back under control just as it landed on the boy's shoulder. It burned through to the skin and he yelped.

"I can do a lot more than that, boys," she said. "Who's next?"

She conjured a glittering cloud of sparks, letting them swirl before her. The boys' eyes widened as they backed away.

They hurried off, glancing over their shoulders as they went. Once they were gone, Ilyana doused the flames. Turning to the girl, she asked, "Are you all right?"

"I'm fine. Thanks for scaring them off."

"Here, let me help you." Ilyana reached for some of the papers that lay scattered on the floor.

"No, no," the girl said. "Please, it's all right. I can take care of this mess myself." She hastily shoved notes, diagrams, and what appeared to be a letter into her bag. She crumpled papers in her haste.

The girl turned to Ilyana. "Thanks again for helping me, uh..."

"My name's Ilyana. And you are?"

"Emira. Well, I guess I'll see you around." Emira hurried off, leaving Ilyana standing there, shaking her head in bewilderment at her odd behavior.

From that day forward, though, Emira seemed to regard Ilyana as her protector, sitting with Ilyana at meals and walking with her to classes. This made Ilyana uncomfortable at first, but as she learned more about Emira, she began to understand her a little better, and eventually she became quite fond of her. From their conversations, she found out that Emira's parents were being held captive by the rebel army. She told Ilyana that coming to the Academy was the best way she knew to help free them.

At that time, the rebels were becoming even more brazen, and their occasional skirmishes against the kingdom threatened to blow up into full-scale war. Kidnappings and other crimes were becoming more and more common as they became bolder; tales of crimes of the worst sort were told in whispers in the halls of the Academy. Emira's parents were just two of the many unfortunate victims of those first steps toward civil war.

The group of water mages had nearly reached the hilltop.

Ilyana smiled once more at Emira, whose lips merely twitched as she tried to return the smile. "It's all right, Emira. We'll do fine. Remember, once our shield is up, no weapon can touch us."

"I wish I could be as calm as you, Ilyana. It would be so much easier for me to do what I have to do." Again, Emira attempted a smile, but it looked more like a grimace. Ilyana's heart went out to her. Emira did not have the temperament for battle, yet she was needed here. Her power in water magic was not strong, but she had an ability that was crucial to their success against the enemy: she had the rare ability to join the powers of others, and to magnify their strength to more than they could accomplish individually.

They reached the top of the hill. A slim young man stood there, sandy hair falling into his eyes in such a way that he was constantly brushing it away with the back of his hand. Despite her nervousness, Ilyana felt her heart quicken, a smile lighting her face. Nyell turned to her and returned the smile. Some of her tension eased.

Ilyana had known Nyell for as long as she could remember. They were from the same village, and their families often visited with each other. She had been delighted when he arrived at the Academy only a week after she did. It was comforting to have a familiar face around.

Nyell had discovered he was a water mage right after Ilyana had left. He was eager to come to the Academy, though his parents hadn't wanted to let him go so soon. But he had insisted, promising to write to them every week and visit as often as he could. Perhaps seeing the futility of arguing with their headstrong son, they relented. Ilyana had smiled when he told her about it. She wondered if her being at the Academy had anything to do with Nyell's impatience to leave home.

To have two mages come from the same village was unusual. The Academy, which housed any who had manifested magical ability, was home to no more than fifty students at a time. Of those, most had only the merest hint of power; they were there more for the prestige attending the Academy gave them than to pursue a career in magic. Ilyana and Nyell, though, were both powerful in their respective magics. Ilyana often wished that Nyell was a fire mage, too, instead of a water mage. She felt a bit sorry for him; to have such power only to spend his life using his magic to water crops. Fire magic, she felt, led to much more exciting career choices.

Her first two months at the Academy had been busy ones; she worked hard during the day and slept poorly at night. Somehow, despite being so busy, she and Nyell had found time to socialize, and they became even closer than they had been back at the village. His friendship helped Ilyana feel as if the workload she had taken on was a bit less onerous.

She had been so determined to strengthen her magic that she stayed awake into the early-morning hours, pushing herself to learn more, and to practice her exercises, until she dropped from exhaustion. It was gratifying to feel her power grow stronger by the day. She delighted in the new things she could accomplish, and the ease with which she could now control her power. Professor Alderin was likewise impressed with her progress, and proclaimed her to be one of the most powerful students he had ever seen.

And then, just as her worries about her magic faded, disaster struck.

~~~~~

"I'm tired, Candace. I think I'll head up to bed," Owen stood up and stretched, yawning as he did so.

The two had eaten at the local pizza place. Candace had been too preoccupied to say much to Owen's attempts at conversation, and had mostly sat in silence, idly picking at her food. Once they had returned home, they plopped down on the couch and flipped the TV on.

"Okay, Owen. I'll probably be up in a bit. I'm not all that tired right now."

"Well, I guess I'll see you in the morning then. Good night." Owen bent down and kissed her cheek.

"Good night," Candace replied absently, still staring at the television.

Owen stood a moment, sighed, and left the room.

Candace had been finding it difficult to fall asleep lately, but, after aimlessly flipping channels for a few minutes, she was surprised to feel drowsiness overcome her. She decided to follow her husband up to bed. Her movement disturbed the dog, which had been curled up beside her on the couch. He jumped down and waddled into the kitchen. He looked at her expectantly, tail wagging.

"Oh!" she said, glancing at his empty food dish. "I forgot to feed you your dinner, Butch! I'm so sorry." As she filled his food and water bowls, she marveled at how, in her forgetfulness, she could practically starve the dog, yet he still loved her unconditionally. She crouched down and placed the bowls in front of the hungry animal. She knelt down next to the dog, scratching his head a few moments while he ate, then heaved herself back to her feet, turned off the light, and went upstairs.

She walked down the hallway and paused at the bedroom door. Soft snores were coming from within; she wondered how Owen could always fall asleep so quickly, while she would often toss and turn for hours before drifting off. She reached for the doorknob but paused a moment, hand hovering just above it. Then, she let her hand fall back to her side and retraced her steps back to the nursery door. She turned the handle and stepped inside, shutting the door carefully behind her.

~~~~~

As time passed, Ilyana was able to more consistently control her magic, and it was coming to her with greater ease. She backed off her exercises after a while; since her magic was stabilizing she felt they weren't as critical as they had been. She still met with Professor Alderin on a weekly basis, and every week he told her that her connection to her magic continued to strengthen. Today's meeting would be more of the same. Ilyana sighed. She decided to ask him if they could meet a bit less often.

She knocked on his office door, and he opened the door, a smile creasing his kindly features. "How are you doing today, Ilyana?"

She set her books down on the corner of his desk and sat in the seat opposite his. "Fine, Professor Alderin. My magic's been a lot easier to control lately."

"Excellent. Now that you're making some progress, I'd like to show you another exercise, one meant to maintain your connection to the power. Here," he said, allowing a flame to balance on the tip of his finger. "Conjure a flame, and hold it as steady as you can, like this. Once you've mastered this, we'll work on increasing the length of time you can hold it."

Ilyana nodded and reached deep inside, striving for her power.

It was not there.

Ilyana panicked. She closed her eyes, reaching again for the power, but to no avail. "What's happening?" she asked, her heart pounding. "Why can't I summon the power?"

Concern radiated from Professor Alderin's eyes. "Hmm, well, let's take a look." He pressed his hand against her forehead. He stood there some time, eyes closed, mumbling softly. Ilyana could feel his presence in her mind, giving her the uncomfortable sensation that he was rummaging around in her thoughts, sifting through her spirit. She fought to remain calm. *He'll find it. I know he will. It can't be gone, not when I've worked so hard to keep it!*

Eventually, he removed his hand from her forehead and let out a heavy sigh. He sat back in his seat and locked his eyes on her own, his arms crossed over his chest.

"Oh, Ilyana. I had hoped that we could avoid this." He took a deep breath, and, taking her hand, gave it a gentle squeeze. "I'm afraid... I'm afraid your fire magic has been burned out. We just couldn't stabilize it enough. Sometimes, despite our best efforts, we are unable to save it."

Ilyana jerked her hand away. "No! There must be some sort of mistake!"

The professor shook his head. "I really wish I could tell you differently. But I couldn't find a single trace of your magic." He looked down at his feet. "I'm so sorry."

"No!" She pushed him out of the way and ran, sobbing, down the hall. She threw herself onto her bed and cried until exhaustion overtook her, and she fell into a restless sleep.

In the ensuing days, the Academy became a lonely place for Ilyana. At first, classmates and acquaintances alike offered gentle words of condolence to her, but, rather than comforting her, their words only sunk her deeper into despair. She spent most of her time alone, walking the grounds of the Academy, doing her best to avoid others.

She had written to her mother, to tell her of her misfortune and request a carriage to take her home. Writing that letter was hard; receiving the answer was worse. Her mother's words on the page, written in her precise script, were sympathetic, yet Ilyana could feel the disappointment hidden behind her mother's kind words. Once she was back home, she would have to live every day with the knowledge that she had failed; seeing her mother, a successful and respected mage, would only serve to deepen her shame at her failure. She knew this, even as Professor Alderin insisted that she was not to blame. Without magic, she saw her future as very bleak.

Nyell refused to leave her to her despair. He came to visit her every day after classes were over. At first, Ilyana was annoyed; she just wanted to be left alone. But he patiently listened to her as she railed against her fate, sobbed over her lost magic, despaired of the future that lay before her. She was grateful that she had such a loyal friend, who stuck with her even in her darkest moment.

A week after she lost her magic, she heard that the rebels

had stormed and taken a small city near the northern border, and were now preparing to mount a campaign to the south, where the capital and the Academy stood. The country was now at war, yet Ilyana could not bring herself to care.

~~~~~

The streetlight outside sent its ghostly rays through the slats of the blinds, dimly illuminating the nursery. The room, once filled with all the bustle and noise that went along with a newborn baby, was so still now, the silence a shroud enveloping all that lay within. Here in this room, Candace felt closest to her son. Here too, she knew, another little infant would soon take his place. She knew it was time to get the nursery ready for the new baby's arrival, but how could she when everything in here whispered Gabriel's name? She walked to the empty crib, drawn to the mobile that hung above it, pale and colorless in the feeble light. She reached for the stuffed zebra hanging from one of its arms; the tiny figure swayed gently at her touch. Its name was Zippy, she remembered. She had given silly little names to each of the animals on the mobile. Every night for two months, she had tucked Gabriel into bed, and, while he lay gazing up at the little animals hanging from the powder-blue arms, said good night to each of them by name. That done, she would then wind up the mobile so it would play its tinny lullaby.

Good night, Zippy.

A tear slid down her cheek as she let go of the little zebra. She lifted her fingers to the winding key at the top of the mobile. She could not bring herself to turn it. The mere thought of the little melody it played brought grief welling up again, and she collapsed into the rocking chair and wept.

She cried for some time, and then, overcome with sadness and exhaustion, fell into a restless sleep.

~~~~~

One day, about a month after losing her power, Ilyana was making her final preparations to depart, as her carriage would arrive later in the afternoon, when Takyra entered the room.

"Hmph! About time you were leaving," she said. "All of us were getting quite tired of your moping. Now at least you can go home to whine and complain about the unfairness of it all. It'll give you a new audience to bore with your hysterics."

Ilyana tensed, but then, rather than rage, an icy calm descended on her. She turned to Takyra and said, "You have no idea what I have been through. Perhaps *you* have no heart, but that doesn't mean you should ridicule people for the grief they feel in theirs."

An odd feeling overcame Ilyana, and she felt an alien sense of power rise from within. She had no idea what it was or how to control it. She pushed it away, and it flowed out of her, forming a ball of water that hit Takyra squarely in the face, soaking her. She gasped as the water ran down her body, pooling onto the floor. She shrieked in rage, preparing to lunge at Ilyana. Then she stopped, a puzzled look on her face.

"You... you just used magic against me!"

Ilyana froze, staring at the water dripping down Takyra's face. She had! But it was not fire; it was water. What was happening?

Leaving Takyra, who stood stunned and dripping wet, without so much as a word of apology, she ran out of the room and down the hall. She had to find Professor Alderin. He would know what was happening to her.

"Wait up!" a familiar voice called from across the hall. Ilyana stopped and waited for Nyell to catch up to her.

"Hey, Ilyana. Where are you off to in such a hurry?"

"Oh! Nyell, you won't believe this. My magic is back!"

He was silent a moment, incredulity warring with hope across his features. Then, he said, "Are you sure?"

"Yes! Just ask Takyra. She's all wet from the water ball I threw at her. It's a little odd that it was water and not fire, but I'm sure that will straighten out in time. Oh, Nyell, I'm so happy!"

Nyell looked sober. "Ilyana, from what I've read, it's not unheard of for a mage who has lost her power to regain magic again. But in every case, it's always been magic of a different element. I think your fire magic is likely gone for good."

"No. You're wrong. It's my fate to be a fire mage, fighting on the front lines, not some stupid water mage, good for nothing more than watering some dirt grubber's land."

He looked hurt, then said, "Who knows, maybe someday your fire magic will return." He reached out for her hands, taking them into his own. "But, you know, water mages are extremely important. Without us, farmers would get nothing out of their farmlands. No one could even live in this part of the country; it's too dry. Besides, I like being a water mage. It means I'll never die of thirst out in the desert." He smiled at her.

Tears streamed down Ilyana's face. "No! If I can't have fire magic, then I want no magic at all!"

"Hold on, Ilyana. I think you need to talk to Professor Alderin. If there's a chance that your fire magic will return, he'll know about it."

She shook her head; she already knew what he would say. After all, he'd told it to her often enough.

Once she'd lost her fire magic, it was gone forever.

As the months passed, Ilyana grudgingly accepted that she was indeed now a water mage, though she remained bitter over the loss of her fire magic. She and Nyell grew apart; as a water mage, he had taken great offense to her attitude that his power was somehow inferior. Meanwhile, she butted heads more often with Takyra and was becoming closer than ever to Emira. Emira was a comfort in some ways, but something about her made Ilyana a bit uneasy. She was always willing to listen to Ilyana complain of the unfairness of her situation, but rather than helping her to feel better, Ilyana couldn't help but to think Emira resented it, though she never showed any signs she did.

Professor Alderin, too, continued to be a comfort to Ilyana. He listened to her complaints, saying little. He doggedly pursued teaching her water magic, reminding her that she was just as powerful in water magic as she had been with fire. She tolerated his lessons, and did become quite talented in water magic, but she did not learn to like it, and sometimes her animosity was so great it prevented her from pulling off a spell at all.

Ilyana again pulled her thoughts back to the present. Nyell was speaking. He looked at each of them in turn, eyes grave, and finished up the instructions she had been too distracted to hear by saying, "All is ready. We are waiting only on you now."

Ilyana looked around her. A group of three fire mages stood off to her left, a soft reddish glow surrounding them. Next to them, but outside the spinning red glow of their combined magic, stood another fire mage, whose job it was to keep any retaliatory magic from disrupting the spells. Ilyana looked back at Nyell. He was to be their protector while she, Takyra and Emira cast their spell.

Ilyana faced the other two water mages. She gave an encouraging nod to Emira, who returned the nod with a feeble grin. Over Emira's shoulder, she saw Nyell. He smiled at her, and she managed a smile in return. She felt a little of the tension between the two of them ease.

The three water mages closed their eyes, centered themselves, and drew on their powers. A hazy blue aura appeared around them, faint at first, then becoming brighter, until it resembled a glittering mirage on desert sand. It began to spin, picking up speed until its pattern, which undulated like waves, blurred into a solid wall of blue.

Ilyana felt a nudge in her mind; it was Emira, asking for permission to join their powers together. She acceded, and felt a sudden increase in the pool of power as hers was added to

Takyra's and Emira's. All was silent; the spinning blue aura blocked all sound coming from outside of it. Now, they would concentrate their power and send it out to the sea to gather the water that would then be hurled at the enemy in one great wave.

Ilyana hesitated. She felt the power of the water magic swirling all around her, a great raging torrent, and she felt anger build. *This is not what I want,* she thought angrily, starting to push the magic away. She wanted only the fire magic, but it would never again be hers.

She opened her eyes and saw Nyell looking at her, a look of pride on his face. *He believes in me,* she thought. *He sees me embracing the power and he thinks I've finally accepted it.*

And, in that moment, she realized how selfish she had been; she had been so wrapped up in her own grief that she hadn't been able to see the plight of others, and how her power could help them. Yet she still had magic, and though it was different than what she had before, it was equally important. Perhaps her life was not working out the way she had expected it, but she still had the opportunity to be what she had always wanted to be: a mage. All of her resentment drained away, and for the first time since her loss, she was at peace. Willing now to fully embrace her water magic, she closed her eyes and concentrated harder than before.

Suddenly, the link was broken. Ilyana heard a whooshing sound and felt heat against her face. She heard a scream, and, her concentration broken, her magic flowed out of her.

Someone had just used fire magic. But who? And why were they attacking the water mages?

She was shocked to see Takyra, her arm ablaze, struggling with Emira, a vicious grimace on her face. Emira, looking scared but resolute, broke free from Takyra's grasp and ran to Ilyana.

"Help!" she said, fear plain on her face. "Takyra's trying to kill me!"

Takyra lunged toward Emira, snarling, "You little bitch! How dare..."

Emira's face contorted in fury, and a bright flare shot from her hand, knocking her adversary back. Takyra's clothing burst into flames and she fell to the ground, screaming. Emira smiled, a grim expression that held no mirth, as she strode over to Takyra, who was now sobbing with pain. One more time, Emira held out her hand, and she blasted the fallen mage with another ball of flame. Takyra's whimpers died off, and she lay still as tongues of flame licked at her charred skin.

Ilyana was frozen with shock. How could Emira do this? And how was it she had the ability to use fire magic? No one had the ability to do more than one kind of magic, unless they had, like her, lost one kind and gained another. It made no sense.

Her gaze shifted between Takyra's still form and Emira, who was now only a few feet from her. As Ilyana took an involuntary step back, regret flickered in Emira's eyes. "I'm so sorry, Ilyana. This was the part I was dreading most."

She saw the faint reddish aura surround Emira once more. *Again, fire magic,* she thought. *How can she...?*

She took a deep breath. How Emira could wield the power was not important; all that mattered was that she had to be stopped. She pulled deep from her magic, preparing a spell to immobilize this woman she used to consider her friend. She dodged just as the traitor loosed her spell, but the fire did not miss her entirely. She felt searing heat scorch her shoulder, and frantically slapped the fire out, burning her hand in the process. She clenched her jaw, resolving to keep her concentration despite the pain.

"Why, Emira?" she said through gritted teeth.

Emira's face darkened. "Why? Because if you succeed, I am lost. My family and I will be nothing in the eyes of your country." She lunged at Ilyana.

Ilyana stepped quickly to one side, managing to only be hit

by a glancing blow from the other mage's fist. "What do you mean?" she said, rubbing the cheek where Emira's fist had landed. "I thought your family was being held captive by the rebels. We are trying to save them, aren't we?"

"Your so-called rebels *are* my family! They sent me here to sabotage any magic used against them. If they are defeated, I'll lose everything!

"And you," she spat, "you and your 'Oh, poor me! I lost my magic!' Ugh... I got *so* sick of hearing you feel sorry for yourself. There were so many times I just wanted to *throttle* you, tell you what a selfish bitch you were.

"But I have more important things to worry about than some poor little mage who lost her power." Emira grinned, and the coldness in that face sent a shiver down Ilyana's spine. "There's no way I'm letting you kill any more of my countrymen. See them down there? Once I take care of you, and then the fire mages over there, there's nothing to stop them from taking this hill. And once they've taken it, with all of her most powerful mages dead, this country will be ours."

Ilyana listened in disbelief. Then, she once more reached for her power. It surged within her, only this time there was no anger—only sadness. She lifted her hand and said, "I'm sorry, but I can't let you do this."

Just as Emira prepared to release another fireball, Ilyana shot a glistening spear of magic toward her. It slammed into the traitor, instantly encasing her in a sheath of clear ice. Her face, pressed up against the crystalline casket, was frozen in mingled surprise and horror.

Ilyana eyes widened as she saw what she had done. The still, glistening form reminded her horribly of an ice sculpture and she turned quickly away, running over to Takyra. The water mage's face was scorched almost beyond recognition. Ilyana listened at her chest; she heard no breathing, no heartbeat. She was deeply shamed; she had suspected Takyra of being a traitor immediately, even though she had no reason to, other than that she disliked her.

At that moment, she saw Nyell on the other side of the barrier. He pounded against it with his fists, his face contorted in rage and fear, shouting something Ilyana could not hear past the glowing blue wall. She let go of the magic, dropping the luminous barrier that separated her from the outside world. Nyell rushed to her.

"Ilyana!" he cried, pulling her roughly to him. "I felt so helpless. I tried to help you, but I couldn't reach you!"

She held him for a moment, feeling the unconditional love that, deep down, she knew had been there all along. Then, she gently pushed him away. "There is no time, and there's still a job to be done."

"No," he said, shaken. "You can't. One mage can't do it. You'll drain all of your power, and with it your life. I won't let you do that."

She looked deep into his eyes and her resolve wavered. *I could just walk away,* she thought. *No one would fault me for it.* She was sorely tempted. But then she remembered that if the battle plan failed, the rebels would overrun the capital, throwing the entire country into chaos. What would be left for her then, but a life on the run? She knew that, should the rebels gain control of this country, they would certainly consider her and Nyell enemy combatants, and would likely punish them accordingly, as an example to the populace.

She knew then what she had to do.

She reached for Nyell's hands, taking them gently in her own. "I have to do this, Nyell. Saving this country, making her whole once more, is something I'd gladly give my life for. You and I are the only water mages left. Perhaps we will fail, but I could never live with myself knowing that I did not try."

A tear slid down Nyell's cheek. "Let me help you, then. We can do this together."

She pulled her hands gently from his. "No, this is something I must do myself. Remember, it's your job to guard me."

Nyell swallowed hard and nodded. He reached for her suddenly, pulled her close once more, and kissed her. Ilyana held tightly to him for a moment, overwhelmed by her love for him, and again pulled away. "I have to do this," she said again. "Will you protect me?"

He stood a moment, grief and pride warring across his face. Then, he nodded. "Always, Ilyana." He took her hand, and they walked together to the top of the hill.

The assault was well underway. The fire dragon already herded the rebels toward the shore. She had no time to lose.

She reached within herself, setting up the shimmering blue barrier between herself and the world. Concentrating hard, she gathered every bit of power within her, her entire body trembling with the effort. She knew it was too much, but what was her life compared to the survival of her country? She knew that if this land fell to the rebels, her life was as good as lost anyway. Everything depended on this spell.

The azure aura around her intensified as it spun around her. When she had gathered all she could, she sent the power out over the waves, gathering the water together until it bulged against the horizon. She could see the soldiers on the beach as they watched the water recede from the shoreline. They milled about, unaware of what was about to befall them.

Ilyana shook with effort. She worked to pull in more water, using the last of her power. This was all she could do. She hoped it was enough.

Then, she let the magic drain out of her, and the blue aura around her slowly dissipated. She watched as the dome of water flattened, a wall of water spreading out across the horizon, growing taller as it sped toward shore. The rebels on the beach saw what was coming and panicked. They ran in all directions, their shouts drifting up to the ears of those who watched, fascinated, from the hill. The wave, by now a forty-foot-high wall of water, slammed into the beach. It rolled out onto the plain, swallowing everything and everyone in its wake. Ilyana could hear screams of terror as the water engulfed the enemy force.

Then the water receded, carrying the soldiers out to sea. As they drifted further out, the men's cries for help became thin and pitiful. Then, all Ilyana could hear was the crashing of waves onto the beach.

She dropped to her knees. She had done it. She trembled with exhaustion; as the last wisps of her power leached from her, she fell to the ground. Through a dark haze, she saw someone run to her, kneel beside her, cry out her name. She longed to reach up, to touch Nyell's face, to tell him it was all right. She tried to tell him it had been worth it to save their country, to make her free of strife once more, but she couldn't move.

A buzzing sound filled her ears. She felt, very faintly, the pressure of Nyell's lips against hers, the wetness of his tears falling onto her cheek. She had done her duty; now it was time to rest. *Our country has been reclaimed from the enemy*, she thought. *She is whole once more.*

~~~~~

Candace woke with a gasp.

It had been the same dream again, she was sure of it, yet something had been different this time. Her feelings of anger and helplessness were gone, replaced by calm; she felt whole now, and more at peace with herself than she had in a long time.

She lifted the blinds. Sparkling dust motes, swept off the slats as they stacked together, danced in the early-morning sunshine. Candace surveyed the brightly lit room. It seemed so empty. She placed her hand on her swollen belly; a light kick responded to her gentle pressure.

She felt a sudden, unexpected rush of affection toward the little one who lay within. *Here I have someone to fill this empty space, if only I will let her.*

Candace again placed her hand on the mobile hanging above the crib. The little animals that hung from it danced at her touch. She took a deep breath and wound the key. She stood there for some moments, fingers trembling slightly, both dreading and yearning to hear the little lullaby. Then, she let go of the key.

She wept as she listened to the sweet little melody. She hoped that her baby girl would find the lullaby just as soothing as her little boy once had.

She heard the soft squeak of the door opening behind her. Owen stood in the doorway. A smile lit her tear-streaked face as she went to him. She rested her head against his chest, reveling in his closeness.

He started a bit, not used to the display of affection. "Were you in here all night?" he asked, raising a hesitant hand to stroke her hair.

"Yeah, I fell asleep in the chair." She took a deep breath. "I know I haven't been that pleasant to live with lately, and I'm sorry. Thank you for putting up with me."

Owen held her at arm's length, hands on her shoulders. "I'm sorry, too. I haven't been as understanding as I should have been."

"You know," said Candace, with a slight smile, "pretty soon we'll have a new baby living in this room, and there is not one bit of pink in here for her! How about we go out and get something appropriate for a little girl's room?"

Owen grinned back at her. "You're right! How about a new mobile? We could get a pink one."

Candace glanced at the mobile. Its melody was now slowing. "Oh, I don't know. I'm pretty sure she'd like the old one just fine. I think maybe just some pink paint for the walls and a few little dresses should do it."

"It's your call." Owen held out his hand to her and together they left the room, the music slowing to a stop as they descended the stairs.